THE
MIDNIGHT
BELL

Also by Jack Higgins

JACK HIGGINS

THE MIDNIGHT BELL

HarperCollins*Publishers*

This novel is entirely a work of fiction.
The names, characters and incidents portrayed in it are
the work of the author's imagination. Any resemblance to
actual persons, living or dead, events or localities is
entirely coincidental.

HarperCollins*Publishers*
1 London Bridge Street
London SE1 9GF

www.harpercollins.co.uk

Published by HarperCollins*Publishers* 2016
1

A catalogue record for this book is available from the British Library

ISBN: 978 0 00 816027 2

Printed and bound in Great Britain by Clays Ltd, St Ives plc

FSC™ is a non-profit international organisation established to promote
the responsible management of the world's forests. Products carrying the
FSC label are independently certified to assure consumers that they come
from forests that are managed to meet the social, economic and
ecological needs of present and future generations,
and other controlled sources.

Find out more about HarperCollins and the environment at
www.harpercollins.co.uk/green

For Madeleine Cameron
With love and grateful thanks

The bell tolls at midnight,
but only when Death requires it.

—Irish proverb

WASHINGTON
AND
LONDON

AN EAST WIND with driving rain and sleet pushed across the airport as the Gulfstream landed. It was immediately approached by a security limousine from the White House, which Blake Johnson, alighting from the plane, was surprised to see was being driven by his longtime secretary, Alice Quarmby. He opened the passenger door, tossed his valise inside, and joined her.

"What are you doing here?"

"Protecting your back, you idiot," she told him, as she drove away. "You were supposed to bring Jake Cazalet back with you from London, and here you are, alone. I'm a nervous old broad when it comes to my boss, so I'd like to know why."

"Sorry, Alice, it's for the ears of the President only."

"Well, it better be good. With his second term coming up, he needs to show who's in charge, and here's former President Jake Cazalet—a fine president in his day, mind you—dining with the Prime Minister and giving interviews to the media as if he's the official mouthpiece for American foreign policy. You know the White House isn't pleased about that."

"I know—but enough about that. Anything else come up?"

"Apparently, the President has made a new friend."

"Really? Who?"

"A Colonel Samuel Hunter. I did some research—don't ask me where. He has a decent black-ops record in the army, nothing spectacular, and since then, he's spent five years with the CIA, where he runs a Special Projects Department. He gets around a lot."

"So what's the 'special project' he's come up with that appeals to the Oval Office?"

"The President has become interested in the private-army business since you were last here."

"Mercenaries?" Blake was amazed. "What on earth for?"

"The new name for them is private military companies, so you might as well get used to it. It seems they've been having some success in Mali, and South African companies have been busy recruiting."

"With plenty of casualties, no doubt?"

"No doubt. And some units have apparently done very well supporting the Nigerian Army in its struggle with al-Qaeda."

"Aided by the military supplies we pump in there?"

"Not in Nigeria, I think. My research suggests the CIA wouldn't touch this one with a barge pole if left to their own devices."

"Like that, is it?" Blake said.

"That's what they say, but who knows?"

"Exactly," he said. "You're an old cynic, Alice, but somehow you always get it right."

"Blame it on the White House, Blake. I've been there longer than anyone else. It breeds cynicism."

THEY WERE MOVING along Constitution Avenue toward the White House, where they found demonstrators in spite of the hour and the heavy rain.

"Try the East Entrance," Blake suggested. Alice did, and a Secret Service man on duty saw to the Mercedes, then escorted them to the President's secretary, who delivered them to the Oval Office and withdrew.

The inclement weather outside had darkened the room, and yet the President kept it in shadow, glancing up from papers now and smiling hugely.

"There you are at last. And you, Alice, it was way beyond the call of duty for you to pick this rascal up at such an hour."

"I guess it's gotten to be a habit, Mr. President, after all these years."

"You're the wonder of the world. Now, if you would, go and get yourself a coffee while Blake and I talk."

Alice withdrew, and the President called, "Join us, Colonel Hunter. I'd like you to meet Blake Johnson."

Hunter emerged from the chief of staff's office, a man much as Blake had expected, around sixty, with a mustache, tanned face, and an expensive suit of blue flannel.

He held out his hand briefly. "Your fame precedes you, Mr. Johnson."

"Colonel," Blake said formally.

Hunter's smile was false and dismissive as he turned to a more important quarry. "As I was saying earlier, Mr. President, we must present our opponents with the unexpected and seize the day. It's been one of the greatest precepts of warfare since Roman times."

The President turned to Blake. "Would you agree?"

"My experience of warfare was being up to my armpits in some swamp in the Mekong Delta in Vietnam, so I guess I never had time to find out," Blake said.

Hunter was annoyed and let it show. "We all have to move with the times," he said to Blake. "Modern thinking, that's what we need. For instance, I'm surprised that a man in your position has an elderly woman as his secretary. How computer savvy can she be?"

"She could write the book on the White House," Blake said. "She's better than any computer."

"And apparently has been poking her nose into Langley's business illegally for her department's purposes," Hunter said.

"That would be my personal security department," the President said. "It's called the Basement. Blake Johnson runs it, and Alice Quarmby has served every president in office since the Basement was first conceived."

Hunter apologized hurriedly. "Of course you are right, Mr. President. Still, this unauthorized accessing of CIA files—it's disturbing."

"You may be right, Colonel, but as I am the president, I'm the one who'll make the decision about it. If you'd show the colonel out, Blake."

Blake was at the door in a moment. Hunter followed, hesitated, and turned. "And what we discussed, Mr. President—about Havoc and the support system?"

"We'll see, Colonel," the President said, and as Blake closed the door, he added, "Come and sit down and bring me up-to-date. Did you bring President Cazalet back?"

"Unfortunately, no, Mr. President. He said he's agreed to deliver a lecture at the London School of Economics about terrorism and ISIS, and he can't leave just yet."

The President frowned. "You did give him the envelope that contained the presidential warrant ordering him home again?"

"Of course. He said he was going to leave, but then Downing Street informed him that they'd all be attending the lecture—so he felt he had to stay. The profits, by the way, are going to charity—the Children of Syria."

"So how can I possibly complain about that?" the President said, then laughed reluctantly. "Damn you, Jake Cazalet, you've left me wrong-footed on this one."

"Actually, Mr. President, if I could make a suggestion?"

"By all means."

"Why don't you send a message to the Cabinet Office congratulating the Prime Minister and President Cazalet on their joint efforts—and announcing that the U.S. will match the money raised for the Children of Syria. That way, it's as if you'd been a part of it the whole time."

The President was smiling now. "What a great idea. I'll see to it at once. With one stipulation."

"What would that be, Mr. President?"

"You climb in that Gulfstream, return to London tonight, and don't show your face back here without him. When he's finished his gig, I want him back, and no arguments, even if he is a billionaire. Let's have a drink on it." The President was smiling as he rose, went to a cupboard, and produced a bottle of scotch and two glasses, one of which he handed to Blake. "Sit down for a moment."

The President settled onto a couch. "I imagine you think I'm crazy, being so concerned about Cazalet, but I can't help thinking about what happened last year." The President had sent General Charles Ferguson, the head of the Prime Minister's "private army," and his people to Cazalet's house on Nantucket, so that Cazalet could thank them on the President's behalf for the success of a recent operation. But al-Qaeda assassins had been waiting for them. "Charles Ferguson, Sean Dillon, Captain Sara Gideon, and Cazalet himself, they could all have died."

"Well, they didn't," Blake said. "None of it's your fault. Besides, Sean Dillon is the most dangerous man I've ever met. They picked the wrong target."

"But they'll try again. Especially after Dillon and company shot the al-Qaeda Master behind the attack."

"I agree with you there. I've a feeling in my gut that al-Qaeda won't let us forget that," Blake said. "Which is why we've spent so much time keeping in touch across the Atlantic."

"My Basement," the President said. "And the Prime Minister's private army." He shook his head. "United by a common purpose and yet so far away from each other."

Blake finished his drink and stood up. "Not in the world we live in, not these days. I'd better get going."

"Of course. Take care."

Blake turned. "Always do, Mr. President," he said, and left.

The President sat there, thinking of what Blake had said. *Not in the world we live in, not these days.* For a moment, he was touched by despair, but that would never do. There was work to be done, and he sat at the desk and started to go through his papers.

FRANK DOLAN, once a master sergeant in the Rangers, now Hunter's personal assistant and chauffeur, was waiting for the colonel as he left the White House, an umbrella high against the pouring rain.

"Everything go according to plan, sir?"

"Sergeant, some truly crazy people work in there, and that includes this president, his security guy, and the old bag working for them."

"That must be her dozing in the Mercedes over there," Dolan said, as he started to drive away. "I looked him up. Blake Johnson, right? Decorated three times in Vietnam."

"Hell, they gave medals away like candy in those days," Hunter said.

"He was FBI for a while, too. Took a bullet meant for Cazalet when Cazalet was a senator."

"Well, bully for him," Hunter said, staring out. "Washington in the rain. I loathe it."

"Have we anything special planned this trip, sir?"

"London. I want to have another look at Hans Weber's Havoc operation, the one working out of that old RAF base at Charnley. Maybe he's found more planes from the Second World War."

"More ghosts on the runways like those Dakotas of his. Piston engines, not even jets," Dolan said.

"But just the thing for African rough spots. If they break down, they can be repaired just like you'd repair an old car, whereas a jet plane in the middle of Gambia would stand there and decay."

"So there really could be money in these old planes?"

"More than you could imagine. It would depend on how they were handled, of course."

"Some of the country the private military companies operate in is pretty rough. I imagine that's why you're interested in Havoc."

"Why, Sergeant Dolan, you know my involvement in the company would preclude that," Hunter said. "Not to mention my connection with the CIA. But if national security is at stake, well, we must be prepared, don't you think?" and he laughed harshly.

AT THE AIRPORT, the Gulfstream waited in the rain as Alice and Blake parted. He'd told her of the President's worries, and she nodded.

"I think there's something else, too," she said. "Even at sixty-five, Jake Cazalet is still full of incredible energy and, more than that, a touch of wildness. You never know what he's going to do next. Presidents aren't supposed to behave like that, even former ones."

"I think I could mention a few who did, Alice, but you're right—he's unpredictable, likely to charge right at danger."

"So bring him home safe," she said.

He kissed her on the cheek, nodded to the flight attendant, and then ran to the Gulfstream. A few moments later, he was settled in his seat and peering out of the window, but Alice was no longer there.

The Gulfstream climbed very fast toward the Atlantic, leveling at forty thousand feet, and the second pilot visited the kitchen area, emerged with three coffees on a tray, and passed one to Blake.

"Six hours to arrival if we're lucky. Storms threatening in the mid-Atlantic, so belt up if you want to sleep."

Blake, however, didn't feel like sleeping. His quick return to London might cause some surprise, so he realized he should give them a heads-up. There was one person available day or night at the Holland Park safe house, so he produced his Codex and called Roper. In spite of the hour, he knew that Major Giles Roper would be seated in his wheelchair in the computer room checking his screens, searching for intelligence. And Tony Doyle, the military police sergeant on night duty, would be near. A Jamaican Cockney born in London, Doyle had joined the army to see the world but had got no farther than Belfast and the IRA. Now his mission was to take care of Roper—and supply him with endless tea, whiskey, and bacon sandwiches.

Roper had his phone on speaker so Tony could hear. "What's going on, Blake? I've heard of quick returns, but this is ridiculous."

"The President wants Cazalet back the moment he's available, so he's sent me to make sure. He worries about the free spirit gathering too much publicity."

"He's worrying too much," Doyle called. "Jake's doing just fine."

"For a man who was once leader of the free world, Tony," Blake called back, "he might just consider stepping away for a while and making himself less of a target."

"Maybe you're right," Roper said. "But it will be great to see you back here. I'll let you get a little shut-eye and check in later to see how you're getting on."

IT WAS QUIET except for the drone of the engines, and Blake lay back and dozed, thinking how first al-Qaeda and then ISIS had altered the world. International terrorism of the most murderous kind was the name of the game now, al-Qaeda disrupting the lives of millions, each of its branches controlled by an anonymous leader known as the Master. Ferguson and his people had been responsible for the death of two Masters, so al-Qaeda would want their revenge.

He got up and went to the kitchen area for the bottle of Bushmills Irish Whiskey he knew was kept there. As he opened it, rain hammered on the fuselage of the Gulfstream and there was the roll of distant thunder. He tossed his drink down and his Codex sounded.

"Who is this?"

The voice on the other end of the line was not one he knew. It was cultured and mature, an older man, the English perfect with only the slightest of French accents. "Ah, there you are, Mr. Johnson. A dirty night to be crossing the Atlantic. I trust the President was in the best of health when you left Washington?"

"Who the hell are you?" Blake demanded, coldly aware that he probably knew the answer to that one already.

"Ah, don't tell me you didn't know I'd be calling sooner or later. There are debts to be paid. I intend to see they are."

"So you're the new Master?" Blake said. "I was wondering when another one would turn up. A voice on the phone trying to justify al-Qaeda and international terrorism. You guys never stop trying, do you?"

"And never will. I'm certainly not the easy marks my predecessors were. Technology changes by the week these days, and even the great Major Giles Roper will find me hard to handle. As for Ferguson—tell him it's a different world. His time is done. Come to think of it, never mind. I'll tell him myself."

"I'm sure he'll look forward to that."

"And Jake Cazalet? Get him home while you can. His time is running out, too. Oh, and say hello for me to the lovely Captain Sara Gideon. I understand she has a birthday coming up soon. Give the captain my sincere good wishes and tell her I'll see her soon."

Blake called Roper and told him what had happened. "God knows what Ferguson is going to think."

"Easy to ask him," Roper said. "He's staying in the guest wing. Were you surprised by the call?"

"No, I've always thought al-Qaeda would seek revenge. We've cost them two Masters already, so what would you expect?"

"Is the conversation recorded on your Codex?"

"Of course."

"That should have Ferguson awake faster than a cold shower. We can all listen."

Ferguson answered five minutes later. "Morning, Blake, are you linked in?"

"Ready and waiting, General."

"So let me listen to what he's got to say."

When it was finished, Ferguson smiled. "Cheeky sod. Run it through again."

Roper complied, and this time Ferguson didn't smile. "He's going to give us trouble, this one. The smooth approach, the familiarity, all designed to mask his true self."

"I agree," Roper said. "But he can't believe his charming approach is going to fool anyone, so what's his game?"

"Maybe it's just meant to confuse," Blake suggested.

Ferguson said, "He's a clever bastard, I'll give you that. And well informed. Sara's birthday, for example. Use the secure link to let all our people know a new Master is back to plague us and alert the Cabinet Office, Security Services, and MI5. I think that's it."

"What about President Cazalet, General?"

"Oh, certainly, him, too. Call him at the Dorchester. Ask him to join us for breakfast. But not a word on the matter to the White House. It's exactly the kind of thing they want to avoid."

"Leave it to me, General."

"I fully intend to, because I'm going back to bed for a couple of hours." He turned to Tony Doyle. "As for you, Sergeant, when it's time, drive up to Farley Field and pick up Blake Johnson."

"My pleasure, General," Doyle told him.

"Drive carefully, you rogue. The hint of a scrape and I'll have your stripes."

Ferguson went out, and Doyle turned to Roper. "So we're going to war again, Major?"

"So it would appear; I can smell the powder," Roper said.

Doyle left, and Roper poured a large scotch, tossed it back, and lit a cigarette. The he pressed the master switch by his right hand, turning on everything in the computer room, and he sat there, brooding over dozens of screens.

"Don't worry, Master," he murmured softly. "I'll find you in the end. I always do."

ON THE LONDON WATERFRONT, fog had descended early, rolling in across the Thames at Wapping, a mile downriver from Harry Salter's place, the Dark Man, where an old pier jutted out from Trenchard Street, an early Victorian pub standing back from it.

There was a motor launch painted blue and white tied to the pier with two chains, giving it a permanent look yet allowing the launch to ease itself in the five-knot current that was running that morning.

The name of the boat was *Moonglow*, and the fact that the painted sign hanging outside the pub indicated that the landlord's name was George Moon amused many people. It didn't bother Moon, though. His family had owned the pub since Queen Victoria's reign, which made him proud, and he liked sleeping on board the launch as he had the night before. But now there was work to be done, which meant a visit to his office.

He went up the steps from the pier, a small insignificant balding man in steel spectacles clutching his raincoat across his body, an umbrella over his head, and approached the front door of the pub. Two notices faced him, one of which said CLOSED FOR THE WINTER, the other, MOON ENTERPRISES LIMITED, and as he approached, the door was opened for him by his cousin Harold, a hard, brutal-looking man with the flattened nose of an ex-boxer.

"Late this morning, George. Posh geezer called twice on the house phone in the last half hour. Said he'd call back."

"So it will keep," Moon said. "I've told you before, you worry too much. I'd turned my mobile off."

"I just wanted to make sure you didn't miss out on anything tasty," Harold told him.

"I know, sunshine." George tweaked the big man's cheek. "Now get me a mug of scalding-hot tea and an Irish whiskey, and we'll wait for your posh geezer to turn up again."

It was quiet in the bar, everything peaceful, bottles lined up against the Victorian mirrors behind the bar. This type of establishment would usually be a thieves' den for serious drinkers and drug users, but Moon had long since knocked that on the head. Development along the Thames had opened a whole new world, and his portfolio was considerable. Life was good.

His mobile sounded, and he answered, "Moon Enterprises."

"How grand that sounds, Mr. Moon."

Harold had been right, a posh geezer indeed. Moon beckoned, putting his mobile on speaker so Harold could listen.

"Who is this?"

"A Master who is looking for a willing servant. I've just deposited seventy-five thousand pounds in your bank account as evidence of good faith. There could be other payments later."

"Do me a favor," Moon said. "Go away and die somewhere. You think I believe that?"

"I'll call you again in fifteen minutes. If you say no, I can cancel the deposit, but as I can't envisage your being that stupid, I don't think it likely. I suggest that you check with your bank."

"A crazy one, that," Moon said, turning to Harold.

"How do you know?" Harold said. "You haven't been in touch with the bank."

"Okay, just to keep you happy. Waste of time though."

He made the call, shrugging, and within minutes received the astonishing news. "I can't believe it," he said hoarsely to Harold. "What's this geezer's game?"

"George, I couldn't care less. All I know is it's real money. Here, let me get you another whiskey," Harold said. "Put a little lead in your pencil for when he gets back to you."

Which the Master did as Moon was drinking it. "Satisfied, Mr. Moon?"

"Who wouldn't be? So who are you and what do you want?"

"What I want is your experience of the London underworld, like your family before you. Generation of thieves and river rats. How did Charles Dickens put it? Those who made a living finding corpses in the Thames on behalf of the River Police? There is not a criminal enterprise you've failed to touch on."

"And proud of it," Moon said.

"You've been especially busy running booze and cigarettes from Europe—but no drugs, you're too cunning for that, which is one reason I chose you. You've also done well with warehouse developments by the Thames, while Cousin Harold can haul in hoodlums by the score any time they're needed."

"And happy to do it, mister," Harold called.

Moon said, "Okay, you know a lot about me, so what?"

"I know everything about you, my friend, even the fact that some years ago you were employed by Russian military intelligence, the GRU, making yourself useful in many ways right here in London. Remember your recognition code? 'The midnight bell is ringing'? MI5 would have been interested. You could have got twenty-five years for treason."

Moon was transfixed. "But how could you have known that?"

"You've heard of al-Qaeda, I'm sure. Our information system is as good as the CIA's—better!—and I can access it by pushing a button."

"So this is a Muslim thing?"

"Is that a problem?"

It was Harold who cut in then. "No problem at all, Master. Whatever you want, you get."

"That's good, because if I didn't, I'd have to have you killed. Anyway, your first job for me will concern Harry and Billy Salter."

Moon brightened up. "We have history, us and the Salters."

Harold said, "What do you want us to do? Smash their restaurant up?"

"Not yet. Something more subtle. Give them just a hint of what we can do."

"You can leave that to me," Harold told him. "Mayhem is my specialty."

"I'm delighted to know you can spell it," the Master said.

"Well, I can, and it will be a pleasure to give the Salters a black eye."

"To a fruitful association, then, gentlemen. I'll be in touch."

MOON SAID, "He's gone, but I can't say I'm happy about working for a Muslim."

"Didn't you tell me that we had a great-grandfather who was an Indian seaman who jumped ship in the Pool of London?"

"True."

"Then stop being racist, join me in the kitchen, and I'll cook you breakfast."

"I wonder where he lives," Moon said.

"I wouldn't mind betting that he'd rather you didn't know. Besides, it could be anywhere—London, Madrid, Timbuktu!"

"You think so?"

"All you need these days is a coded mobile, and you can cover the world."

HAROLD WAS RIGHT, of course, for the Master did move frequently, for obvious reasons. At that moment he was living in Paris on a furnished barge next to the other barges moored on the Quai des Brumes on the Seine.

The Master thought the business with the Moons had gone well.

Despite a certain criminal cunning on their part, they had missed the fact that he had taken complete control of them. They'd sold their souls to the Devil, which amused him. Just like Faust. Life was all about power.

Things had gone well so far, and he could proceed with confidence to the next step, but there was always the unexpected in life—there'd just been a death in the family of the other people relevant to his plans. For the moment, he hesitated, waiting for God to select the right time to move for, as in all things, there was only one God and Osama was his Prophet.

But he decided the time was now, and he took out his coded mobile and made a call to Drumore House in County Down in Ulster, still the old family home, in spite of a certain decay, of the Magee family.

Finbar Magee, seated at the breakfast table in the farm's kitchen, pushed away his plate and reached for the half glass of whiskey that his cousin Eli had shoved over to him.

"Who the hell is bothering me now?" Finbar said, taking out his mobile and putting it on speaker.

Eli, white haired and bearded, was pouring tea. "Answer it, for God's sake."

Finbar did. "Who the hell is this? I'm not in the best of moods."

"Well, you wouldn't be," the Master told him. "I've heard about the accident that killed your wife. You're being treated very unfairly. Come to London, and I'll help make it right."

"That takes bloody money, ye madman," Finbar shouted.

"Which is why I've placed twenty thousand pounds in your bank account for traveling expenses."

"Damn you, I've no time for jokes." Finbar switched off. "Did you hear that idiot?"

"I did, but I didn't hear you calling the bank to check the situation," Eli said.

Finbar stared at him, frowning, then did just that. Minutes later, he was staring wild-eyed at Eli. "It's true. The money's been deposited."

"Then you'll have to hope he calls back."

In the same moment, the Master did. "Are you happy now?"

"Why should I be?" Finbar said. "But how do you know about the accident, and why should it concern you?"

"I represent an organization that has had problems with a certain General Charles Ferguson and some people who work for him, including an IRA assassin named Sean Dillon."

"That bastard!" Finbar slammed his clenched fist down on the table. "May he die before I do, so I'll have the satisfaction of knowing he's dead."

"I can imagine. I also know about the unfortunate business concerning your sons some years ago when he left one of your boys crippled for life. He's given you a very rough time."

"Too bloody true," Finbar said, and shook his head. "How do you know so much?"

"Because I represent the most powerful organization of its kind in the world, al-Qaeda. Our access to information is limitless, and the money I have given you is just the beginning. I know you've got your phone on speaker—this concerns your cousin Eli as well."

"And if I say no?" Finbar asked.

"That would prove how stupid you are, and I would have to arrange for your disposal."

Finbar laughed harshly. "Well, we can't have that. I'm in, and that includes Eli."

"I knew you were a sensible man. Who knows, we might even solve the mystery of the *Maria Blanco* and its cargo."

"You know about that, do you? Twenty-five million pounds in gold bars when it was taken. God knows how much that would be worth today."

"A lot," the Master said. "It could have kept the IRA going for years, and they let it slip through their fingers."

"I think it was Dillon, the bastard. Could it have been?"

"Supposedly, he was in the deserts of Algeria at the time training new recruits for the IRA. But you never know for sure with a man like Sean Dillon."

"So what do I do now?"

"Get yourself to London, and I'll be in touch. But remember that you belong to us now. It would be unfortunate if you forgot."

The Master was gone in a moment, and Eli said, "What was all that?"

"It was about us being in the money again, so happy days, old son. I'm on my way to London."

AT THE SAME TIME, Sean Dillon was driving his Mini into the Holland Park safe house in response to Roper's call about the arrival of a new Master and Ferguson's suggestion of a breakfast meeting.

He went straight to the computer room, which was empty, but

the sound of voices and laughter sent him through to the canteen, where Maggie Hall had provided breakfast and Tony Doyle was helping her serve it.

Blake was there, and Sara had brought Dillon's cousin Hannah, and Harry and Billy Salter arrived, both in black tracksuits. Hannah was young, only nineteen, but she had grown up in an IRA family and knew how to handle a gun. She was also studying at the Royal College of Music, but Dillon worried sometimes that she was just a little too attracted to the outlaw life.

As for the Salters, they were gangsters who had discovered they could make millions legitimately in London these days—and young Billy had even gone so legit, he'd joined MI5.

"Turnup for the books, this, but the smell of your cooking always drives me potty, so let's get to it, Maggie," Harry Salter said.

They all started to eat, and Blake asked, "So what does everyone think about another Master on the scene?"

"I'd like to shoot the bastard," Harry said, with feeling.

"You can hear a recording of him in the computer room," Roper said. "What's your take on all this, Billy?"

"As long as I have room for a pistol in my pocket, I'll manage."

"And you, Sean?" Sara asked.

"Well, it isn't Afghanistan, where you won your medals, Sara, more like Belfast City during the Troubles, and I survived that."

There was a somber moment as if no one knew what to say, and then came the sound of a car arriving outside, where it had started to rain. A moment later, Henry Frankel, the cabinet secretary, walked in, a navy blue trench coat draped over his shoulders.

He kissed Harry on the head. "Restore me to sanity, you old

devil. No matter how well I do my job, it's hell down there: Sunni or Shia, ISIS or ISIL, what is Hamas up to now, what is Iran going to do, will Yemen survive, is Palestine going to blow up again?" He threw up his arms.

"Take it easy, Henry," Roper said. "You'll give yourself a heart attack."

"Giles, I may be cabinet secretary, but I'm just another bloody civil servant, a kind of superior office boy, passing to the Prime Minister news about what's going on in the wider world and it ain't good. Terrorism is creating havoc everywhere, we're facing one war after another, and it all looks as if it could get worse. Our most senior politicians are beginning to feel that they can't cope. Take the people I just left. There was Sir Charles Glynn, Director General of MI5; Ferguson representing your lot; the home secretary; the man from Scotland Yard; Uncle Tom Cobley, I swear; and we mustn't forget Jake Cazalet."

"So where is this tirade leading us?" Roper asked.

Jake Cazalet walked in at that moment and answered. "They don't know what to do anymore, except to allow you people to shoot what we hope are the villains. The news that al-Qaeda has raised its head again in the shape of a new Master went down like a lead weight considering that the last one was barely dead."

"I imagine it would," Blake said.

Sara turned to Frankel. "Have a decent breakfast, Henry, and remember what Somerset Maugham said. 'To dine well in England it's necessary to have breakfast three times a day.'"

Henry laughed. "Ah, you always find a way to cheer me up. I shall follow your advice religiously."

"So what's Ferguson up to at the moment? Still at Downing Street?" Dillon asked.

"Ministry of Defence. An ad hoc committee with interested parties discussing how to keep things from getting out of hand."

"Why aren't you on it? Good God, Jake, with your experience as a soldier and president."

"Don't worry, the Prime Minister has made me a special advisor. I'll find excuses to avoid going back to Washington, won't I, Blake?"

"That'll be the day," Harry said. "So we really do have to stay close?"

"Within reason."

"We do have the Dark Man to open, but I suppose young Hasim can manage in a pinch. He's shown a lot of promise, that boy, and Dora thinks the world of him."

"Then there's things to be done at Harry's Place," Billy said.

"Have you got a wedding or something?" Sara asked.

"One or two things, that's all, but stuff needs organizing. We can get back here soon enough if you have a problem."

"Well, I do," Dillon said. "I just heard yesterday that a dear friend of mine has been killed in a car crash on a visit to Ulster. A drunken driver was responsible. I need to pay my respects to the family, so I'll have to go out for a while."

"No problem," Roper said.

Dillon nodded, staring into space, and Hannah said gently, "Is it help you need?"

There were others listening, as Dillon said, "And you the girl to see it. When I came to live in Kilburn with my father, my mother being dead, our next-door neighbors were Finbar and Eileen Magee, her the kindest woman I ever knew, him a drunken, unpleasant swine, a con man and petty criminal who had been to prison often."

"So what did all that lead to?"

"Twin boys named Tad and Larry, who attended the same school I had, though twelve years later."

"So what went wrong?" Sara asked. "Something obviously did."

"The Magees, like me, came from County Down, had been a family of substance in earlier times, and they owned a farmstead above Drumore Bay. A cousin, Eli Magee, farmed it for them and ran a big old launch named the *Maria Blanco* from the jetty below in the bay."

"Was Finbar IRA?"

"They wouldn't have him. He was a braggart who claimed to be IRA to his sons and encouraged them to visit, which Eileen didn't want because there was bloodshed and war over there. There were lots of guys like him, claiming a false glory when all they were doing was driving a truck by night, hauling groceries to supermarkets, booze to pubs, and delivering orders from the chief of staff on the way to local commanders."

"Backed by documents that would satisfy the police?" Sara said. "If they were stopped?"

"Of course, but carrying a weapon was out because of the danger of police searches." He shrugged. "It was a kind of IRA postal service delivering mail to its troops."

"And you would know," said Hannah.

"Of course, I'm the fella who'd dumped a promising career at the National Theatre two years earlier because his father, in Belfast for a family funeral, stumbled into a firefight between paratroops and an angry mob, and was shot by mistake. It was the Provisional IRA for me, the Provos, next stop, and I'd have thought you'd agree with that, Hannah, after what happened to you and your parents."

"Nobody could understand more, Sean, and a hell of a choice to have to make."

Sara said, "But what did Eileen think of Finbar's persuading his sons to visit him in bandit country?"

"Her worst nightmare came true because the RUC began sniffing around Finbar, the man with the sons from London who kept visiting him."

"I'd have been surprised if they hadn't. What did it lead to?"

"He produced a Browning handgun from his pocket one night just to give himself the right kind of macho image, drunk as usual. Refused to stop for a police car, crashed in the chase."

Hannah said, "So ten years in the Maze Prison?"

"No, because he was drunk, he had a problem handling his gun, and the police opened fire."

"They shot the bastard?" Hannah said.

"No, but they did hit Larry Magee twice, one in the right leg, the other in the back, a legal response to attack, but as the police had done the shooting, it was an awkward one. They solved it for the moment by dropping the boys off at the local cottage hospital."

"So obviously Finbar was arrested," Sara said.

"Of course, but the doctors at the hospital, knowing which side their bread was buttered on, but not what to do with Larry, approached the IRA chief of staff for County Down, Hugh Tulley, who sent a top enforcer to clear things up, which he did."

"Would that happen to have been you?" Hannah asked.

Sara cut in. "What did you do?"

"The IRA had plenty of money in those days, plus the right connections. I stole the boys from hospital one night, drove them to the home of a good friend, who flew us out to a small airfield in Kent. Using our connections, I'd been able to arrange a discreet private hospital to receive a young man who'd been in a car crash abroad, back injured, leg broken."

"Very clever," Hannah said. "So Ulster, the gunplay, never happened?"

"And Eileen?" Sara asked.

"Forever grateful."

"Which only leaves Finbar," Hannah said. "What happened to him?"

"Nothing," Dillon said. "The RUC never brought a charge. They found him too useful as an informer."

"The bastard," Hannah said.

"Yes, he was and still is." Roper smiled. "But at least it leaves us with Captain Wonderful here, who rights all wrongs."

"Not really, Larry was crippled for life," Dillon said. "But at least Eileen got her boys back home."

Billy cut in. "All these years, Dillon, and you never mentioned you knew the Magees." He appealed to Hannah. "They were the most famous gangsters in London when they were active."

"Gangsters?" Hannah was astounded.

Harry said, "He's right, Hannah. Only the best for them. Suits from Savile Row, shoes from Lobb's, one of the nicest houses in Curzon Street, not too far from the Dorchester, which you've got to admit is rather convenient. The Green Harp near Shepherd Market, one of the best gaming clubs in London, with Tara Place on the upper floor specializing in Irish cooking."

"Which I haven't sampled since the improvements," Dillon said. "But intend to."

"What a story, Dillon, you're always full of surprises. Come on, Billy, we've got work to do," Harry told him.

Billy stood up, and said, "And Finbar, what's happened to him?"

"Eileen was over in Ulster to discuss legal matters concerning the Magee farm, where he'd been living for years. He picked her up at the railway station, drunk as usual, had one of his crashes, and managed to kill his wife. Cuts and bruises where he was concerned, but it appears he'll walk free."

"Dear God." Hannah crossed herself. "Damn him to hell."

"A truly dreadful man," Sara said. "But still their father, that's the problem. What do you think the brothers will do?"

"I haven't the slightest idea," Dillon said. "I don't even know whether the funeral's today or tomorrow. I'm going to see Tad and Larry now. How often do you see me in a black suit, but this one is just in case."

"Can I go with you?" Hannah asked. "Mine's dark blue, but acceptable."

Roper said, "It's okay by me, but if there's a funeral, I want you back here as soon as it's over."

Dillon grabbed Hannah's hand, they hurried out, and Roper turned to the Salters. "You are the only two I can accept living out, so off you go."

Harry grinned, said, "Let's move it, Billy," and they were gone.

Blake, Henry Frankel, and Jake Cazalet had been talking quietly. They turned expectantly. "The guest wing can meet your needs unless you'd care to return to the Dorchester," Roper said.

"I'll hang on here for the moment," Blake told him. "Any word from General Ferguson?"

"He'll be here as soon as he can. Begs your indulgence."

"How wonderfully British of him," Cazalet replied. "So let's have tea or something and resume our conversation."

"I'll join you in a few minutes." Roper moved out into the computer room.

He was followed by Doyle with a mug of tea and a bacon sandwich on a small tray.

"You haven't eaten a thing, sir, too busy talking."

Sara came in, and at the same moment Roper's Codex sounded. He picked it up but didn't answer at once, saying to Sara, "We need to talk about Highfield Court, your grandfather, and Sadie. Obviously, it's a concern. Just give me a minute."

He raised the phone in his hand. "Giles Roper. Who is this?"

"You know me as the Master. I thought it time we had a chat."

Tony Doyle was shocked. "It's him, all right, Captain Gideon. I recognize his voice from the recording."

"Go and get the others now," she said, and shoved him out of the door.

"A pleasure to hear your voice, Captain Gideon. I'm a great admirer."

The others came in, Henry Frankel leading. "What in the hell's going on?"

"Ah, the reinforcements have arrived," the Master said. "Not necessary. I'd intended to speak to each of you individually, but I'm happy to tell all of you together: You'll get no warning of the gun that barks at you from the darkness when you least expect it or the car bomb that will launch you into eternity."

"I'm trembling in my boots," Henry Frankel told him. "I can hardly stand."

"Ah, Mr. Frankel. Your partner must have a permanent smile on his face. You're such a funny little man. Why is that?"

"It's the only way I can cope with the prospect of being bored to death by a creature like you."

"Ah, you have claws. I'll have to think of an answer to that. I'll let you know next time."

"And when will that be?" Roper asked.

"Whenever I want, wherever I want. I can find you, but you cannot find me. I have a network of true believers and criminals who will do anything for money. I am invisible."

"So there you are, gentlemen," Henry Frankel said. "On top of that, he won't be happy until sharia law rules the roost at the Old Bailey."

"An interesting thought," agreed the Master.

Jake Cazalet said, "Do you think the people of the free world are going to stand by and just allow all this to happen?"

"Oh dear, the voice of America speaks. Go home, President Cazalet, while you will can."

"Or what? You'll declare jihad?"

Charles Ferguson, alerted by Tony Doyle on his arrival, had eased in quietly behind them and heard enough to realize what was going on.

"Why, yes. You have earned jihad," said the Master.

Ferguson called, "Charles Ferguson here. On me, too, then?"

But the Master had switched off. There was quiet, then Ferguson said, "I think a drink is in order. Let's all go get one, sit down, and decide what we've going to do about this creature."

IN THE BARGE on the Quai des Brumes in Paris, the Master sipped coffee and considered the call. He had enjoyed baiting Ferguson and company at Holland Park, but it was time to get to business. He should speak to the new Army of God man at Pound Street, Yousef Shah, freshly arrived from Oxford University, where he had lectured in comparative religion.

As Dr. Yousef Shah sat at his desk in the office of the Army of God Charity, beginning the task of familiarizing himself with his many duties, he was shocked at what the quiet voice had to say when he answered the phone.

"There is only one God and Osama is his Prophet."

Yousef Shah's reply was automatic. "Osama is risen."

"This is the Master, wishing you well. Has the Grand Council in Paris warned you about what you will be up against in this appointment, supplied you with details of our particular enemies here?"

"Such material has been supplied to me in full, and I've already started to work through it."

"You will find strong backing in the Army of God and the Muslim Brotherhood. Those numbers we gave you—call upon them in a time of need and the people will follow your orders without argument because they know the word of Osama is behind you."

"May his name be blessed," Yousef Shah answered automatically.

"And may it be so, but remember at all times that there is a particular danger there. We have had two Masters killed because of the activities of a British intelligence group led by Major General Charles Ferguson."

"I shall take care at all times, I promise you, particularly with these people."

"The blessing of Osama go with you," the Master told him, and hung up.

Yousef Shah sat there, thinking about the call, then reached for the information file he'd been given and started to look for Charles Ferguson. He read the information he was seeking, then phoned the Brotherhood's special number and identified himself.

"A house called Highfield Court at the end of South Audley Street. The people are Jewish, the name Gideon. Check the situation at night thoroughly, and I do mean thoroughly."

"At your orders, Imam."

He sat back. He had no idea what he had done or intended, but it was a beginning.

UNAWARE OF THE HIGH DRAMA they had left behind them, Dillon and Hannah drove toward Hyde Park as it started to rain.

She said, "What exactly did the brother do? Not drugs, I hope."

"No, Eileen wouldn't have stood for it, and her voice was law in the home, especially after the marriage broke up and Finbar cleared off to Ulster."

"Good for her."

"Only an idiot chooses that game these days when ten or fifteen years' hard time is what you draw."

"But what about the other things?"

"Eileen's family were bargees who worked the Thames from

one end to the other and stole anything they could lay their hands on. A way of life."

"I suppose to young boys it must have seemed normal," Hannah said.

"Booze and especially cigarettes have always been much cheaper in Europe than Britain, where they're heavily taxed, so that's where they started, working for other smugglers until they saved enough for their own boat. The people in that game would raid other boats, there was open warfare, and the legend of the Magee brothers was born. A tough life, but that's the way they all started on the Thames, even Harry Salter."

"So they were thieves?"

"Still could be as far I know. Tad's the hard man, Larry the brain. A few years ago, there was a rash of robberies in London involving gold, diamonds, and stuff like that, millions disappearing into the maw of Europe. Scotland Yard believed the Magees were responsible but could never prove it, and it's too late now. They're living on their reputation, part of the elite, too well-off to have to steal anymore."

"What about women in their lives?"

"Tad was deeply in love some years ago, but she died of a brain tumor. He's never taken another woman more seriously than a night out. As for Larry, I suppose the back-shooting took care of him."

She was uncomfortable and it showed. "I suppose so, but I can't wait to meet them."

"I tell you one thing. They're going to love you," and Dillon turned out of Park Lane into Curzon Street, drove halfway down, and paused for the gates of the magnificent Georgian town house to swing open. He drove inside and parked beside an Aston Martin.

"What a contrast," Hannah said, as she got out. "Your Mini and this Aston Martin."

"Indeed so, but my old Mini is supercharged, and Tad Magee has been trying to buy it for years."

They approached the front door, which opened, and a white-haired woman of sixty or so wearing a belted white smock over a blue dress stepped out smiling.

"I was hoping you would come, Sean," she said, as she opened her arms to him.

He turned to Hannah. "Molly Ryan, a friend from my youth and the housekeeper here."

Hannah held out her hand. "It's grand to know you."

Molly embraced her lightly. "What a lovely Irish girl. Where did you find her, Sean?"

"This is my second cousin, Hannah Flynn, she's at college in London. Her uncle and I were young boys together in Collyban. Served in the Provos later."

"My respects to him, my dear. He's well, I trust?"

"Dead," Hannah told her. "A UVF hit man finished him off."

It was amazing how Molly's face hardened. "May he rot in hell. But never mind—come away in and meet the boys. They've known Sean all their lives."

She led the way, they followed, and Hannah was enraptured. The furniture, the carpeting, the pictures on the walls, it was serious art by any standard. An archway gave way to a conservatory crammed with tropical plants, small palm trees at the back, the two Magee brothers in elegant black suits seated at each end of a glass table, dark hair and tanned faces, with the look of highwaymen from some romantic tale about them.

Molly advanced, smiling, Dillon following. "Cheer up, darlings, for haven't I got Sean Dillon with his cousin, Hannah Flynn. She's at college here in London, although I don't know what's she studying."

Hannah, who had held back, now showed them, with a touch of bravado, for there was a Bechstein grand piano beside the archway, the lid open. She remained standing, leaned down, and played one-handed the opening bars of a rather dashing Italian sonatina she was fond of.

Larry Magee pushed himself up in an instant, leaning on his walking stick, then came forward and held out his hand. "I don't know where Sean's been keeping you, but that was a wonderful intro."

"Do you play yourself?"

"I did my poor best to please my mother but never got far and nowhere near your standard."

"You wouldn't, and her studying at the Royal College of Music," Dillon told him.

"Well, I'm pleased to hear it and hope to see a lot of you. I'm Larry Magee and the facsimile at the other end of the table is my twin brother, Tad, a fearsome creature with a bad reputation." Magee smiled and gave her his hand.

"I'd tell you where to go, brother, but there's a lady in the room,"

Tad said. "Please join us, Hannah. I see you're walking wounded, like Larry. With Sean involved, that smells like the Troubles to me."

"Car bomb," she said. "Took my parents and left me with the stick."

"Are you from County Down, like Sean here and my own family?"

"No, I have a horse farm at Drumgoole in the Republic. Inherited, of course, and my aunt Meg is running it while I'm at college."

"And what will you do when the concert halls start calling?" Dillon inquired.

"I don't think that's likely."

"Well, as a man who has played good barroom piano all my life, I'd say it's pretty certain."

Molly, who had slipped out, returned now with coffee, which she poured out for everyone. "Is there anything else, Tad?"

"I don't think so. Get yourself ready. We're due at the church in an hour and a half."

She retired, and Dillon said, "Kilburn?"

Tad nodded. "Mary and Joseph in Flood Street. It was her church for all those years, good and bad, so it seemed fitting. The present priest is a nice boy, but I've got old Father Sharkey to agree to take the service. Eighty-five, but he's up for it. The organist's in hospital and there's no choir available, which is unfortunate."

"I can manage the organ," Hannah said. "I've been playing the one in my parish church in Drumgoole since I was fourteen. I can't help with the choir. Was there any special piece of music your mother liked to hear?"

It was Larry who answered. "'Danny Boy.' She used to sing it around the house when we were boys."

"I remember it well," Dillon said.

"Then 'Danny Boy' is what you get." Hannah turned to Dillon. "We'd better be off. We need to change into something suitable."

"We'll go to my place," Dillon said. "There's a boutique around the corner that can find something for you."

Tad moved out ahead and went upstairs; Larry escorted them to the front door and opened it. "Our lawyers have made it clear to us that my father will be charged with only the minimal offense of drunk driving. That means he walks free."

Dillon said, "It stinks, but there's nothing to be done about it."

"I could have him taken care of."

"Oh, no, you don't." Hannah grabbed him by the lapels and shook him. "I imagine Special Branch at Scotland Yard will already be waiting to see if anything happens to him. Your mother wouldn't like it, but they'd love catching a Magee at last."

Dillon said, "Finbar's not worth putting yourself in harm's way over, Larry."

"I know, but he's never been able to get his head around the mystery of what happened to the *Maria Blanco*. Convinced you had something to do with it."

"So how could I be in two places at once?" Dillon asked. "But never mind that. We've got a funeral to go to."

He took Hannah down to the Mini, and they scrambled in. She said, "What was that all about?"

"It's between me and my God, cousin," Dillon said, and drove away.

———

THE RAIN HAD STARTED at the house just as Tad, Larry, and Molly were about to be picked up by their limousine. A quick check indicated that there were sufficient umbrellas and waterproofs on board, so they moved on.

"You'd think the Almighty could do better than this," Tad grumbled. "The grave could flood."

"Your mother would have said don't be blasphemous," Molly told him.

"I can't help it, Tad. Let's get inside and do right by her," Larry said, and they got out quickly, pushing into the shelter of handheld umbrellas, making for the church door held open for them and moving in to find Dillon waiting. There was a good turnout, older people from another time who had known Eileen Magee well and remembered her kindly.

It was incredibly peaceful. Mary and the Christ Child in the chapel just inside the door, and as Hannah moved into that great hymn, "Abide with Me," the undertakers started up the aisle to present the coffin to Starkey, Molly and the brothers keeping to the left, the bearded man who was Finbar Magee pacing them on the right.

Everyone sat as Starkey started the service. There was a hush as he extolled Eileen's virtues and gave the blessing and the prayers for the dead, and then a wonderful thing happened. The organ started up, playing "Danny Boy," and Hannah's voice rose with it, and not one person moved until her music died away.

Molly was crying and so were others as people made their way out. It was still raining, and the undertaker whispered to Tad, "A bit of water in the grave, sir. We'll take care of your mother tonight back at the Chapel of Rest and see what tomorrow brings."

Hannah had closed up the organ and came across. "Best I could do."

"And bloody marvelous," Larry said. "Wasn't she, Tad?"

"You really are quite a girl, Hannah." Tad put an arm around her and kissed her cheek. "We're very grateful, and please tell Molly to stop crying."

A voice echoed from the right, and they turned to see Finbar standing by the confessional boxes. "And what about me, your father? I came to face the shame of it, didn't I, or doesn't that count?"

"You devious bastard, I don't believe you," Tad replied. "You're lucky I allow you to leave this place still walking. Never show your face here again."

Larry added, "Get back to Ulster while you still can. That's sound advice. You're not wanted here and never will be."

"Then damn the lot of you and go to hell," his father replied, pushing his way through the thickening crowd and disappearing.

Larry turned to Dillon and Hannah. "Is there any chance we could have supper together?"

"Another time," Dillon said. "But my masters call, and like a good boy, I obey. Sorry I can't explain."

"Seriously? We're not supposed to know you've been working for British Intelligence for years now?"

"Okay, but we've got a real crisis facing us, believe me. We'll see you when we can, but for the moment, it's all hands to the pumps."

"Which includes me," Hannah called, as she followed Dillon to the Mini, jumped in, and they drove away.

"I like that girl," Larry said.

"So do I." Tad nodded. "A very special lady." He sighed. "Let's get out of here." And he led the way to where Molly waited in the limousine.

DILLON TURNED INTO PARK LANE, driving toward Marble Arch, and Hannah said, "When you were speaking at Holland Park about the Magees at Drumore, you said that the *Maria Blanco* was a big old launch tied up to the jetty and used by Cousin Eli to fish from. I get the feeling there's more to it than that. Why don't you tell me what all the fuss is about?"

"God help me, girl, why are women so persistent? You won't leave me alone until I do, will you?"

"Absolutely not."

"Then shut up and listen. I was called to Belfast and told by the Army Council that I was needed in Algeria by the Gaddafi training camp to help with new recruits for the IRA. I'd trained there myself, and so had my good friend after me, Daniel Holley, who you've not had a chance to meet."

"Is he a Provo?"

"Oh, yes, but of a special kind. A Protestant."

"Sweet Jesus." She was shocked. "And what kind of a Provo would a damn Prod be?"

"The kind whose sweet young Catholic cousin was raped and

murdered by UVF scum, so he executed the four who had done it. There was nowhere for him to go except to join the IRA after that."

"Mother of God," she said.

"But enough of his background. He works for Ferguson like the rest of us do, so you'll be meeting him one of these days. He's partner in a shipping line out of Algiers. He's half Irish, and his mother is a decent Catholic woman from Crossmaglen, but never mind that. Do you want the rest of the *Maria Blanco* story?"

"Of course I do."

"Hugh Tulley got word from an informer that one of the Belfast banks was sending twenty-five million pounds in gold bullion to Dublin concealed in a meat wagon that would be passing his way. A common enough trick in those days to avoid holdups."

"So he decided to have a go?" Hannah said.

"You could say that. A brisk gunfight on a country road with night falling that left three policemen in plainclothes dead, Tulley wounded, and two of their own dead. The alarm was raised all over County Down, and the RUC swung into action."

"So what happened next?"

"Tulley thought of Eli, on his own at Drumore, Finbar being in the Maze, and the answer to his problem seemed obvious. Get to Drumore as fast as possible, transfer the bullion to the *Maria Blanco*, and take to the seas."

"And did that work?" she asked.

"With difficulty, because of people's wounds, but they made Eli, a man of enormous strength, help them. They intended to sail away, but it became obvious that Tulley and one of the other men were close to death and they were all bleeding."

"What did you do?" Hannah asked.

"Well, you have to remember that the RUC did not know where they were, so if they took Eli's Land Rover, there was hope for them at the cottage hospital nearby, where the nuns were kind."

"And come back for the bullion later?" Hannah asked. "That seems a thin chance to me. What about Eli? What was he up to?"

"Not much. They found some old-fashioned shackles in the boathouse hanging on a peg with two keys, which they were careful to take with them when they left him chained."

"And Tulley's boys?"

"The first roadblock was enough, and they held their hands up."

"And Eli?"

"The police found him, still shackled. He said he heard the boat's engines and managed to peer through a crack in the wall planking and glimpsed a shadow in the wheelhouse as the *Maria Blanco* moved out to sea."

"And Tulley and company?"

"He was crippled. They were in the Maze together with Finbar when the legend of the *Maria Blanco* and its cargo was born." Dillon shrugged. "The RUC looked at every possibility, turned the criminal underworld in Ulster inside out, but never got a hint, and that's the way it is to this day."

"I bet it is. So what happened to Eli?"

"Well, as he'd been a victim, life went on, Finbar serving his time in the Maze for another year, obsessed with the knowledge of what had happened. I think it was the fact of it all having taken place in Drumore and, because of that, having it somehow slip through his fingers that got to him."

Hannah nodded. "I can see that." She was frowning. "Sean, I hope you don't mind my saying that you seem incredibly knowledgeable about the whole business. Did you by chance have anything to do with it?"

"Thank God I didn't," he said cheerfully. "Booked out of Belfast on the afternoon plane to London Heathrow, which I left the following morning on the ten-thirty flight to Algiers."

"You wouldn't lie to me?" she said.

"Of course not. You can't be in two places at the same time. So let's leave the mystery of the *Maria Blanco* to continue to torment Finbar."

"That's all very well, cousin," she replied. "But I think it will continue to torment a lot of people, including me. Twenty-five million in bullion, how much will that be now?"

"I wouldn't think about that; it will ruin the rest of your day."

Dillon laughed and turned into the safe house at Holland Park to find Ferguson's Daimler parked there, and as he and Hannah got out of the Mini, Ferguson, Cazalet, and Blake emerged from the main entrance.

Ferguson said, "Everything go all right at the funeral?"

"Not really," Dillon said. "The father turned up, drunk as usual, and distinctly not wanted."

"Always bad news, Finbar," Ferguson said. "But we've been having a further development here. The Master's on the phone again.

Roper will fill you in. Henry Frankel's returned to Downing Street, and we're off to join him and the Prime Minister."

"Is there anything I can do?" Dillon asked.

"Yes, actually. Since you're an old IRA hand, the Prime Minister may value your opinion on al-Qaeda and ISIS and the possibility of them hitting the streets of London. If you can spare us the time, that is?"

Dillon, at his most Irish, said, "God save you, General, for giving me the opportunity to serve."

"Get in, damn you," Ferguson ordered, which Dillon did.

Ferguson turned, a smile on his face. "Impossible man, but what can one do? You'd better go and report to Major Roper, Hannah."

He climbed in beside Doyle, the Daimler moved away, and Hannah turned and went in.

ROPER, SMOKING A CIGARETTE, a glass of whiskey in his hand, leaned back in his wheelchair, Sara sitting beside him enjoying a coffee.

"Where's Dillon?" he asked.

"The general decided he should accompany them to Downing Street and that Sean might be useful because of his IRA experience."

"Well, Dillon could certainly write the book on that."

Hannah jumped to Dillon's defense. "He had reason enough. His father died in a firefight in Belfast, so he was fighting a just cause."

"So was I, defusing bombs all over Belfast, the kind that murdered your parents and crippled you."

"I thought he was your friend." Hannah was angry, face flushed.

"But he is," Roper said. "Also an enigma. Fought the revolution worldwide, found it just as easy to work for the Israelis as he did the PLO. Learned Arabic when the IRA sent him to one of the Gaddafi training camps and discovered he had a gift for languages, and now he speaks several."

She looked bewildered. "I didn't know all of that."

"And you probably don't know this," Roper said. "His attempt to blow up the Prime Minister and the War Cabinet almost succeeded. That was during the Gulf War."

Hannah took a deep breath. "Damn him, he even plays the best barroom piano I ever heard."

"A lively lad."

They were on their way in to lunch, but they got no farther than the door when an alert call sounded. "Hang on," Roper said. "Ferguson wants a word."

Ferguson's face came on the screen from his office on the third floor of the ministry. Hannah could see paneled walls, a picture or two, and a mahogany desk that somehow suited Ferguson's personality. Henry Frankel and Dillon sat on either side of him.

Frankel said, "Just to let you know that President Cazalet has made it clear he intends to honor his speaking commitment, so we'll need to keep the security high. He's at Downing Street now with Blake Johnson, and I'll be joining them soon."

Sara said, "I imagine the White House will be annoyed that he's not returning to the States."

"Perhaps," Ferguson told her. "But these are troubled times, and good friends need to stand together."

"So what do we need to do? It's like we're going to war."

Dillon cut in. "Someone once said that in war all a soldier knows is his own small part of the front. Al-Qaeda may be all over the world, but this is our part of the front. We've disposed of two Masters already, and now we have a third. Our battle is to give him what we gave them."

"Well said, Sean," Ferguson said.

"There you go," Dillon said. "Calling me Sean again."

"On your way, you rogue," Ferguson told him. "And don't forget to check underneath your car for bombs."

"As if I would," Dillon said, and the screen faded to black.

"ANY QUESTIONS?" Roper asked Sara, but it was Hannah who replied.

"If we're going to war, who exactly are we going to war with?"

"You've got your studies," Sara told her. "Nobody's suggesting you should get involved in this."

"But I live with you," Hannah said. "For four years. That was the deal. I think I managed to prove myself last year when the going got tough."

"You have a point," Roper said. "And I know you also break the law by carrying a gun in your pocket. But your primary responsibility is the Royal College of Music, and don't you forget it."

"I won't," Hannah said. "But to take care, I need to know who the enemy is."

"All right," Roper said. "Besides the new Master, our own small part of the front, as Sean put it, has to do with the Muslim Brotherhood and the rascals at the Pound Street mosque. They had a go at us when Imam Hamid Bey was in charge there. His death was none of our doing—a car crash—but a new man has just moved in there. His name is Yousef Shah, an Oxford graduate and an unknown quantity. We're going to be keeping a very close eye on him."

"If I meet him, I'll remember to give him Sean's favorite greeting," Hannah said. "God bless all here."

Roper laughed, and said to Sara, "I think she'll do just fine. But speaking of security, if we're a target, then so are those close to us, probably. I think it's time you checked in with your grandfather, Sara."

SHE DID, but it was Sadie Cohen, the housekeeper, who answered the phone. "So you've finally remembered where you live."

"We've been really busy, love," Sara told her. "Things aren't looking too good at the moment. General Ferguson was wondering whether you and Grandad would care to move in with us for a while just in case anyone might show an unhealthy interest."

"You could be offering the Dorchester, but it wouldn't do you any good. He's on his way to Leeds. Some important person has taken ill, tickets sold out, could Professor Rabbi Nathan Gideon step in. He said he'd call you."

"Well, he didn't."

"He has a lot on his plate."

"I'm sure, but never mind. We can't leave you alone. It won't do, not the way things are at the moment."

"So you and Hannah won't be here tonight?" Sadie asked.

"Well, that is the general idea."

"Leaving the house with no one in it? What nonsense; I haven't the slightest intention of doing that. Now you take care of yourself, and we'll see you when we can," and she cut off.

Sara said to Roper and Hannah, "I can't leave it like that. I must go and try to make her see sense," and she made for the door.

Roper called, "Just watch your back."

Hannah took the silenced Colt .25 from her pocket. "I'll take care of that department."

"Yes, but who's going to watch your back," Roper said. "You're getting to be worse than Sara. Tell her to use the Land Rover and take care."

Which sent Hannah running out of the door smiling.

THE LATE AFTERNOON RAIN came with a sudden rush at High-field Court that sent Sadie Cohen running upstairs to see that no windows were open. She checked all the bedrooms, finishing with Hannah's, where she found one open a little.

"Naughty girl," she muttered. "Typical."

Not that she meant it, for she had come to realize for some time now that Hannah was the daughter she'd never had. Hannah, who'd lost her mother and father to the car bomb in Northern Ireland that had killed them and crippled her, returned her affection completely. The fact that she was Catholic and Sadie Jewish was irrelevant.

Sadie slammed the window down, peering out because this was her favorite view, high up on the fourth floor of the house, the American Embassy in Grosvenor Square no more than a couple of hundred yards away.

It never failed to please, and she looked down at the garden, which was at its best, flowers in season, poplar trees swaying, but then she frowned at a flash of yellow down there. A man in an oilskin jacket stepped out of the rhododendron bushes, stood there in the rain, then stepped back into cover.

Sadie went downstairs, entered the kitchen, opened a large wooden drawer, and took out a sawed-off shotgun and a packet of cartridges. She loaded the weapon quickly, then went out in the hall, approached the front door cautiously, and waited, the shadow of a man outside.

Her Codex sounded, and as she pulled it out one-handed to answer, the shadow vanished from view.

"Sadie Cohen," she said.

"Hi, love," Hannah replied. "Sara and I are on our way. Should be with you in fifteen minutes."

"You'll be welcome," Sadie told her. "Because we appear to have a guest in the garden. Could be others, too."

"Remain inside," Hannah told her. "Intruder," she said to Sara, and called Roper. "Where's Dillon?"

"When he turned up and found you gone, he said he'd join you," Roper told her. "I'll check and tell him to put his foot down."

"Dillon's on his way," she told Sara, who said, "That's a comfort. I bet it's the Brotherhood. They've tried before, three or four pretending to be seeing to waterworks or drains or something like that."

Hannah produced her Colt .25 and checked it. "Well, the bastards can bring it on as far as I'm concerned."

"I couldn't agree more, love." Sara was smiling. "Isn't it great to be a woman?"

"Absolutely," Hannah told her.

"So as the great Bette Davis said, 'Fasten your seat belts, it's going to be a bumpy night,'" and Sara put her foot down hard as they roared away.

SADIE TURNED OFF the hall light, but as the darkness had increased considerably and very quickly, she switched on the garden lights. The conservatory was in darkness, and she stood there beside the Schiedmayer concert grand in the study, waiting and watching.

There was some sort of movement out there. She waited, then switched on the conservatory lights, illuminating two men in yellow oilskin uniforms peering in the window.

They backed away hurriedly into the darkness, and Sadie was filled with fury, turned the key, and flung open the door.

"Who the hell are you?" she called. "Get out of this house." She went down the terrace steps, cocking the sawed-off. "I'll shoot without hesitation," which she did, firing one barrel into the night sky.

One of the men jumped out of the thicket behind her, grabbing at her wrist, forcing the sawed-off up, and tearing it from Sadie's grip. A second came to his aid, trying to control her as she kicked, and two more men in yellow oilskins ran in through the open gates to help them.

The Land Rover arrived just after that, swerving in, Sara braking so hard that she sprayed gravel over everyone. She slid from the driver's side, drawing her Colt, and Hannah joined her on the other side, weapon in hand.

"All right," Sara cried. "That's enough."

The one who had picked up the sawed-off said, "I don't think so, Captain Gideon. If you and the girl don't put down your weapons, I will blow your housekeeper's head off."

On the instant, Hannah shot off the lower half of his left ear.

He cried out, blood spurting, and dropped the shotgun, and Dillon seemed to slide in at the wheel of the Mini at the same time, spraying another wave of gravel.

"My goodness, but you girls have been having fun," he said, as he got out.

"What kept you, cousin?" Hannah demanded.

One of the men reached down to grab the shotgun, and Dillon kicked him in the face. The man fell over, and the others cried out in protest.

Dillon said, "Line up and shut up, or someone else could lose half an ear." He turned to Hannah. "There you go, stealing my favorite party trick."

"It runs in the family," she told him. "The way they treated Sadie, they got what they deserved."

"On that point, I wouldn't argue with you." Dillon turned to the lineup. "Who's going to tell me who sent you, although I don't expect to be surprised."

They stared at him stony faced, and no one said a word except Dillon, who told them exactly what he thought of them in harsh but fluent Arabic. They stared at him in astonishment, and he returned to English.

"So let's try again, and I would suggest that one half ear a night is enough."

The man with the ear bleeding into the handkerchief he held against it said, "Imam Yousef Shah, although I suspect you know that."

"As it happens, I do, so what would your name be?"

"Hamid Abed."

"Well, keep better company is my advice. Take them to their van, Hannah. Send them on their way, and you have my permission to shoot anybody who makes a false move. Keep an eye on her, Sara, while I help Sadie indoors. She's shaking."

Hannah shepherded them outside to their yellow van and waited for them to scramble in. Hamid still held the handkerchief to his ear as he turned to her.

"You use that gun like a soldier. Who taught you to do that, memsahib?"

"The Provisional IRA," she told him.

"Allah preserve me." He was shocked. "And the leg? You are crippled?"

"Car bomb," she said. "When it comes down to it, you lot are just beginners. Off you go, Hamid Abed, and try to behave yourself in the future."

The van drove away; Hannah turned and walked back to Sara, who said, "What was that all about?"

"He wanted to know where I learned to shoot."

"And you told him the IRA?"

"Which shocked the hell out of him. He called me memsahib; I thought that was Indian?"

"So it is, and I'm surprised," Sara told her, as they entered the house. "Their attitude toward women is different from ours, so when they meet someone like you and me, they don't know how to handle us."

"They'll have to learn," Hannah said, and followed Sara in, pausing at the umbrella stand, helping herself to one of the several walking sticks.

"Leg bad tonight?" Sara asked.

"You could say that." Hannah grinned. "One cripple to another. You, too?"

"Yes, it's an absolute bastard. The fruits of war."

"Ah, for that I can only offer you this." Hannah handed her a walking stick. "On the other hand, for the hero of Abusan, a Military Cross goes with it."

Sara gave her a hug and a kiss on the cheek. "Bless you, Hannah, for being you. I'm beginning to wonder how I ever got by without you. Let's go and see what Sean's up to."

The door of the rabbi's study stood open; Sadie had lit a fire in the magnificent Georgian grate. Dillon sat at one side, speaking to Roper, and he paused.

"Sadie went off to the kitchen to make tea and coffee. I think she's upset," he said.

Hannah had turned and was already on her way. Sara said, "We'll handle it," and hurried after her.

Sadie was sitting in a high kitchen chair sobbing, Hannah's arm around her. "It's okay," Hannah told her. "I'm here now, and so is Sara."

"I'm so sorry," Sadie said. "I got the shotgun to chase them away, even fired a round into the sky, but it didn't stop them. I was terrified, thinking they might be ISIS and knowing what terrible things they've done."

"Well, Sara and I soon put them in their place," Hannah said. "And as we know exactly who was responsible for the attack, we'll be able to do something about it."

Sadie brightened at that. "True enough." She took a deep breath. "Go and see Sean in the study, and I'll follow you with a trolley."

Dillon was putting logs on the fire when they joined him. "How is she?" he asked.

"Nerves shot," Sara told him. "Thank God we were able to get to her in time."

"Too true, but I won't allow it to happen again. I've just made that clear to Roper."

"And what did he say?"

"Ferguson is still at Downing Street but sends his best. He'll be with us soon, so let's have a drink or sit down and have a cup of tea Irish-style and relax."

At that moment, Sadie wheeled in the trolley, obviously trying to be brave. "Tea up. I've managed salad sandwiches and scones. Oh, I forgot to say 'God bless all here.' Is that right, Sean?"

"Sadie, you're the wonder of the world."

THE DAIMLER WAS ON THE ROAD, Sergeant Doyle at the wheel and Ferguson, Cazalet, and Blake Johnson in deep discussion, when Ferguson's Codex rang. He answered, his smile changing to a frown.

"Roper," he said. "Let me put it on speaker. He has rather dramatic news for us."

Roper then gave them a detailed account of the events at Highfield Court.

"The bastards," Blake said. "Those Brotherhood guys."

"I agree," Cazalet told him. "But no match for a woman who is one of the few to be awarded a Military Cross in the British Army."

Charles Ferguson chuckled. "Or an even younger one raised all her life in a household that was a hotbed of the Provisional IRA."

"What do you want to do?" Roper demanded.

"We'll call round to see them," Ferguson said. "First—get me Imam Yousef Shah on the line."

There was a pause, and then, "Shah here."

"Charles Ferguson. I shouldn't think any of the theology departments at Oxford would be too proud of you tonight, you and your Brotherhood."

"I have no idea what you're talking about. The Muslim Brotherhood has no connection with this mosque. You must look elsewhere for whatever disturbs you."

"A nice turn of phrase, Imam, but I was actually considering what might be the best way of disturbing you."

"I appreciate the warning," the imam told him. "But take care—

my appointment in Samarra could be yours. May Allah go with you."

He went off, and Roper said, "Shakespeare would have loved him."

"Good point. But we'll be off to Highfield Court. Oh, and do a favor for me. Tell Sadie we're coming and make it clear we aren't expecting dinner or anything. She takes her hospitality very seriously, you know."

"What a hypocrite you are, Charles," Roper said.

"A fault I readily admit," Ferguson told him. "But so useful in this game we play, Giles."

IT WAS TWO O'CLOCK in the afternoon in Washington when Alice Quarmby, summoned by the President, arrived at the Oval Office.

"Do you have the slightest idea what it's about?" she asked the secretary.

"Afraid not. It might be a minute, though. Colonel Hunter's been in there for forty minutes."

"Then it's me for the powder room, Elsie. Be right back."

IN THE OVAL OFFICE, the President was sitting behind his desk, Hunter standing as he talked.

"The use of private military companies in the recent ISIS attacks in Mali certainly proves their worth."

"As glorified security men, protecting business or preventing the theft of Muslim treasures, yes, I'll grant you that. Meanwhile, the

French flew a hit force of marines in a fleet of aircraft all the way from Paris by night and caught ISIS with its pants down. Rather more impressive, I'd say."

There was little Hunter could say to that, but as he turned to leave, the President said, "Actually, there's something you could do for me, Colonel. You're heading for London now, right?"

"Yes, sir."

"Now do me a favor and help Blake watch out for Cazalet over there. Don't let them know, just be my extra eyes and ears. He's putting himself in harm's way. Too public, Colonel. I want him back here where we can protect him. The damn fool seems to court death every time he speaks in public."

"Yes, I can see what you mean, Mr. President. I'll take care of it."

"Excellent. You may need some extra authority, so I've made you a presidential aide with a pass to prove it. Don't forget to call on the ambassador. He'll be expecting you but won't know why. Elsie has an envelope for you on the way out, and I'll phone you from time to time. Remember: This must stay secret, even from the ambassador. Philip Hardy is a good man but has a mind of his own."

"Of course, Mr. President, I understand perfectly now."

Alice, standing in for Elsie for a few moments in the outer office, had heard everything as Hunter stood with the door ajar. She ducked into the filing cupboard a second before Hunter emerged from the Oval Office and Elsie entered.

"I believe you have an envelope for me?"

"Yes, I do, Colonel," Elsie said, and passed it to him.

He hurried through the maze of corridors that was the White House, opening the letter and taking out the card and marveling at the gold edges with OFFICE OF THE PRESIDENT OF THE UNITED STATES and COLONEL SAMUEL HUNTER, AIDE TO THE PRESIDENT underneath in bold black print.

When he got to the car and climbed in the Mercedes, he could hardly breathe.

Dolan said, "Are you okay, Colonel?"

"Never been better." Hunter passed the card. "Read that."

Dolan did, then said, "But what does it mean, sir?"

"Our ticket to prosperity."

ONCE HUNTER WAS out of the way, Alice was called into the Oval Office, where she found an angry President behind the desk.

"There you are, Alice. Any word from Blake, any at all?"

"I'm afraid not, Mr. President."

"Damn his eyes. I'm worried, Alice, for both of them. These ISIS bastards are capable of anything."

"So it would seem, Mr. President."

"All right, but if you hear anything—anything at all—get right back to me immediately."

"Yes, Mr. President." She returned to her desk, but she knew what she had to do. She had known Blake too long, and it was not, after all, being a traitor to her country, so she called him on his Codex, unaware that he was driving to Highfield Court with Cazalet and Ferguson.

"Alice," he said. "What's cooking at the White House?"

"I had a call from the Oval Office earlier. We need to talk, Blake."

He switched to speaker, gesturing to Cazalet and Ferguson. "Why, Alice, what happened?"

"The President sent for me," she said. "And he was really concerned that he hadn't heard from you. But there's something else. He had a visitor. I was in the outer office and overheard some of his private conversation with Colonel Samuel Hunter, that CIA guy who's interested in private military companies and this Havoc outfit."

Charles Ferguson tapped Tony Doyle on the shoulder. "Nice quiet spot, Sergeant, pull over."

Doyle did. Ferguson nodded to Cazalet and handed him the phone. "Jake here, Alice, not trying to trick you or anything. General Ferguson and I just happened to be sharing a car with Blake. Do you trust me?"

"Of course I do, Mr. President."

"Then tell us exactly what you heard and everything you know about this Colonel Hunter."

She did as she was told, and when she was finished, Cazalet said, "Brilliant. Try not to feel too uncomfortable about telling us. You've served your country, believe me."

Blake took the phone. "Take care, love. You never did a more important thing."

"Carry on, Sergeant." Ferguson sat back as they moved away. "I disliked Hunter straightaway. Now I know why."

"We'll have to watch our backs with him," Cazalet said. "And I'd say that Havoc project of his is worth checking on."

"Oh, it shall be, old boy," Ferguson said. "Just leave it to me. I have the perfect man in mind," and he took out his Codex again.

―――――

DANIEL HOLLEY WAS POUNDING alongside the Seine, which was his habit when in Paris. He had a superb furnished barge, which he was running toward now, Notre Dame on the far side of it, hauntingly beautiful in the floodlight. His Codex sounded, and he paused to answer.

"Good evening, Daniel. It's Charles Ferguson intruding into your life again."

"Well, if that means doing something about ISIS and the bloody mess they've made of this city, I'm your man."

"Not directly, but there's something that might be related. Can you come see me?"

"I'll be with you tomorrow."

IN LONDON, the four men who had attacked Highfield Court stood before Imam Yousef Shah in his office at the Pound Street mosque. No one had helped Hamid Abed, and the handkerchief he held to his ear was soaked with blood. The man who stood behind them was enormous, addressed by the imam as Omar. A leather pouch filled with lead shot swung in his right hand, and he monotonously slapped it into the palm of his left.

"So, Hamid Abed," the imam said. "You let your comrades down by betraying me."

"Not so, Imam. It seemed obvious that the target knew who was behind the attack. This warfare must have been happening between Captain Gideon, her friends, and the mosque for some time."

"Which is none of your business, as I will show these fools here, that they may demonstrate to others the punishment that awaits all traitors."

He nodded to Omar, who struck Hamid violently with the leather pouch, sending him crashing to the floor unconscious.

Omar kicked him several times as the others watched, terrified. He said, "What do you want me to do with him, Imam?"

"Beat him thoroughly, Omar, then throw him in the river. The Thames is tidal, and few bodies that go in appear again. It'll be a warning from Allah that all wrongdoers must be punished if they transgress. Take these other wretches with you so they will learn, and speak to me when you are finished, for there is no more to be done."

UNCONSCIOUS IN THE POURING RAIN on an old wharf in Battersea, Hamid barely felt the pain of the blows while the others watched in horror as Omar gave him a last kick.

"So, a final lesson for all of you," and he heaved Hamid up and tossed him into the Thames. "There he goes, food for the fishes."

THE RIVER CHURNED, the sky echoing the thunderclap above that brought Hamid Abed back from the dead, a vivid flash of lightning illuminating the river. Ships were anchored on each side, old warehouses rearing into the night as he raced by, for there was a five-knot tidal current taking him out to sea fast.

It was the Thames that was saving him now, its icy grip freezing the pain from the terrible beating, leaving him completely numb, but he was conscious when the current took him toward one side of the river and deposited him on a set of ancient steps.

In great pain, he hauled himself up to a dim light that was bracketed to the decaying walls of an old warehouse above a sign that read ST MARY'S STAIRS. For a moment, he was dumbfounded, but then he laughed helplessly. Saved by the Mother of Christ, but that was all right because she was in the Koran, too.

What it all meant, he did not know, except that, leaning against the wall under the sign, he realized two things. He was seriously injured, and if he fell into the hands of the Brotherhood again, he was a dead man. On the other hand, he was assumed to be dead already, but there was no way he would get help from his own people. Too afraid of ISIS or the Brotherhood.

He stood there, coughing blood in the rain and looked up at the sign. St. Mary had saved him once before in spite of his being a Muslim. Maybe she could do it again? His foot kicked a wooden pole on the floor, perhaps from a brush. A staff to walk with up the alley toward the main road, and so he started, a hand braced against the wall to help him.

THE MOMENT THE DAIMLER drew up in the drive of Highfield Court, Hannah had the front door open, and Ferguson and the others rushed inside out of the rain, where a profound smell from the kitchen indicated that Sadie had been busy.

She came down the corridor to greet them wearing a kitchen smock, wiping her hands on a towel.

"There you are," she said. "I thought we'd lost you."

Ferguson kissed her on the cheeks. "Would we do that to you, Sadie? I can't believe you've been cooking after what you've been through."

"Yes, you can, you old rogue, but it's nothing special, considering the number at the feast. You'll just have to put up with what a Jewish lady manages to come up with when she tries spaghetti Bolognese."

"Ecstasy, I'm sure," he said.

"Well, a glass of champagne first would be nice."

She vanished toward the kitchen, and Sara said, "We'll go in the study and be comfortable. I'll light the fire."

"Where's Hannah?" Blake said.

"Slaving in the kitchen, helping Sadie like a decent Irish girl should. Ah, here's the footman, come to serve the champagne," and Dillon entered pushing the drinks trolley.

THE MEAL WAS as excellent as everyone had expected, and afterward, over coffee and tea, the situation was discussed.

"The problem is the nighttime," Cazalet said. "I think Blake and I should come up from the Dorchester and move in for the night. Would that suit?"

"That would be fantastic," Sara said.

"Then can we say that's a given?" Cazalet asked Ferguson.

"Very generous of you, Mr. President. I'm sure Sadie will be delighted."

"With what?" she said, walking in with a fresh pot of coffee.

"You're going to have lodgers, my dear," Ferguson told her, and the front doorbell started to ring.

"Now who in the hell can that be?" Dillon said, and he was out of the study in a moment, a Colt .25 ready as he approached the door, followed by Hannah, pulling out her own gun and running to cover him.

She was like a different person, calm and assured, her weapon ready in both hands as he reached for the key to open the door.

She said, "Take care now, Sean, and don't be dying on me. I've lost enough from my family."

"Yes, well, I'm cleverer than that, girl." He pulled the flap of the letterbox open.

"Who's there?"

The voice was broken, strange, and very slow when it said, "My name is Hamid Abed, and I seek the memsahib that she may show me mercy."

"Holy Mother," Hannah said. "That's the man I shot! But what would he be doing here?"

"We'll soon see." Dillon, gun in hand, opened the door, and Sadie screamed.

The light from the hall showed the terrible beating Abed had taken, blood all over him, and Hannah pushed Dillon to one side and kneeled.

"Who did this to you?"

"The imam at Pound Street. He had me whipped and broken, thrown in the Thames by Omar Bey, the man they call the Beast."

"Forget him now, you are safe with me, but why call me memsahib?"

"I was in the Pakistan Army, like my father before me, but my grandfather and his father were in the Indian Army under the Raj, memsahib." He laughed. "I was thrown into the Thames to die, and a miracle took me to St. Mary's Stairs. Mary, the Mother of Jesus, is in the Koran. There was nowhere else to go, so I came here. It was a long walk in the rain."

"I understand, and there's no need to worry." She glanced at Ferguson. "General?"

"I've already called Maggie Duncan at Rosedene, my dear. An ambulance is on the way."

MAGGIE DUNCAN HAD BEEN MATRON for many years at Rosedene, a very special medical establishment that offered only the best of treatment to those damaged in their service to Charles Ferguson's organization. Her boss was Professor Charles Bellamy, considered by many to be the finest general surgeon in London.

Hannah had accompanied Hamid in the ambulance, and after a discussion of what had happened with the others, Dillon and Sara followed in the Mini.

"It doesn't look good, Sean," Sara said.

"About as bad as it could, dear girl." His voice was angry and the harsh Ulster accent plain. "Omar the Beast is it, the imam's hit man. I'd like to meet that one."

He swerved slightly, and she said, "Easy, Sean, your time will come, God willing, or mine."

He glanced at her, frowning, then turned the Mini into the entrance to Rosedene and parked.

MAGGIE DUNCAN MET THEM as she came out of her office in reception. She was dressed for the operating theater.

"That bad is it, Maggie?" Sara asked.

"That man's condition is appalling, multiple fractures, damage to many organs, a ruptured kidney. Frankly, I don't even know how he made it to you."

"He had a pole of sorts, which I suppose he found somewhere on St. Mary's Stairs, and he used it to help him walk. All very biblical, Maggie."

"Over the years, Sean, I've often put this question to you—when is it all going to end?"

"You're a good and honest Christian, Maggie. Book of Revelation. Behold a Pale Horse, his rider was called Death, and Hell followed close behind."

"The Apocalypse?" she said. "You surely can't be meaning that?"

"And why not, when people are meeting a bad end in every bloody country on earth?"

Hannah appeared suddenly, crashing through the swinging doors that led to the medical units. "He needs you, Matron, as quickly as possible."

Maggie pushed straight through the door, and Hannah turned to Dillon and Sara, and slumped down beside them. "He hasn't got a hope in hell."

Sara said, "Miracles can happen, love. Bellamy is an extraordinary surgeon."

"I know he is, but I also know the smell of death well from my childhood in an IRA household, the boys turning up bleeding all over the place with the SAS on their tails and only the village doctor to do the best he could for anyone wounded."

The door opened, and Maggie, splashed with blood, said wearily, "He's going, Hannah. I'm so sorry."

Hannah was on her feet and darting past her. Dillon and Sara hesitated, and Maggie led the way to an operating theater at the far end of the corridor, where they were able to observe through a window. Hannah stood beside the bed, and Bellamy was there, his theater scrubs stained with blood. Maggie said, "It was one thing after another. The professor really fought for him, but . . . just a minute. What's happening?"

Very slowly, Hamid raised his right arm, which was swathed in bandages, and Hannah held his fingers, and his lips moved, and then his head lolled to one side as he died, the alarm calling in more staff, and Dillon and Sara turned and went back to reception.

"A bad one, Sean," she said, as they sat. "I saw plenty killed in Afghanistan, but some things you never get over."

"You could say that. If this Omar the Beast was standing in front of Hannah, she'd empty her gun in him."

Before Sara could reply, the entrance door swung open and Ferguson entered, face grim, followed by Tony Doyle.

"Has he gone?" he asked.

"I'm afraid so," Sara told him.

"I thought he might." He offered a folder to Dillon. "Roper looked up this Omar Bey for you. MI5 have him on file."

Dillon opened it, and Sara leaned over to look at the enormous animal that Omar Bey appeared to be. "My God," she said. "A monster."

"He's certainly murdered a number of fellow Muslims, but Scotland Yard got nowhere with those. There's a total unwillingness amongst the Muslim community to get involved," said Dillon.

"I can believe that," Ferguson said. "But we'll keep the file, Dillon. It may prove useful."

Hannah joined them, looking bleak. "So that bastard gets away with it?"

Dillon passed her the file. "I don't think so. That's what he looks like."

She glanced at the photo in the file, then closed it. "What happens now?"

"I've already alerted Mr. Teague and his disposal team," Ferguson told her. "They'll be here shortly."

At that moment, Teague walked in, a tall, distinguished-looking man in black overalls whom Hannah had met previously.

Her voice shook as she said, "So this is the best we can do for him, the ovens?"

"Most Muslims would expect cremation," Teague told her, "and I have a Muslim cleric to call on. All will be proper. Hamid Abed will not pass over alone."

Sara said, "Shall we go together, Hannah?"

Teague glanced at Ferguson, who nodded, and said to the women, "If that is your wish, then go now, there is always a certain urgency to this business."

Hannah turned to Dillon. "Sean?"

He shook his head. "I'll see you later."

Teague already had the door open, and they brushed past him and were gone, and he stepped out after them.

Ferguson shook his head. "I'll never understand women."

"But thank God for them," Dillon said. "I'll have to get moving. My place is at Holland Park tonight, I promised Roper."

"Then you'd better be off," Ferguson said.

Dillon went out fast; the Mini roared, the noise fading in a remarkably short time. He had left the Omar Bey file on the coffee table. Ferguson was slipping it in his briefcase when Tony Doyle peered through the door.

"Highfield Court, General?"

"Not needed, Sergeant. President Cazalet and Blake are staying the night. You can take me to Holland Park. I need to have a word with Professor Bellamy, so I'll call you when I need you."

ROPER HAD TRIED to contact Dillon for quite some time without success, so it was obvious that the Irishman had turned off his communication system and that meant he was up to no good.

Roper sat there, thinking about this. It was raining hard, drumming against the windows in the darkness outside.

"Damn you, Sean," he said softly. "Don't do this to me."

At almost the same moment, Dillon's voice came in loud and clear. "Have you been trying to get in touch?"

"Of course I have, a bad business, the whole thing."

"You could put it that way, but there's a certain element of farce to the whole affair. I mean, who is the enemy? The imam? He can't be touched. He's a cleric, and shooting him would cause a riot."

"Of course it would. You got the file I sent you?"

"Yes, and I must say MI5 have done an excellent job. Omar Bey rides around in a yellow van provided by the Brotherhood, lives in a tenement behind Rangoon Wharf, and eats late most nights at Patel's, a Pakistani restaurant at the other end of the wharf. He parks his van outside. I'm looking at it now."

"Waiting to put a bullet between his eyes?" Roper said. "That's crazy, Sean."

"Who said anything about a bullet? The rail at the edge of the wharf is old and wooden. I've opened his van with my keys, gained access to his steering and braking system, and locked the driver's door again."

"My God, but that's diabolical," Roper said.

"Well, let's hope it works, because he's just emerged from the restaurant and is hurrying through the rain to reach his van. Now he's getting the door open and heaving himself inside. Just listen."

Roper could hear the van's engine starting in the background as Dillon held up his Codex, but the heavy drumming of the rain reduced the sound so much that he couldn't tell what was happening until Dillon spoke again.

"Bloody marvelous. He swerved to the right, went straight through the railing, and nosed down forty feet into the Thames."

"Then get the hell out of there," Roper said. "Before you're seen."

"Giles, nobody's come running out of the restaurant because

they haven't heard a thing, and I'm already retreating through a maze of backstreets to where I parked the Mini a quarter of a mile away. I'll see you soon, old son."

Dillon held his arms up into the night, rain battering his face, then started to run.

AT HOLLAND PARK, Ferguson was troubled and restless. So much had happened, so many things to take into consideration. He slept with difficulty and was not in the best of spirits when he awakened and discovered it was nine-thirty, with heavy rain still beating against the window.

He felt old beyond his years, with a foul mouth and a splitting headache, but thank God for the swimming pool and the steam room, so he pulled on a tracksuit and slippers, and went downstairs.

It was unusually quiet, which surprised him, so he moved toward the computer room and found Maggie Hall looking anxious along with the chef and several members of the kitchen staff, all peering through the half-open front door and talking nervously among themselves.

"What on earth is going on?" Ferguson demanded.

"It's Major Roper, General," Maggie told him. "There was a special delivery, a very nice suitcase President Cazalet left here not long ago. Major Roper isn't happy."

"Then what in the hell are you and your staff hanging around here for?" Ferguson said. "Back to the kitchen, the lot of you."

Which they did, and he helped himself to the umbrella from the stand at the door, ventured outside, raised it, and hesitated at the spectacle before him. The safe house's Subaru was parked in the opening in the pouring rain, its tailgate raised, giving Giles Roper some sort of shelter as he leaned forward to examine the contents of the open suitcase inside the car. Staff Sergeant Tony Doyle stood beside him holding an umbrella to give him as much protection as possible, his own combat cape streaming with rain. Ferguson took a deep breath and went to join them.

"It would be an insult to ask what you're doing," he said.

"I'm certainly not wasting my time, General, but then I was warned."

"What's that supposed to mean?"

"Sergeant Doyle and I were enjoying a cup of tea when we heard a vehicle drive in and out of the courtyard. He investigated and returned with what he found, the suitcase. A few minutes later, the Master called. Sent his respects to President Cazalet and said I didn't have long."

"The bastard," Ferguson said. "It's not just talk, I presume?"

"I'm afraid not," Roper said. "As I advise you to make clear to whomever is driving through the gate now."

He carried on, and Ferguson hurried across to the Mini as Sara and Hannah got out. He spoke briefly to them, explaining the situation, and they started forward.

"Don't be stupid and get inside," Roper said. "If there's one thing in this life that I'm an expert on, it's bomb disposal. Thirty years of the Troubles in Ireland got two-thirds of the people in my business killed and put others like me into a wheelchair."

Hannah looked dreadful, but Sara took her arm. "We'll leave Major Roper to it. He's got enough to worry about."

Ferguson said, "What about the Howler, Giles?" The Howler was an experimental gadget Roper had acquired many years ago for bomb control.

"I've got it here, but nothing is a hundred percent, General," Roper told him. "It's got real power, but harnessing it takes patience and a lot of know-how. The man who created the Howler was a genius, no doubt about that. It does about eighty percent of what he intended, and that requires real effort and ability. You could argue it's better than nothing."

"Why couldn't he finish it?" Sara asked.

"Because I shot him dead," Roper said. "But if you don't mind, I really have to get on with it. It takes a lot of concentration."

THEY SAT IN the dining room drinking tea and coffee, the atmosphere grim, Maggie Hall hovering anxiously in the background. An hour later, Roper rolled in, Tony Doyle following behind.

Roper pushed the Howler across to Ferguson, who took a deep breath, and said, "All done?"

"Oh, yes. The Master is going to be so disappointed. A tricky business, mind you. I can't think of anyone else in the business who could have handled it."

Hannah said, "Why did you say that?"

He ignored her for a moment, and said to Maggie, "Irish whiskey in my tea, I think I've earned it, and bacon and eggs." She hurried away, and he turned to Hannah. "Where were we?"

"You know damn well where we were."

"Oh, that." He smiled, but in a way no one had ever smiled at her before, the eyes dark and empty. "An old story, my love, when the world was young and someone like me could believe he was invincible because he'd shot dead two IRA assassins who'd ambushed him and had a Military Cross for it."

"But I thought you received the George Cross," Sara said.

"I did. That was for dismantling the Portland Hotel bomb, which took me nine hours and even longer for the Ministry of Defence to honor me."

"Which still doesn't explain the Howler," Hannah put in.

"One of the cleaners at my billet, a nice Protestant girl named Jean Murray, told me that her brother, Kenny, was studying electronics at Queen's University and was working on a thing he called a Howler that would enable him to switch off any kind of electronic control system. The possibilities were obvious concerning bombs, and I asked to meet him."

"So what happened?" Sara demanded. "Do I smell some sort of scam here?"

"The Howler was real enough, but Jean and Kenny were IRA, and it was a kidnap plot, the purpose of which was to squeeze the juice out of me about the secrets of the British Army's bomb-disposal units."

There was silence, then Sara said, "Well, as you're still here, you obviously handled the situation."

"They were amateurs, really. Searched me, lifted my Browning, and missed out on the ankle holster with a Colt .25 loaded with hollow-point cartridges. Kenny was taunting me, a gun in his hand, when I shot him dead."

Hannah crossed herself, and when she spoke, it was obviously with some difficulty. "And Jean Murray?"

"I left her with her brother and returned to the unit."

Hannah was obviously experiencing difficulty with the whole business. "And did you ever see her again?"

"Oh, yes, the following morning, when I was leaving my billet to attend a staff conference at the Grand Central Hotel and found her waiting for me outside. I stopped to speak to her, and she showed me a black plastic control.

"She said, 'You wanted the Howler, so here it is,' and held it high for a moment. 'But your real present is in that shopping bag under your seat.'"

"God in heaven," Hannah said.

"So she blew herself up into heaven or hell, depending how you look at it," Roper said. "Crippled me pretty effectively and placed me in a wheelchair for the rest of my life."

There was a dead silence, broken only by Maggie pushing in the breakfast trolley. Roper looked down at the eggs and bacon.

"Having said all that, I suppose things could be worse," and he started to eat.

The others followed him as Maggie served them, subdued by what he had said. It was his Codex sounding that broke the ice. He switched it on and the Master spoke.

"Ah, you're still with us, Major Roper? You must be as good as everybody says you are!"

"That's quick, damn you," Roper said. "How on earth do you do it?"

"I've told you before. Our people are everywhere. That's why we will win and you will lose, my friend. It is inevitable."

"Why don't you go to hell, mister?" Hannah called.

"Master, Hannah, not mister, and as for hell, I have been there during my lifetime and it wasn't nice. Allah protect you."

He switched off. Roper said, "A considerable nuisance, that man. What are we going to do about it?"

"Nothing we can do until you find him for us, Giles," said Ferguson.

"Easier said than done, General. Trying to penetrate the al-Qaeda network is the same as trying to penetrate the highest levels of the CIA."

It was Hannah who broke in. "I thought you were Major Giles Roper, king of cyberspace, never been known to fail. Where'd he go?"

Sara almost choked on her cup of coffee, but Roper ignored her. He chuckled, and then the chuckle turned into a full laugh. "Thanks for the challenge, Hannah. I accept it gladly. I'll run him down if it's the last thing I do. And since I don't want it to be the last thing I do, I suppose I'd better get on with it."

He pressed a button, reversed his wheelchair, and went out. Tony Doyle said, "I'll see if he needs anything," and left.

Dillon walked in wearing a terry-cloth robe, his hair damp, face flushed. "Breakfast over?" he said.

"Good God, where have you been?" Ferguson demanded.

"I didn't go to bed until the early hours. I was busy making sure that the bastard Omar Bey came to a bad end in the Thames at the wheel of his van. I thought Roper would have told you."

"Well, he didn't," Ferguson said, and Sara interrupted. "You're sure, Sean?"

"Absolutely. No bullet between the eyes, General. He drove straight through the railings on Rangoon Wharf."

"With a little assistance from you."

"Of course."

"Bad cess to him and good riddance," Hannah said.

"Ah, the fierce one, my cousin," Dillon said to Ferguson. "But what would you have us do next?"

"I presume our American friends are still at your house," he said to Sara.

"Yes, they are," she said.

"Go and check on them. Should Johnson and Cazalet have to leave for any reason, I don't want Sadie to remain in the house alone. You must bring her here."

"She's stubborn enough to say no, General, and probably so will Grandpa when he gets back."

"Well, Dillon will never stand for that, but we'll cross that bridge when we come to it. Anyway, you go back and assess the situation."

Sara started out, and Hannah said, "What about me, General?"

"I don't know," Ferguson told her. "Aren't you supposed to be at the Royal College of Music practicing scales or something?"

"Very amusing, sir," she said. "But it happens to be the autumn holiday."

"Well, I suppose you could practice here. Perfectly good piano over there. Dillon plays it all the time." He turned to Dillon. "Don't you?"

"I do indeed, but not like she does."

"Oh, sort it out, Sean, I'm expected at Downing Street."

"There he goes, calling me Sean again when he needs something, Hannah."

"Complete nonsense," Ferguson said, and went out.

"So," Hannah said. "What do we do, cousin?"

"Oh, something will turn up," he said. "I'll go and make myself presentable."

KILBURN, THE IRISH QUARTER in London since late Victorian times, was famous for its pubs, and the Green Tinker was one of the best, its landlord, Pat Ryan, a popular man who in his youth had served in the IRA for several years but all that was behind him now. Trouble was the last thing he needed, particularly when it was called Finbar Magee, who had been at the height of drunken rage the previous night, cursing his sons to hell at the bar, challenging other customers to fight with him. It had taken four members of staff to handcuff him and put him in a back room to sleep it off.

Head barman Jack Kelly had looked in to ascertain Finbar's situation and returned to find Ryan drinking tea at the bar and reading the *Times*. He glanced up.

"How is he?"

"Terrible. You should have got the police this time. It can't go on."

"I couldn't do that to Tad Magee's father."

"Who was mouthing Tad off terribly last night, cursing him and his brother, Larry, making serious threats. You and the Magee brothers go back a long way, Pat. Together in the IRA in your youth."

"True enough, though not to be mentioned."

"So give Tad a call and get something done once and for all."

Ryan said, "I suppose you're right. Pour me a large Bushmills Irish Whiskey, and maybe another, and I'll give it a go."

IN NEED OF a change of clothes, Dillon was being driven to his cottage, Hannah at the wheel of the Mini, when Tad contacted him on his Codex.

"Sean, are you doing anything?"

Dillon switched over to speaker. "Nothing special."

"I need a favor. I know you can fly jets, but what about a twenty-five-year-old Chieftain in excellent condition?"

"I know it well," Dillon told him. "A real airplane."

"So you could fly one?"

"Tad, I can fly a Boeing if I have to. What's the story?"

"I have a Chieftain, beautiful specimen, piston engines, operating out of a small flying club called Barking in Kent. Unfortunately, the pilot I normally use is out of the country, and I need a flight to another small airfield called Dunkelly in County Down."

"Would this be for an illegal purpose?" Dillon asked.

"Only if we throw my father out of the plane when we are over the Irish Sea. I'm kicking him out of London, and serve the bastard right. When an Irish pub in Kilburn can't put up with his drunken ways, it's time to go. Can you help?"

"Of course I can."

"Then meet me at the Green Tinker in Kilburn."

"When would you like me?"

"As soon as possible," Tad told him. "Is that okay?"

"Not as long as you don't mind Hannah being with me. She's with me now."

"That's all right by me."

"We'll join you at the Tinker soon."

"When would that be? I want him out of London before tonight."

"Then how about this? If you can get him to this Barking place, we'll meet you."

"Are you sure you'll find it?" Tad asked.

"That's what sat navs are for," Dillon told him. "We'll see you there."

He switched off and turned to Hannah. "Any objections to a flying visit to County Down?"

"Not that I can think of."

"Excellent, then punch in Barking airfield and away we go."

THEY STOPPED AT a village pub for soup and sandwiches, and carried on to Barking, finding it little more than a hamlet. The tiny airport, as with most such places outside London, was a relic of the Second World War, with a single runway, an aging flight-control office, and a couple of shabby hangars. There were a couple of dozen aircraft parked, mainly single-engine, the rather splendid twin-engine Chieftain to one side.

Dillon saw a Land Rover with Tad beside it talking to Pat Ryan and Jack Kelly from the Green Tinker and Finbar standing to one side looking dangerous.

He got out of the Mini and approached them. "God bless all here."

"Good to see you, Sean," Pat Ryan said.

"My cousin, Hannah Flynn," Dillon said, as she limped up, leaning on her stick.

It was apparent then that Finbar was handcuffed, and his face was twisted and ugly.

"Cripples now, is it, Dillon? But that's about all you're fit for."

Everyone was shocked, but before Dillon could make a proper response, Hannah had produced her Colt .25 from her right-hand pocket and jammed it into his mouth, splintering Finbar's teeth.

"This weapon is not only silent but also fires hollow-point cartridges. You'll be dead in ten seconds if I decide to pull the trigger, and I've done that several times, as Sean Dillon will tell you. I've also survived a car bomb that destroyed my parents. Walk softly around me, or I will shoot you. Nothing more's certain. Now get on the damn plane and behave yourself, or I'll open the door over the Irish Sea and shove you out myself."

Finbar's mouth gaped; he turned to the plane and heaved himself inside. To the others who were gazing at her, including Tad, Dillon said, "She plays great piano, too, but you know what they say about Provos."

"Once in, never out," Tad said, and the others nodded, including Dillon, as they watched Hannah mount the steps into the plane.

A man in brown overalls was approaching from the flight-control office. "Ready to go, Mr. Magee?"

"That's it, then." Tad shook hands with Kelly and Ryan. "We'll get off. I'll beg a lift from Sean and Hannah when we get back."

"Any time, Tad, you know that," Pat Ryan said.

"Is that it, then?" Dillon asked Tad, as they went to the plane. "No one's asked to see my pilot's license, no flight plan. What's going to happen when we land at Dunkelly?"

"Someone will check the engine and refuel for the trip." Tad smiled. "Sean, you did the same thing for me and Larry all those years ago when we got shot up by the RUC and you needed to get us to England."

"That was then, this is now," Dillon said.

"Some things never change," Tad told him. "So be grateful."

Tad led the way up the steps, found Hannah in a seat up front, Finbar farther back holding a cloth to his mouth. Dillon closed the airstair door and then went forward, brushing past Tad and Hannah and entering the cockpit with its double seats. Everything seemed to be in order, so he checked out the wind and weather with the man in the flight-control office.

"I'm ready to go. How does it look?"

"No wind to speak of, possibly heavy rain on your first approach. Tad said you are a very experienced pilot."

"You could say that."

"Then you'll see this aircraft has been fitted with a much more advanced navigation system than the original. I've inserted all the usual flight details necessary to reach Dunkelly. If you check the folder I've left you on the right-hand seat, you'll find it's simple."

"I'm feeling unnecessary already."

"I can see how you would, but in a way, a lot of pilots are these days."

"Whatever happened to romance and high adventure, but thanks anyway."

Opening the cockpit door a crack, Dillon bellowed, "Here we go, so belt up," then started to move toward the end of the runway. He turned, giving the engines full throttle, and rose above the trees as he eased back on the control stick, his spirits lifting as they always did.

ABOUT FORTY-FIVE MINUTES LATER, Hannah appeared with coffee, sitting in the left-hand seat as she offered it to him and opened a tin box of assorted biscuits. Dillon put the plane on automatic pilot, drank the coffee, and sampled the biscuits.

"They don't seem to have heard of tea," she said. "Sorry about that."

"Not your fault, and all that tea to look forward to in County Down."

"Spoken like a true Irishman."

"Who lived in London from the age of twelve and only returned home at nineteen when his father met a bad end in the Troubles. A funny old life when you look at it. How are Tad and his father getting on back there?"

"Well, Finbar's not speaking too well, which is my fault entirely."

"You've nothing to reproach yourself for. The things he said were unforgiveable."

"The point is, what are you going to do about it? Dump him on Eli?"

"I don't know. His responsibility for his wife's death is impossible to deny," Dillon said. "Only a quirk in the law allows him to walk free. He's an easy man to hate and always has been. Tad and Larry have no time at all for him now."

"Which still doesn't deal with my original question," Hannah said.

"I certainly don't have an answer, but perhaps Tad has one." Dillon nodded. "Some sort of solution. I'll go back and see how they're getting on."

He got up, and Hannah said, "What are you doing? You can't leave me. Who's going to fly the plane?"

Dillon pointed to the instrument panel. "See that button? It means the plane is on automatic pilot. Don't touch it. I'll be back."

——————

FINBAR'S FACE WAS a nightmare covered in dry blood. That he was in considerable pain was obvious, and he glared at Dillon, eyes full of hate as he nursed the glass of brandy and soda that Tad had given him.

Dillon said, "How are you?"

It took an effort, but Finbar could speak slowly. "How do you think, you stupid bastard? I'll make you pay, you and that little whore. She'll be begging for mercy by the time I've finished with her. As for you, Dillon, you'll never see the *Maria Blanco*, but I will, you see if I don't. What do you have to say to that?"

"That if you try to do harm to my cousin in any way, I'll find you wherever you are, and I'll put a bullet between your eyes."

"Just try it," Finbar said, shaking. "I'll show you."

"You'll show me nothing, you shite. You're a fantasy man, Finbar, and you can't see the difference between fantasy and reality anymore. Keep quiet from now on, or I might really open the door and throw you out."

Dillon moved away and sat opposite Tad, who had been reading a newspaper and now put it down.

"Enjoying yourself, Sean?"

"Not really, but it does raise the serious question of what to do with him. He's your father, that's a fact, but his offenses put him beyond hope. I doubt if a priest could help." Dillon shook his head. "He'll be off to London again when your back's turned."

"Not if I clip his wings for good."

Dillon frowned. "And you think you could do that? How?"

"I don't think this is the right place to discuss it. Later, perhaps."

Dillon nodded, a slight smile on his face. "I look forward to it."

He went back to the cockpit, and Hannah said, "Thank God you're back." He smiled as he sat, and she added, "You look pleased with yourself. What's happened?"

"Something or nothing." Dillon took control again. "Onward to Dunkelly and we shall see."

HEAVY RAIN ENLIVENED the situation considerably as they crossed the County Down coast, but the approach to Dunkelly, a small airfield very similar to Barking, gave Dillon no trouble at all as he landed and taxied to where Eli stood beside a Ford estate car talking to a middle-aged man who was wearing an old leather flight jacket.

They stood waiting as the Chieftain rolled to a halt. A few minutes later, the airstair door opened, and Dillon was first out, followed by Hannah.

Eli gripped Dillon's hand hard enough to make him wince. "By God, but it's good to see you, Sean."

"And you," Dillon said. "This is my cousin, Hannah Flynn. Try not to crush her hand."

The other man held his out. "Billy Spillane, Sean, I run this place. A bloody legend, you are, and no mistake."

Behind them, Finbar negotiated the steps gingerly, his handcuffed wrists out in front of him. Spillane said, "God save us, have you been in another car crash or something? You look dreadful."

"No thanks to that bitch standing there. All her fault."

"What a lying bastard you are," Dillon said, and turned to Spillane. "He got what he deserved."

"Absolutely," Tad Magee announced, as he came down the steps. "I'd have thought you'd have realized that after all these years." He turned to Eli and embraced him. "Good to see you."

Eli's smile was enormous. "And always good to see you, Tad. I got your letter."

"And you saw the lawyer, Michael Strachan?"

"In Belfast yesterday, as you instructed."

"Good man yourself, so let's take ourselves off to Drumore House and see if the old place is still standing. Stick him in the rear of the estate car, Eli, and we'll join you. I'll drive."

"Like hell you will," Finbar cried, and kicked out, but Eli squeezed him around the neck with his enormous hands, and a few seconds was enough for Finbar to end up in the rear seat gasping for breath.

"Excellent," Tad Magee said. "Let's get moving," so the others got in and he drove away.

HANNAH WAS ASTONISHED by Drumore House as she took a walk with Dillon under a borrowed umbrella after the others had gone in. The rain fell, there was the Irish Sea rolling out beyond the boathouse and the jetty below, waves flowing in.

Dillon smoked a cigarette with what was obviously conscious pleasure as he looked down at the tide coming in.

"You love all this, don't you?" Hannah said.

"Well, I am a County Down man, my love," Dillon said. "Born in Collyban farther along the coast from here, raised by my mother's brother, Mickeen Oge Flynn, when she passed on and my father went to Kilburn to make a future for us. He did finally and had me join him when I was twelve. Having said that, I didn't think much of Collyban, but I've always liked it here."

"It's not the decrepit old place I'd expected," she said. "Substantial building, eighteenth century from the look of it, and soundly built."

"You're quite right," he said. "The Magees have a history. They were squireens, a nice estate in the county and prosperous with it."

"I thought there might be something like that," Hannah said. "It's a special place, the cliffs on the other side wrapping around."

"And dangerous. Deep water closer than you would imagine, a jagged coastline, caves that can drown you if you don't get out in time. Although I was older than Tad and Larry, I enjoyed some great holidays with them."

"I bet you did." She smiled, and the rain increased into a solid downpour on the instant.

"Sorry about that," Dillon said. "I'm afraid that the rain around here is particularly Irish and has a habit of doing exactly what it wants. We'd better go in."

TAD AND THE OTHER TWO were seated at the huge old kitchen table. He was drinking tea at one end, a folder of paper in front of him. Eli was shoving logs into the ancient oven, and Finbar sat with handcuffed hands wrapped around a large glass of beer.

When Dillon and Hannah entered, Tad said, "There you are. We've been waiting for you."

Finbar said, "What the hell do those two have to do with anything?"

Tad ignored him. "Join us, Sean, and you, Hannah."

"What's going on here?" Finbar demanded.

"If you shut up, you'll find out," Tad told him, as Sean and Hannah sat down, Eli facing them, solemn as a judge, his craggy old face giving nothing away.

Tad opened the folder, took out several documents, and spread them on the table." Ten years ago, my mother approached Larry and me in great distress because life had become unbearable with your drunken ways. You were in constant debt, besieged by creditors, and she begged us to help in some way, which we did, paying over the odds through our company for the small house in Kilburn."

"Did that make you feel good or something?"

"Not particularly. Since you carried on in exactly the same way during the years that followed, we had to do the same thing for this place."

"You seem to have forgotten that in both cases you put your mother's name on the properties," Finbar said.

"And you expect to inherit them?"

"Of course I will. I was her husband."

There was a pause, and it was Hannah who spoke. "What a truly despicable creature you are."

"You shut your mouth, you bitch," he said. "I was her husband; I'm entitled."

"Don't worry," Tad said, and picked up one of the documents before him and held it up. "Have you read her will lately?"

Finbar glared at him. "I've told you, I was her husband, so I'm entitled to inherit."

"No, you're not," Tad told him. "She cut you out of her will a long time ago. The house in Kilburn was sold, so you've no decent base in London anymore. If you attempt to stay, you'll have a nasty accident one night, I promise you."

"You can't do that," Finbar said, but for the first time, there was an uncertainty in his voice.

"I suggest you stick to County Down," Tad said. "I don't know what you could do to make a living, but perhaps the new owner of Drumore House will find you something to do." He smiled across the table. "Would that be possible, Eli?"

"I'd say it would depend on how he behaves," Eli said.

"Eli?" Finbar croaked. "She left this estate to him?"

"Actually, she left it to me," Tad said. "But I'd rather keep it in the family, and Eli has agreed, so as soon as I've signed this deed of transfer that Sean and Hannah will witness, it goes to Mr. Strachan in Belfast to put through court."

He pushed the document along the table, rolling a pen with it, which Hannah caught, did her signing, and passed it to Dillon, who did the necessary, then pushed it back to Tad. Then he reached across the table and shook a massive hand.

"Good luck, old son."

Hannah joined in. "I'd say this wonderful place deserves you, Eli."

He smiled, and Tad pushed a key across to him. "The hand-cuffs if you want to release him now, but don't trust him, not even a little bit. He'll never forgive you for having what he sees as his. Promise you'll take what I say to you seriously."

Eli didn't say a word, simply went to Finbar and unlocked the handcuffs. Finbar stood there, rubbing his wrists. "Bastard," he said. "I'll fix you for this if it's the last thing I do."

Eli swung him around, giving him a kick in the backside that sent him staggering into the corridor, then returned to the others.

"That's the way," Dillon told him. "Show him who's boss and keep it up."

Eli sat down. "There is something I have to tell you about Fin-bar," he said to Tad. "Something serious." He turned to Dillon. "It involves you also, Sean. He was on a phone call, and the man on the other end described you as an IRA assassin working for General Charles Ferguson in London."

"Who the hell said that?" Dillon demanded.

"It was the day before the funeral; we were in here at breakfast when Finbar's mobile rang. He was in a bad mood and answered, turning his phone on speaker. It was a total stranger, who said he felt Finbar had been treated very unfairly in the matter of his wife's death and had put twenty thousand pounds in his bank account so that he could go to the funeral."

"That's incredible," Hannah said.

"No, it's not," Dillon told her. "There's more to it, isn't there, Eli? You heard everything, so tell us. This is important. More than you could know."

———

ELI HELD NOTHING BACK, telling them everything he could recall of the exchange between the Master and Finbar. Tad sat there taking it all in with extraordinary calm, turning to Dillon when the big man was finished.

"I suspected you were in intelligence of some sort, Sean, but this takes the biscuit, and you, too, Hannah? That's extraordinary."

"It just sort of happened," she said. "There are a lot of bad people around these days. But music is still of prime importance in my life."

"And so it should be," Tad said. "You have a remarkable gift for it."

"Which I won't let her forget," Dillon said. "You don't need to worry about that, but let's consider the present. You're involved with the wider situation, Tad, whether you like it or not. The people I work for out of Holland Park have been up against this Master business before and have enjoyed some success, but whoever the individual is, he's controlled by the al-Qaeda Grand Council. Their knowledge is amazing. They seem to know everything there is to know about everybody, so be prepared. It can be unnerving if the Master decides to call."

"What about ISIS?" Tad asked.

"Rubbish as far as AQ are concerned. There is only one God, and Osama is his Prophet, that is their creed above everything."

"All very complicated," Tad said, and at that moment, Dillon's phone rang.

When he was with Hannah, he'd got into the habit of leaving it on speaker, and the Master's voice echoed clearly. "There you are, Mr. Dillon. You have been active. Good morning to you, Hannah, and welcome, Mr. Magee. You have been busy, too, I must say, as opposed to your father, who I see is no longer center stage. I had promised to help him solve the mystery of the *Maria Blanco*, but not now. He can stew in his own juice."

"That's his problem," Tad said, "and I think you'll find me an entirely different kind of man to deal with—not that I plan to deal with you at all, you shite."

"Tsk, temper, temper. Who knows? In the world we inhabit today, anything is possible. We'll be in touch, Mr. Magee. Have a good flight."

Dillon switched off, and Tad said, "Incredible."

"Yes, quite a performance," Dillon said. "But you heard the man. Let's say a fond farewell to you, Eli, and get back to the airfield. Don't take any crap from you-know-who, and you've got my phone number so you can let me know if you hear from this guy again. We'll get off now, up into the wide blue yonder. Just give us a lift back to the airfield."

ON THE QUAI DES BRUMES, the Master opened the door leading out to the stern of the barge.

The awning stretched tightly, rain pattering down, and he stepped out, a cup of coffee in his right hand, and stood there savoring the damp smell that was a mixture of the rain and the River Seine. He loved it all completely and never tired of it.

But there was work to be done. What a stupid fool Finbar Magee had turned out to be, but his son was obviously an entirely different proposition. The gangster was still there, lurking under the surface, the hard man waiting to move in spite of the Savile Row suit and the Aston Martin. He would have to be careful there.

And Samuel Hunter. A dishonest man by nature in spite of the medals. He reviewed what he knew. On a previous visit to London, Hunter had discovered the old RAF base at Charnley in Essex, where Hans Weber operated half a dozen Dakotas. Weber traded mainly with West Africa under the rather grand name of Havoc International, shipping cargo, mostly to Ghana and Nigeria, and then carrying on to Mali to pick up any general cargo needed in France and England.

But Timbuktu had been invaded by rebels operating under the black flag of al-Qaeda, ignorant tribesmen unaware that Timbuktu had been a center for Islamic learning for hundreds of years. The books and manuscripts in its libraries were worth many, many millions, especially on the black market, although it was an affront to Islam to sell them.

Over champagne and an excellent meal at the Hilton in Park Lane, which he regretted later, Weber had let the cat out of the bag by telling Hunter how he had already smuggled out some early manuscripts of the Koran, passed them to the right dealers in London, and cleared one hundred thousand pounds, leaving some dealers begging for more.

It had been obvious to Hunter that by increasing the cargoes and loading a Dakota to full capacity several millions could be made out of such valuable items, and he was determined to have his way in spite of Weber's reluctance.

The truth was that Weber was regretting his involvement and desperately tried to get out of it by changing his mobile and moving out of his usual hotel into a one-bedroom flat in Hatherley Court in Bayswater that was owned by a cousin.

None of this had helped as Hunter had sent an e-mail to Charnley airfield indicating that he was on his way to London.

The Master smiled and punched in some numbers on his phone.

In Bayswater, Weber sat in despair by the window in his pajamas, drinking coffee for his breakfast, the rain pattering against the window, and then the ancient house phone of the flat rang. He stared at it for a minute or so, but as the ringing persisted, he picked the phone up, and the Master said, "So there you are, Mister Weber. It's not Colonel Samuel Hunter, which I'm sure is a relief to you."

Weber was stunned. "Who is this?"

"Most people call me the Master."

"I've never heard of you. Master of what?"

"Never mind that for the moment. Let's deal with you. You own a small aircraft company operating out of an old RAF base at Charnley in Essex called Havoc International. A rather grand title."

Weber said, "You need something like that to impress the sort of people I have to deal with."

"Of course, the African trade, Ghana and Nigeria."

"That's right."

"Yes, those old Dakotas are perfect for that kind of thing," the Master said. "A remarkable aircraft. Many have been flying since the Second World War, perfect for the desert trade."

Weber said, "That's right, but where is this going?"

"To Timbuktu and Mali and rebels under the black flag claiming to be the followers of al-Qaeda. In fact, they're a murderous rabble who shame the ideals of Osama bin Laden whose name be praised."

Weber said carefully, "Look, who are you?"

"I serve the holy cause of al-Qaeda. There are others like me who serve the movement all over the world."

"But what do you want with me?"

"To save you from yourself, Herr Weber," and here the Master broke into German. "You have behaved dishonorably in trading on false documents supplied by dishonest government officials in Mali. You have been guilty of removing precious Muslim relics and selling them to unscrupulous dealers in London. Most Arab countries would execute you for such offenses."

Weber was sweating now, and replied in English, "Many of these things were being burned, destroyed by the mobs."

"A poor excuse, but let me move on to the arrival of Colonel Samuel Hunter on the scene, and the man Dolan, his servant. Villains of the first order under the guise of representing the President, although I'm sure he would be as disgusted as the rest of us at such behavior."

Weber said, "He damn well would be if he knew what they were up to. Okay, I've been a complete fool, I admit it, but Hunter is something else again and it's driving me crazy. He's insisting we run things as a major operation, and I don't know where to turn."

"But I do," the Master told him. "Al-Qaeda will not allow this wretched man to succeed, but for the moment, it's essential that he believes he has the upper hand and we must fool him completely. Does this appeal to you?"

"Absolutely." Weber's spirits lifted at once.

"Excellent. If you have a pen available, I'm going to give you a very special number. Write it down and destroy it later when you've memorized it. Hunter will keep getting up to no good, I'm certain, and it would be useful to know what."

Weber produced a pen, listening as the Master said the number, writing it on his left wrist. "And you trust me with this?" he asked.

"You may have been a fool, but you're not a bad man, which Hunter is, beyond question. You became a victim, hiding there in Bayswater not knowing which way to turn. Now you have power, a belief in yourself that Hunter is not aware of."

"You've saved my life," Weber told him. "He could be here at any time, and I expect he'll want to get moving at once."

"Tell him it's proving difficult to procure the right trading documents from those dishonest government officials in Mali and that he'll have to wait."

"Thanks for the advice. You know, I was in despair. You're a great man."

"There are many people who would take exception to that description," the Master told him.

"All I can say is that I was in despair and now feel as if I've been resurrected."

"Rather biblical, that." The Master laughed. "My son, who was dead, is alive again, but for the present, I must go."

Weber replaced the phone, his hand shaking slightly, smiling now as he thought about Hunter. "Right, you bastard, just bring it on and we'll see where it gets you," he murmured, and went to have a shower.

———————

THE CHIEFTAIN LANDED at Barking after a perfect flight, and a little more than an hour later, the Mini dropped Tad at the Curzon Street house, then carried on to Holland Park.

As Dillon and Hannah entered the safe house, the sound of laughter took them into the computer room, where they found Roper, Tony Doyle, and Daniel Holley sharing a bottle of champagne together.

"Sean, me boy," Roper roared. "Daniel only got here half an hour ago and brought us a bottle of Krug. You haven't met Sean's cousin, Hannah Flynn, Daniel."

"No, but I've heard only good things about her."

Holley leaned down and kissed her gallantly on both cheeks, and Roper said morosely, "Another bloody Provo for you, Hannah, a rare bird this one. A damn Protestant."

"Whose mother was a decent Catholic woman from Crossmaglen and don't you forget it," Dillon told him.

"Oh, shut up and help us finish this champagne. We'll need help because this is the second bottle, but you can amuse us with an account of what happened in the Emerald Isle."

"Well, Tad Magee really put the boot into Finbar," Dillon said, as Tony Doyle filled glasses.

"And how did he do that?" Holley asked.

Dillon had just raised a glass to his lips, and said to Hannah, "You tell them."

So she did, not leaving out a thing, and when she reached the matter of the estate ending up in Eli's hands, Roper roared his approval and raised his glass. "Finbar Magee has been a bastard of a man all his life. His drunken driving killed his wife, and due to the vagary of the law, he walked free. Tad Magee could have had him put down for good."

"He didn't need to," Dillon said. "He's turned him into a dead man walking. Killing him would be easy. Is Ferguson in the house?"

"Yes, but he's resting," Roper said. "The Prime Minister was speaking in the House of Commons last night. Didn't finish until midnight, then there was a meeting of the Action Committee at Downing Street. It was three o'clock in the morning when he got back here and announced he was going to bed. Before he could, I had to put a call from the White House to him. Another hour there. He's been sleeping ever since because he's got Cazalet speaking at the London School of Economics at three-thirty, which they've estimated could take three hours if we include questions. I have to check on him in an hour."

"What's he trying to do, kill himself?" Holley demanded.

"No, he isn't," Dillon said. "All this upheaval is meat and drink to him. He's a tough old bird, and he'll die in harness when he's ready and not before." He turned to Roper. "Are we all expected to join in to hear what Jake Cazalet has to say?"

"No. All the seats have gone, and we'll be surrounded by security—some of Scotland Yard's finest, plus MI5 and a sprinkling of SAS. They should be able to handle even the worst that ISIS could offer."

"Well, I imagine they would," Dillon said.

"On the other hand, the American ambassador, Philip Hardy, is to hold a reception this evening at the embassy in Cazalet's honor. We are all invited, except you, Tony. General Ferguson will expect you, as a good chauffeur should, to sit in the driver's seat of his beloved Daimler, guarding it with your life while watching a movie on your tablet."

"Well, thank you very much, Major," Tony Doyle said. "For some reason I thought that's how it would be. I wonder why?"

It was Hannah who replied. "Well, at least you can eat with us, Tony. I don't know about the rest of you, but I'm starving. I'm sure Maggie Hall can provide us with a late lunch if we ask her nicely, so let's give it a try," and she got up and led the way out.

MAGGIE, AS USUAL, managed to rise to the occasion: turtle soup and shepherd's pie backed up by a mixed salad. Fat strawberries to follow, doused in cream, and the inevitable coffee.

As they sat there talking, Ferguson walked in, smartly dressed in a dark blue suit that shouted Savile Row, a gleaming white shirt, and a Guards tie. He looked remarkably well.

"So there you are, Major," he said to Roper. "You all seem to be having a jolly time, I must say."

"Well, you look amazing, sir," Sara said. "I don't know how you do it."

"It's what I keep the sauna, the swimming pool, and gymnasium for, Captain. I trust the rest of you use them with similar success. At the moment, I'm in search of my chauffeur. Make sure the Daimler is fit to play, Staff Sergeant, and wait for me." Doyle was on his feet at once and disappeared outside. "So you and Hannah are back in one piece?" Ferguson said to Dillon. "You must tell me about it, but later."

"You need to know, General. The Master had apparently been manipulating Finbar. He also spoke to me, Hannah, and Tad Magee."

"My goodness, he has been active," Ferguson said. "We'll discuss it later. I've arranged a videoconferencing chat with the Algerian foreign minister that should be coming through in the next ten minutes or so. Sorry to inconvenience you, Major Roper."

"No problem, sir," Roper said, and went out at once.

"It seems you left the minister a rather hurried note that you intended to visit us, Daniel," Ferguson said to Holley.

"Yes, because he was away on a trip up-country."

"He was interested in your mention of Mali and would like to know more, which is why he's asked for an opportunity to speak to you directly here."

Holley was joint owner of the biggest shipping firm operating out of Algeria and had dual nationality. He was also a special envoy for the foreign minister, with a diplomatic passport.

"Then we'd better get in," said Holley. "I see no reason why the rest of you shouldn't observe."

They were only just in time, for in minutes the foreign minister came into view, middle-aged handsome in a good suit and military tie.

"That's a Sandhurst tie," Sara whispered.

"It would be," Holley whispered. "He was a cadet and afterward served in the Algerian Army."

The foreign minister said cheerfully, "So you got there safely, Daniel. Good flight?"

"Yes, sir."

"It would be; those Falcons are wonderful planes. But to get down to business, General Ferguson has spoken to me about this firm, Havoc, that uses Dakotas for rough trade in Ghana and Nigeria, and tries to get away with anything it can in Mali. Those foolish rebels there, operating under the black flag, have been plundering the mosques and ancient centers of learning of wonderful art, books, and treasured histories of Islam, destroying much through ignorance. I will not have what has survived fall into the wrong hands. Can I trust you to deal with everyone connected with this Havoc firm? I'm sure you will find a solution."

"Absolutely, sir. I'm happy to be of service, and I know I'll get some help from my friends here."

"Excellent, that was all I wanted to check. I leave it in your hands, then. Take care, Daniel, and all of you. Hard times, but we'll survive."

The screen faded.

"He seems a pretty decent sort of chap," Sara said.

"You mean for a Muslim?" Holley commented.

Sara was immediately angry. "The Muslims I killed in Afghanistan—and there were many—were angry men determined to kill me and my comrades any way they could. The fact that they were Muslim was no more important a factor than a British soldier being Roman Catholic or Protestant or, like me, a Jew."

"Calm down, both of you," Ferguson said. "These are hard and difficult times, but if we can't pull together, we'll go under. Now, I've got to go, but I'll see you tonight at the American Embassy. No weapons allowed on the premises, and I expect nothing but good-will from all of you. That's an order."

He went out, and Dillon said to Sara, "Too much champagne, my love, but having said that, I take his point."

"I'm tired of the whole bloody business," she said. "We got rid of Saddam and Gaddafi, then Osama bin Laden, and it hasn't made any difference because we've now got ISIS. In Afghanistan, when our convoy was ambushed, I was wounded and crippled for life, but I managed to kill around forty men with a heavy machine gun, so they gave me the Military Cross. These days there are British insurance lawyers who'd offer to sue me for damages if asked."

"You're absolutely bloody right," Holley said.

"Take Ferguson's advice," Dillon told her. "Take advantage of the swimming pool, sauna, and gymnasium."

"Do you mind if I join you?" Holley asked her.

"Why not," she said, and he followed her out.

Roper put the kettle on. "I'm going to make a pot of real tea just for you if you'll join me, Hannah?"

"Of course I will." She held the lighter for him when he produced a cigarette. "Why was she so upset?"

"Two reasons, my child," Dillon put in. "First, it's been a long, long war."

"And second?"

"She and Daniel were a serious item."

"Oh dear," Hannah said.

"Indeed. Things got in the way. This is the first time they've met in more than a year."

"Well, all I can say is he seems to be absolutely lovely to me."

"He's one of my best friends," Roper said. "A Yorkshire and half-Irish Protestant with a Catholic mother and a first-class honors degree from Leeds University. In Belfast, studying for an MBA at Queen's, he was walking his sweet young cousin to her lodgings one night when they were kidnapped by entirely the wrong sort of people from the other side in the conflict. He was beaten and tied up, and she was raped and murdered by four men."

Hannah was truly horrified. "I can't believe it."

"I haven't finished. He managed to free himself, grab a pistol one guy had left lying around, and shot all four dead."

"And after that?"

"She was from a Catholic family in Crossmaglen, her brother very important to the Provisional IRA. Daniel needed a refuge from the other side and the law. He took the oath and was sent to one of the Gaddafi training camps in Algeria. He's served the Cause ever since, a Provo to the hilt and a brilliant mind, which has made him millions over the years."

Hot angry tears flowed, and Hannah wiped them away with her sleeve like a child. "That's the most dreadful thing I have ever heard of."

"It shaped his life, but it's history now, so as the tea's gotten cold, would you be offended if I asked you to obtain some more, nice and hot, from the kitchen?"

"What an idiot you are," she said, and went out.

———

AT THE SAME TIME, Colonel Samuel Hunter and his bully boy Dolan were in a cab, having just arrived at Heathrow. Hunter told the driver to take them to the Park Lane Hilton and sat back, relaxing for a moment.

"You've got to admit it. London's the place to be these days."

"Can I ask you, Colonel, why you picked the Hilton?"

"I like a run every morning, first thing; it's been part of my makeup since I was a cadet at West Point. It's why I'm in the shape I am. Hyde Park, on the other side of Park Lane, is a particularly pleasant place to exercise in. In fact, the Queen's bodyguard, the Household Cavalry, indulge their mounts there, enjoying a gallop each day."

"I suppose it's nice for the tourists," Dolan said.

"Which we definitely are not. That's another reason to stay at the Hilton. It's only five minutes' walk away from the Dorchester, where Cazalet and Johnson are staying."

"Are you looking to follow Cazalet around?"

"Nothing too obvious. I was reading the *New York Times* on the plane and there was a write-up saying he's making some sort of speech at the London School of Economics this afternoon. It also said that the American ambassador is having a reception in Cazalet's honor tonight. The President told me to let the ambassador know I was in town, and I imagine it'll be easy enough to get an invitation." Hunter took out his mobile and made the call to the embassy as they came to Marble Arch.

It felt strange, but he breathed deeply as he spoke. "This is Presidential Aide Colonel Samuel Hunter. I've just arrived at Heathrow on official business for the President, and I'm calling on the ambassador as a courtesy. Please notify him that I'm staying at the Park Lane Hilton."

Dolan said, "We'll see what that produces."

"A result, I'd say. I've booked us a Mercedes through the hotel, Dolan, so you'll have to play chauffeur again."

"And what about Weber?"

"No problem. He'll have to do as he's told or else. I'll give him a call now. That'll be a nice surprise for him."

Weber was still at the Bayswater flat and was shocked to hear Hunter's voice on his mobile so soon and even more dismayed to be told that the colonel was already in London.

"A nice surprise for you, Hans, but I managed to get away a couple of days earlier than I thought. We're booking in at the Hilton now, and we'll come down to Charnley to visit you later."

"I'm in London at the moment, had to come up on business," Weber said, his heart sinking.

"Well, you'd better get back down again so we can talk," Hunter said, and switched off, only for his phone to ring again, the American ambassador himself. "Philip Hardy, Colonel, welcome to London."

"Why, that's very kind of you, Mr. Ambassador," Hunter told him.

"I trust the President was well when you left him?"

"In excellent form, I assure you, sir."

"A special day for us," Hardy said. "We have President Jake Cazalet delivering a most important speech about the ISIS threat, all seats taken, I'm afraid, but perhaps you might join us at seven this evening for a reception in his honor being held at the embassy."

"So kind of you to ask; I'll be delighted to accept." Hunter switched off, turning to Dolan. "So that's taken care of." The cab was just pulling into the Hilton. "So now we book in, unpack, have something to eat, then get down to Charnley and sort Weber out."

MEANWHILE, WEBER WAS CHECKING his left wrist and calling the Master.

The call was answered on the instant. "So soon, my friend?"

"Yes, he just called. I told him I was in London on business, and he told me to get back to Charnley so we can talk. What do I do?"

"As he says. Return to Charnley, listen to his demands, then point out again that bargaining with corrupt officials in Mali takes time and that it's impossible to land there without such documentation. Having discovered the value of what's going on, the officials involved are demanding a fortune. I'll be interested to know what his reply will be."

"I'll see what he says, but he's a hard bastard at the best of times. A thoroughly self-serving individual, and the Dolan man is an animal."

"That is not the strength but the weakness of people like that," the Master told him. "We'll speak later when you know where you are. Stop worrying, my friend, you've got me to do that."

Weber, feeling suddenly empowered, did just that. Pulling on an anorak in case of rain, he hurried downstairs to his car and set off for Charnley.

HANNAH WAS STILL with Roper and Dillon in the computer room when Sara and Holley returned, fresh faced.

"I trust you enjoyed your ablutions," Roper said. "But things have been moving along. The dubious Colonel Hunter and his bagman sergeant have been logged through Heathrow and booked into the Park Lane Hilton."

"So convenient when he wants to be able to keep an eye on Cazalet at the Dorchester," Sara said.

"He's not a nice man." Roper nodded. "A proper bastard in every way, which MI5 confirmed big-time. You'll be meeting him tonight, he's been invited to the reception, but then he would be. It's protocol, but there's nothing to do about that."

"Well, I for one would like to know what makes him tick," Holley said. "Which at the moment, appears to be Charnley airfield and the ghostly Dakotas, so I have a suggestion. At Farley Field, only twenty minutes away by car, I have one of my most prized possessions, my Falcon jet. I could fly a plane like that to this Charnley place in fifteen minutes or so and find out what goes on there. I'd only be following the Algerian foreign minister's orders. I can take passengers if anyone fancies the flight."

"You can rule me out, too complicated," Roper said. "But the rest of you might find it fun. Pretend you're an enthusiast, Sean, who's got a thing about old Dakotas. You're just friends having an afternoon out."

"Sounds good to me," Sara said. "I'm up for it if you are, Hannah?"

"Of course she is, so let's get moving," Holley put in. "We'll see you later, Giles."

They left on the run, there was laughter outside for a while, doors banged closed in the Land Rover, and away they went, leaving Giles Roper alone in his eternal wheelchair.

HANS WEBER HAD a good run to Charnley in his old Volkswagen before getting out to open the main gate, for he'd closed the place for a week until he could work out for certain what was going to happen. He walked back to the VW to slide behind the wheel when, with a sudden roar, a Falcon swooped overhead, circled the airfield, and dropped in with great skill to one side of the two Dakotas parked beside a handful of small planes.

As Weber got behind the wheel of the VW and drove to investigate, the Falcon's airstair door opened and Holley and his passengers got out. Weber parked the VW and went to meet them.

"Good afternoon, I'm Hans Weber and I own this place. I'm afraid we're not open, but if I can help in any way." He turned to the Falcon. "A superb aircraft."

"True," Holley said. "But the two Dakotas there. What truly remarkable airplanes. The workhorse of the Allied armies during the Second World War and after. From flying over the Himalayas carrying essential supplies from India to China, to flying every-thing from coal to foodstuffs to keep people fed during the Berlin Blockade in nineteen forty-eight. I hear you run a freight company carrying cargo to Nigeria and Mali."

Weber immediately looked wary. "The odd flight, but there isn't really much call."

"I suppose not," Holley said. "But we'd love to have a look in one of the Dakotas." Before Weber could reply, a Mercedes swept in through the open gates and came toward them, top down, Dolan at the wheel and Hunter beside him.

They both got out, and Hunter said, "What in the hell's going on here? We're not open for business."

Dillon, a brilliant actor since his youth, had no difficulty in as-suming an English accent that was upper class to perfection.

"No need to adopt that kind of tone. It offends the ladies, and we can't have that, can we?"

Dolan advanced on him. "Then you know what to do, you little ponce. Just get back in your fancy plane and clear off before I flat-ten you."

Dillon turned to Weber. "Your partners?"

"In a way," Weber said. "One of the biggest mistakes of my life."

"Then all I can say is I'm sorry for you. Such a pity. One of those Dakotas would have complemented the Spitfire in my collection. Carruthers, you may fly us out of this shocking place as soon as may be."

Sara and Hannah played their parts beautifully, haughty and disdainful as they followed Holley up the steps into the Falcon, Dillon bringing up the rear. Only after the door closed did the two women collapse with laughter, hugging each other, before dropping into their seats.

"Carruthers," Holley called, as he sat down at the controls. "Where in the hell did you get that from?"

"Oscar Wilde or it might have been Noël Coward," Dillon said.

"A powerful performance," Holley told him. "You did well to keep your hands off him."

"I wasn't going to do that. It would prevent me from experiencing the look on Hunter's face when he meets us at the reception."

"Oh, we're all looking forward to that," Hannah called, and then the Falcon roared along the runway, lifted up over the gate, and started to climb.

"WHO WAS THAT?" Hunter demanded.

Thanks to the Master, Weber felt a new confidence. "Oh, just some bloke. He said he collects old planes and would like to get his hands on a Dakota."

"Just a big kid playing with toys." Dolan sneered. "I'd like to kick him right up his backside, and those two posh birds need a real man to take them in hand."

"Which I presume would be you?" Weber said.

"You bet your life it would be." Dolan's eyes gleamed. "I'd show them who was boss."

"Spare us the details," Weber said, and turned to Hunter. "You want a go and I just don't have one moment right now. You can come into the office and examine the documentation. I'm trying every way to get a deal with those crooks in the airport at Mali."

"Then up the price, offer them more," Hunter said. "We can afford it. We'll make a fortune if we can get the right kind of stuff out there into the world market. Everybody's got a price. Find out what theirs is."

"That won't help in this case. Even the villains are Muslims, and as the facts become clear to the general population that the books, the documents, the art, everything looted in Timbuktu, have enormous religious significance, even the bad guys will take it seriously."

"All the more important that you get this done right now, Weber. Don't fail me, or you'll regret it. We're staying at the Hilton. I expect to hear from you soon."

They drove away, and Weber called the Master and told him what had happened.

"This Hunter is a bad man with no honor in him at all, and his sergeant has the manners of a street thug," he complained.

"I couldn't have put it better myself, Mr. Weber. But don't worry, he'll be out of your hair very soon. Men with no honor die with no honor."

THE AMERICAN EMBASSY in Grosvenor Square was no more than a hundred yards from Highfield Court, which is why Charles Ferguson's people gathered there before going to the reception.

Sara and Hannah arrived a couple of hours early to give whatever help was necessary but discovered that they were not really needed.

"I can't compete with the American Embassy for food, and it would be madness for anyone bothered about their career to turn up drunk." Sadie shook her head. "So coffee and soft drinks, I think."

"Totally boring, but sensible, I suppose," Sara told her. "I think I'll go have a shower and change."

"I'll do the same," Hannah said. "We'll see you in a bit, Sadie."

HANNAH WAS BACK some forty minutes later wearing a deceptively simple evening suit of black silk by Givenchy that Sara had insisted on buying for her the moment they set eyes on it in Harrods. Complemented by a white linen blouse and her fashionably short hair, Hannah looked sensational when she went downstairs and found Roper in his wheelchair in the rabbi's study, where a log fire burned brightly.

"My goodness," he said. "You look wonderful."

"Even with this?" She raised the walking stick in her left hand.

"You should try a wheelchair, but I love you enough to say stop feeling sorry for yourself. You, Sara, and I, we share the same problem, and it's a bastard, but you have to make the best of it. So give me a kiss on the cheek, then slide back the partition to the piano room and play something."

So she did, revealing the Schiedmayer concert grand, the conservatory crammed with flowers and plants. To one side was a stand with candles and matches to light them, which she did, aware of cars arriving outside.

There was a step behind her, and she turned and found Sara in the full dress uniform of a captain in the Intelligence Corps, an array of medals on her tunic.

Hannah said, "I've never seen you like that. You look great."

"So do you. We're going to have a special evening, so what do you think of giving it a special start with some vintage Cole Porter?"

As Ferguson entered, leading Cazalet, Blake Johnson, and Henry Frankel, Hannah sat down, but instead of playing Porter, she plunged into one of her favorites, the magnificent and shattering opening of Rachmaninoff's Fourth Piano Concerto. She took it up in a crescendo, cut it off suddenly, then turned on the stool to find them staring in awe.

She felt like a fool for showing off and tried to brave it out. "Of course, when it comes down to it, what Rachmaninoff really needs is a fine orchestra and a world-class pianist."

Ferguson led the enthusiastic clapping, and called, "Make it Hannah Flynn with the London Symphony Orchestra at the Albert Hall, I'll be the first to buy a ticket. Where on earth have you been keeping such a talent?"

"Oh, I have a marvelous teacher, it's all his doing," she said, as others crowded around to congratulate her.

Henry Frankel kissed her cheek. "I wish I were your agent, love, I really do. I'd make a fortune." Then he clapped his hands. "I think it's time we started over to the embassy, everyone."

Tony Doyle stepped behind Roper's wheelchair and led the way out. Sara moved to Hannah's side and hugged her as they went forward. "It was so wonderful, and Sadie cried her eyes out. She loves you like a daughter, you know. But where did all that come from?"

"Henry Frankel asked me that, too, and I said I had a great teacher at college, and that's true, but—I don't know, something's happened inside me. It's like I'm discovering myself."

GROSVENOR SQUARE WAS as busy as it always was when there was a reception at the embassy, with a sizeable police presence and only a few cars allowed to park after being carefully checked. The Mercedes had been one of them when it had arrived earlier and Hunter, resplendent in dress uniform, had gone into the embassy, leaving Dolan to fill his time the best he could.

He was standing on the pavement, leaning on the Mercedes and smoking a cigarette, when he had a shock. Sara, in uniform with all the medals, caught his eye, and then he realized where he'd seen her and the girl walking with her before.

A couple of policemen stepped into the road to hold up traffic for Roper in his wheelchair, the others following him, Dillon and Holley walking together. As they crossed the road, Dillon recognized Dolan and waved.

"Won't they let you in, old boy? What a shame."

He and Holley laughed as they were passed through the security gates to be greeted by American marines.

Hunter's mobile trembled in his pocket with a text that said: *Call me.* He retired to the privacy of the men's room and called Dolan.

"What the hell is so important?" he demanded in a low voice.

"I was watching people going in, and those crazy Falcon people from Charnley were there."

"You must be mistaken."

"No, I'm not. The two women were with the group, one in army uniform. She had medals."

"Did she indeed?"

"The bastard who was interested in the Dakota and his pilot? He saw me, and shouted, 'Won't they let you in, old boy?' He seemed different."

"What do you mean?"

"When he dealt with us at Charnley, he seemed like just a stupid prick, but not this guy. He's trouble."

"You were right to call me."

"What are you going to do?"

"The place is jammed with people, but I'll find them."

"Watch yourself. He and his friends could be awkward."

"In the American Embassy? I doubt it. Maybe I'll be the one to make trouble for these Falcon people. We'll see."

Hunter went back to the crowd, lifted a glass of champagne from the tray of a passing waiter, and went hunting. It didn't take long. The crowd was heaviest where the ambassador stood, people hanging in there, hoping for a word or two with the great man, but their chance tonight was minimal.

With him, though, was Cazalet, with Henry Frankel, cabinet secretary to the Prime Minister, and Major General Charles Ferguson, who also worked for the Cabinet Office. He recognized both of them from CIA files. The four people from the Falcon affair, however, who were there with them, were complete strangers, and so was the man in the wheelchair.

The reason for his ignorance was Alice Quarmby. Back in Washington, she had used the power of the President and the Basement to access the related CIA files and wipe the slate clean. The Prime Minister's private army had ceased to exist, and so had the records of anyone who'd ever worked for it.

Hunter believed Ferguson to be a military advisor to the Cabinet Office as he pushed through the crowds toward the ambassador, who was listening to Jake Cazalet while Dillon and the others made small talk.

Hunter emerged from the crowd. "Mr. Ambassador. A word, if I may."

They all turned to look at him. Noting the uniform, the ambassador said, "How can I help, Colonel?"

"Samuel Hunter, sir, we spoke this morning. I'm an aide to the President, in London on his behalf."

"Behalf of what?" Dillon asked, and turned to Holley. "Aren't you an aide to the Algerian foreign minister, Daniel? What do you do?"

"I must confess—not a lot."

Hunter said, "Well, some of us take our work more seriously than that."

"I'm pleased to hear it," Holley said. "Of course, I'm not an aide, I'm a special envoy. Maybe that's why I have so much fun."

Sara cut in. "Oh, I don't know, darling, I wouldn't have called it fun when you took that army of Tuareg tribesmen all the way down through the Sahara to save the city of Timbuktu from the al-Qaeda rebels."

"What a great story." Dillon smiled. "It's got everything but *Beau Geste*, the French Foreign Legion, and Fort Zinderneuf."

The ambassador said, "Of course, I suppose you started with Desert Storm. Twenty-five years ago. We were meant to have finished with deserts after we toppled Saddam, but it seems to have gone on forever as a never-ending war in Afghanistan. A dreadful bloody place, but then you Special Forces people will have found that out for yourselves."

"Yes, terrible people, the Afghans. Absolute savages," said Hunter.

"Interesting," Holley said. "Which province did you soldier in?"

"Helmand," Hunter answered.

Sara Gideon said, "Why, so did I! Of course, that was before you people took over and set up a base with showers, television, and burgers. Quite a comfort zone."

"Are you suggesting the High Command was at fault to do that, young woman?"

Jake Cazalet, who had been listening to the exchange together with Ferguson and the other guests, intervened.

"She is not your young woman, Colonel, but a captain in the British Army. Her medals speak for themselves, as does her service record: Belfast, Bosnia, Kosovo, Iraq, Afghanistan, plus a Military Cross for bravery in action."

Hunter's astonishment was plain to see. "I don't understand. What did she earn that doing?"

Sara broke in. "Just listen, you stupid man, and I'll tell you. I was in Sangin when a Brigade Reconnaissance Force special-ops unit needed a Pashto speaker to go up to Abusan, where they had a badly wounded Taliban leader who couldn't speak English. Three chaps from the BRF supported me. Wally, Alec, and Frank, who was the sergeant. They were dressed like Taliban and had an old Saladin armored car left by the Russians, now mounted with a heavy machine gun. We joined on the end of a convoy going up-country by night when we were ambushed by a large Taliban force."

There was music and laughter in the rest of the room, but Cazalet, Ferguson, and company all moved closer, not wishing to miss a word.

"The enemy came in yelling and screaming," said Sara. "Alec

started to fire the machine gun, I emptied my Glock, Wally was using his AK until he got shot in the throat. Frank had opened a box of RPGs and started to fire them, one after another. A grenade in return put him down, and the shrapnel wounded me above the left eye. Then Alec went over the side, shot in the head, so I took on the machine gun while Frank, bleeding badly, kept launching grenades."

She stopped suddenly, looking back into some secret place, and Roper said gently, "Go on, Sara, tell us what happened then. I think it would be good for you."

"The machine gun emptied, but I managed to reload with the spare cartridge box and continued shooting. Frank had run out of grenades and was badly wounded in the chest. I'd given him my head cloth to hold against it, and as I resumed firing, I was shot in the leg and held on to the gun to keep from falling over, and then the Taliban started to run away, and I could hear the helicopters, so I slumped down against Frank and waited."

"Did he survive?" the ambassador asked.

"Yes, to receive the Military Cross from the Queen, who told him how grateful everyone was, but that didn't help Wally and Alec."

"But you were awarded the Military Cross also. You're wearing it."

"Quite right, but I received mine from Prince Charles later."

There was a complete silence from everyone until Henry Frankel crossed to her, kissed her on the cheek, and said, "God bless you for opening up like that. I'll never forget it."

Roper said, "I've always loved you, Sara, but even more after listening to you. By the way, in case you're wondering where Hunter is, he eased back into the crowd a short while ago, his tail between his legs."

The ambassador said, "I served in Vietnam at the age of eighteen, with Blake Johnson here."

Blake said, "It was great fun, I don't think. Fighting Vietcong up to our armpits in some lousy swamp in the Mekong Delta. In defense of the American Army, I must say my opinion of that clown Hunter is unprintable. God alone knows what kind of Special Forces he was involved with."

"I'll drink to that, old buddy," said the ambassador. "But if you'll excuse me, I'd better circulate."

Ferguson moved to them. "An interesting evening. I think it's time to discuss what to do about Hunter."

"Tonight?" Dillon asked.

"Not much we can do tonight. Tomorrow at breakfast."

"He seems to have made quite an impression on you," Dillon said.

"I'd like to shoot him myself. What the Algerian foreign minister said to us is true. Hunter's a rotten apple if ever there was one."

"And Havoc?" Dillon asked.

"Another one of his rotten schemes."

"Actually, I don't think Weber's heart is in the Havoc affair anymore," Dillon said.

"What do you mean?" Ferguson demanded.

"When Hunter turned up there with his bully boy sergeant,

Weber didn't like it at all. When I asked if Hunter was his partner, he said he was, in a way, and that it was the biggest mistake of his life."

"Excellent," Ferguson said. "We'll see what comes up tomorrow."

THE NEXT DAY, it was a dark and dismal morning, rain drumming relentlessly against the window, as Sara and Hannah went down to the canteen in search of breakfast. They found Dillon and Holley enjoying poached eggs, bacon, and toast. Sara took the same, Hannah the scrambled eggs, and Dillon offered tea or coffee according to their pleasure.

"No sign of the general?" Sara inquired.

Dillon shook his head. "Roper was finishing as we got here and is back in the computer room."

Holley said, "He told us that Ferguson's hardly been off the telephone for the past two hours, so when you're finished, I suggest we go and find out what's going on."

THEY FOUND ROPER pouring a large Irish into a mug of tea. Tony Doyle was watching, dressed to go in a khaki trench coat against the rain and carrying an umbrella.

"I hope you've had breakfast, Tony," Sara told him. "You might end up asleep in that Daimler."

Ferguson, on the way in, said, "And so he will, if necessary. Go and wait for me outside, Staff Sergeant." He looked at Roper and shook his head. "A bit early in the day even for you, Major."

"I couldn't agree more, General, but I don't worry about it. So much has happened to me, it's a miracle I'm here at all. Not that it matters. Hunter and his sergeant friend do, however. How do you want us to handle them?"

"The problem is that this wretched man is a presidential aide even though we know, thanks to Alice Quarmby, that he's only got one task, to keep an eye on Jake Cazalet."

Holley said, "That doesn't mean he can use his position for nefarious purposes."

"Which this Havoc business at Charnley qualifies as," Dillon said. "MI5 are aware of Weber's little enterprise and the Dakota loaded with Muslim treasures looted in Mali."

Sara said, "So why not arrest Weber?"

"He isn't going anywhere," Ferguson told her. "And we can use him to snag Hunter."

Hannah said, "But why let the bastard in the country at all when we know he's a crook?"

"Too difficult at this point. Too sticky." He shook his head. "An American colonel, a presidential aide, and a CIA operative who we know traffics with arms dealers on behalf of his country but holds out his grasping hand." Ferguson smiled ruefully. "A strange game we play, but our game. Mind you, there's nothing I'd like better than to fly Hunter and his sergeant by helicopter to Afghanistan, leave them to rot in Helmand province, and fly away without a second look. What would you say to that, Captain Gideon?"

"Why, that I'd fly the helicopter for you, sir. You did second me to the Army Air Corps three years ago."

"I remember," he said grimly. "But to be serious, we really must find something to do about the colonel. Any sensible suggestions welcome, so keep thinking. Don't forget that Cazalet's speaking again tonight—this one I expect you all to attend. Let's go, Staff Sergeant."

"There goes a remarkable man," Hannah said. "But one of these days, he's going to drop dead in his tracks if he keeps up this pace. For a man of his age, it's ridiculous."

"I wouldn't try telling him that," Roper said.

CLOSE TO BELGRAVE SQUARE and adjacent to Buckingham Palace Gardens, Hedley Court was the work of one Henry Hedley, a Victorian entrepreneur who had made a fortune out of coal and railways but was more interested in the cause of his fellow men.

It had opened in 1850, a Victorian masterpiece that soon became the home of free thinking. As Benjamin Disraeli, the great politician and future prime minister, said of it: "Never the voice of government of whatever brand, only the voice of sensible people, whoever they are."

The Great Hall at Hedley Court could hold three hundred people and many more than that had turned up in the hope of seeing Jake Cazalet, but only ticket holders were admitted.

A loudspeaker system had been installed so that the speech could be heard by the large numbers who stood outside to listen, which explained the sizeable armed police presence.

The American ambassador, a special guest, sat with the Prime Minister and Cabinet colleagues in the front row.

In deference to Roper's wheelchair, Ferguson's party had squeezed together into a balcony box from where they could observe everything, which explained why Sara saw Hunter and Dolan, still in uniform, sit down at the end of a row that was not too far from the Prime Minister's party.

"Look what the cat's brought in, General," she pointed out. "It won't be long before he and his wretched sergeant are on television. The cameras are operating from the box opposite."

Ferguson glanced down and exploded. "That bloody man is getting everywhere, and it's quite improper for him to be in uniform. The reception at the American Embassy was different."

"I suppose you could say he's making his presence felt," Dillon said, and turned to Blake Johnson. "Don't you agree?"

Ferguson exploded again. "Well it's time somebody took him by the scruff of the neck and dropped him on another planet or something."

"Difficult to arrange, General, but I'll see what can be done," Dillon told him.

There was a sudden quiet as the music played by the television company came to an end, and the Prime Minister, without any fuss, nodded to Jake, and they walked to the lectern together. There was scattered applause.

The Prime Minister said, "Please rise for the American national anthem."

With a great shuffling, the audience complied, and the music soared out, Cazalet with his hand on his heart, the Prime Minister with the same, and when the anthem finished and applause broke out, he waved it down.

"You all know this man," he said. "A distinguished soldier and great president of the United States. I beg you to listen to him," and he returned to his seat.

Cazalet jumped straight in. "Nine-eleven. The London bombing. Both were al-Qaeda, so we went to war with them, and yet al-Qaeda lives on. Sometimes it stands to one side observing the barbarity of new groups such as ISIS, yet there it remains. We thought that the death of Saddam, Gaddafi, and bin Laden would cure the ills of the Middle East, but we never appreciated the extent to which those tyrants had kept the lid on their countries with an iron hand. Now, with Syria, we have an unprecedented refugee problem."

There was silence for a moment, then someone called, "What's to be done about the refugees? Can you tell us that?"

"Even in the remotest areas, people can look at a television screen. They see the best that Western civilization has to offer, and they want it. Europe, the United States, why wouldn't they want to go there, and with America's history of accepting immigrants in large numbers, why shouldn't their hopes be high?"

Hunter jumped up. "This is a disgrace. What gives you the right to even suggest that the United States might consider such people in any way suitable to be admitted to our country?"

There was an angry muttering, but Cazalet waved a dismissive hand. "I knew Damascus before the war. The city had a reputation for being one of the most beautiful and civilized in the Middle

East, and it was. Muslims, Christians, and Jews worked together happily, the stores and restaurants were full, no one fought."

"Don't talk nonsense," Hunter said. "I'm warning about the thousands of migrants who stampede into Europe any way they can like ravenous wolves."

"Including doctors, teachers, and many people with valuable professional experience to offer. I think our country might welcome a few."

"Then all I can say is thank God you are not in the White House now," Hunter told him. "We don't need you."

The angry voices started again, telling him to shut up or get out, but when someone called him a Nazi bastard enough was enough, and two large policemen approached Hunter down the aisle and had words. He tried to argue the matter, but raised voices made their point, and he and Dolan left.

Ferguson said, "And that's a Special Forces colonel."

Roper nodded. "I must check his file again."

Sara said, "It's got to be the greatest work of fiction of all time."

Cazalet was addressing the audience again. "Sorry about that, ladies and gentlemen, the charades are over. Could I have some serious questioning now?"

A young woman a few rows back raised her hand. "Kate Munro, sir. I'm with the *Spectator*."

"I'm flattered," he told her. "That's the oldest political magazine in the country. How can I help?"

"What fascinates me is not so much that you were president of the United States or that your family was rich and your father a senator. It's that you walked out of Harvard—"

Cazalet cut in on her with a smile. "And went downtown to the recruiting office and joined the army for two tours in Vietnam."

"Exactly. Your draft lottery number hadn't come up. You could have avoided it all. You were even wounded twice. Why did you do it?"

The crowd was completely quiet, everyone waiting, and Cazalet started to talk. "The Vietnam War was a bad business. Many Americans didn't agree with it and unfortunately often took their anger out on the soldiers. One morning, I dropped by my dining hall to have coffee and noticed a new student who'd lost most of his left arm, obviously a veteran."

There was a pin-drop silence as the young woman asked, "What happened next?"

"Oh, another student came in and started to give him a hard time. I suggested he leave him alone, but he refused, so I knocked him out. Of course, I was called to the dean's office to be told what a bad thing I'd done to a rather unpleasant bully. I realized at that time, for the first time, really, that I had a different set of values, so I marched into a Cambridge recruiting office and joined up. My mother was a great lady and took it well, my father not as much— he'd been convinced I'd never be able to get any kind of decent career in the future, but he changed his mind when I got shot and received a few medals. It was good for a political career, he used to say." Cazalet smiled wryly. "He never understood I did it because I had to."

"Well, we understand," the young woman said. "Thank you very much for your service."

"To be interviewed by the *Spectator* is reward enough. Now— can we get back to the business in hand? Who else has got a question for me?" A forest of hands was raised instantly.

IN THE END, the evening had to be brought to a close because of the hour, and Jake Cazalet had enjoyed the triumph of a lifetime. Ferguson and the others hung on for a while out of consideration for Roper in his wheelchair.

Sara turned to Ferguson as Henry Frankel and Ambassador Hardy joined them, Cazalet delayed by outstretched hands.

"An amazing speech, it'll be on every front page. The big question I'll bet everyone will be asking, though, is who on earth was the idiot in American uniform who was trying to give him a hard time."

Hardy said, "The one thing I dread is that some newspaper reporter will find out he's actually a presidential aide. The President never did make it clear to me what the colonel was doing in London."

Cazalet joined them at that moment, and Blake Johnson, right behind him, said, "I can answer that, although I'm breaking a presidential confidence."

There was a pause, startled looks were exchanged, and Philip Hardy said, "I'd hate to see you put yourself in a difficult position because of that bastard, Blake."

"I'm not. Yesterday, Jake and I were being driven in General Ferguson's Daimler when my secretary spoke to me from the White House. She had overheard the President and Hunter— the man was only given the appointment to empower him. In effect, he was to spy on Jake and be sure of where he was at any given moment. The implication was that perhaps Jake should pull back on public appearances and realize that he is no longer president."

Philip Hardy laughed out loud. "Well, if that's the general hope, it has just been shattered by the finest speech I've heard in years." He turned to Cazalet and shook his hand. "You surely made me proud to be an American tonight, Jake. We both served as boys in Vietnam, both were wounded, and I just want to apologize for the insults you received from that wretched man while he was wearing the uniform of our country."

"Kind of you to say that, Phil," Cazalet told him. "Sticks and stones to guys like you, me, and Blake."

"Of course," Hardy said, glancing at Ferguson and nodding slightly. "I must leave you now and prepare my answers for the publicity that I'm sure will come my way."

"I'll go with you, Mr. Ambassador," Henry Frankel said. "Just in case there are any questions you may have for the Prime Minister."

They departed, and Ferguson turned to the others. "I don't know about you lot, but I must say that this was quite an invigorating experience. Now we must go home, my friends, and try to rest while we can to prepare for what lies ahead."

———

DESPITE THE HOUR, Weber was not asleep when the telephone rang in his flat, and the Master said, "I imagine you've been watching television."

"I wouldn't have missed it," Weber told him. "What a clown Hunter proved to be. He made a complete fool of himself."

"That's because he is," the Master said. "While Cazalet, on the other hand, was amazing. Having said that, it's very disappointing from al-Qaeda's point of view. The last thing we were looking for was an American hero inspiring people."

"What do you think will happen now?" Weber asked.

"It's a great story, but on the other hand, what does it really mean? Cazalet was a fine soldier and a great president, but those things were then, and this is now. The unfortunate thing is Hunter. It was only his approach to you that brought him to my attention."

"What do you want me to do?"

"Get in touch with me when he approaches you again. He'll be desperate now, and his hope of getting into the illegal Mali trade is all he has left because his little tirade could cause his recall to Washington at any moment. If he approaches you, let me know at once."

"And what will you do?"

"I'm tempted to have him shot, but we'll see."

THE MASTER OPENED the door leading to the stern of the barge on the Quai des Brumes and gazed with pleasure at the floodlit splendor of Notre Dame, a glass of red wine in his right hand. The stupidity of Hunter had been beyond belief, but before giving orders for his assassination, it would be sensible to see what the new day would bring. In a certain way, it would be quite entertaining, and he smiled, finished his wine, and returned inside.

AT THE HILTON PARK LANE, Hunter sat in his suite with Dolan, drinking heavily and watching one news program after another that featured the events at Hedley Court.

"Just look at Cazalet," Hunter said. "Thinks he's so damned marvelous up there on stage. Who does he think he is?"

"I think he knows exactly who he is—and now so does everybody else if they didn't already," Dolan said drunkenly, holding up his glass. "God bless America."

This infuriated Hunter. "Go on, you bastard, get out of here. Who needs you?"

"I'd say you do, Colonel, if only to back up your lies. As I recall, all you were doing in Sangin was administering supplies to the PX."

"I said get out of here," Hunter told him. "So do it or I'll call security."

"I'll be back," Dolan told him. "There's no one else who'd bother with you now," and he lurched out.

Hunter sat there afraid like he had never been. Why had he done it, such a stupid thing and in uniform? Everything had been going so well, and then came the icing on the cake, the totally unexpected appointment as a presidential aide. It had gone to his head and puffed him up and at the same time made him envious

of the man, the medals, the glory, which explained his mad decision to attend the Hedley Court function in full uniform and act
as he had.

He went to bed, slept badly, and was rung at seven by a call
from the American Embassy. "Colonel Hunter, you have a Master
Sergeant Dolan with you on your trip?" a woman's voice said.

Hunter shook his head to clear it. "That's correct, is there a
problem?"

"He was noticed staggering along Park Lane this morning at
about three a.m. He stepped off the pavement and was swiped by
a bus. He's ended up in Marsh Lane Hospital's emergency room.
He had no identification about where he was staying on him but
did have his passport, which led to us."

"How is he?" Hunter demanded.

"It seems he's not good at all, but you can call the hospital yourself. I believe the police may want to have a word with you."

Hunter had walked to the television set while talking and found
himself watching himself on an early morning news show.

"Why would they want me?"

"You'd have to ask them that, I'm afraid, sir."

"Everybody knows he was with me. I should estimate that at
least half the population of London saw me in action on television
last night."

"Yes, Colonel, I'm sorry, sir."

Hunter was reasonably clearheaded by now. "Why would you
be? Who are you?"

"Lieutenant Mary Smith, on attachment to the embassy, Colonel. I'm sorry about what happened to you last night."

"Not as much as I am. I was an unbelievable damned fool, but I appreciate your comments. I'll call the hospital."

Which he did and received what news there was from a ward sister, who made it clear the situation was grave and visitors were not welcome. So that was that. He was tired of the old Hunter, the lies and the subterfuge. He was likely to get a swift recall to Washington, so his only chance to do something about Havoc would be now. Maybe he could think of something legal to do with the Dakotas? He'd better go to Charnley now and find Hans Weber.

AT HOLLAND PARK before breakfast, Dillon was on the way to the sauna when he looked in on Roper and found him sitting on his own, drinking tea and surveying his screens, virtually all of them showing Hunter's attack on Cazalet the previous night.

"That's going to run for a hell of a long time," Dillon said. "I presume it's not gone down well in Washington. I suppose Hunter will be recalled."

"I should imagine so, but no news from the White House yet. And there's something else." Roper told him about Dolan. "I've been in touch with the hospital and was lucky enough to find a doctor on duty who'd been involved. He told me that Dolan is not likely to live."

"What'll Hunter do?"

"I haven't the slightest idea. Daniel's in the sauna. I told him all about it when he looked in a short while ago. See what he's got to say."

The sauna was thick with steam, Holley the only occupant, and he said, as Dillon sat down, "Have you talked with Roper?"

"You could say that. Dolan's misfortune has really stirred the pot."

"Hunter has created an unacceptable situation from everyone's point of view," Holley said. "Remember what Ferguson said last night? That he wished someone would grab him by the scruff of the neck and drop him onto another planet or something?"

"I do indeed," Dillon said. "It would certainly be a good thing from everyone's point of view if he disappeared off the face of the earth for a while."

"Do you mean permanently?" Holley asked.

"A bit drastic, that," Dillon said. "But considering the situation, we shouldn't hang around."

"What are you thinking?"

"You own a Falcon 200, Daniel, one of the finest planes in the business. It needs two pilots, but that's okay because you have me to fly with you. And it seats six passengers, though we'll only have one."

"And who might that be?"

"Colonel Samuel Hunter, who do you think?"

"And what are we going to do, drop him out when we get airborne?"

"They used to do that in Vietnam, Daniel; they don't do that anymore. No, he's expressed considerable interest in Mali, so let's take him there."

"You're crazy," Holley said.

"You've got to go anyway. The Algerian foreign minister made it quite clear that he expected us to do something about Havoc, which means you in particular are expected to do your bit. So let's be practical. Your tanks full?"

"Yes. They always are. A fetish of mine."

"How long to Mali?"

"Six and a half hours."

"There you are," Dillon said. "A walk in the park, old son. We could do the return flight on the same day if necessary. Bamako may be the capital, but I suspect you'll find Timbuktu more romantic, since that's where you played the hero, galloping around dressed as a Tuareg, shooting the hell out of the black-flag crowd."

Suddenly, Holley found the idea so outrageous that it was distinctly appealing. "Damn you, Sean Dillon, the things you get me into. But what do we do with Hunter when we get there?"

"Make him give us details of all the crooked officials he and his people have been dealing with there. Roper would love that, and so would MI5."

"Okay, but what do we do with Hunter when we come back, dump him in the desert?"

"I must say there's a certain appeal to the idea of Hunter alone in the depths of the Sahara, but I think not. Let's just hope the shock makes him mend his wicked ways. Let's get moving," Dillon said. "And tell Roper we're going to take a couple of days off. Ferguson's so busy, we'll be back before he realizes we've gone."

"How do we lay hands on Hunter?" Holley asked.

"We'll drop into Charnley. I have a hunch Hunter will turn up there. If not, we'll persuade Weber to give him a call," Dillon said.

A little while later, Sara drove up in the Mini and walked into the computer room. "Morning, Giles," she said.

"And good morning to you, my love," he told her. "Where have you been?"

"Dropping Hannah off at college. She's on break, but she needs to practice. Four years of hard work lies ahead, and I'm not allowing her to forget it."

"She won't, Sara; she recognizes she's blessed with a gift that must be nourished in spite of her propensity to reach for the pistol in her pocket."

"Have Sean and Daniel had breakfast yet?"

"No, they are in the sauna. Have you heard about that sergeant of Hunter's?"

"No," she said. "What's this?"

"Lying at death's door after being run down by a bus in the early hours in Park Lane. Drunk out of his mind apparently."

"So what happens to the good colonel?" she asked. "Any word from Washington?"

"Not so far. Blake says he's spoken to Alice and she's told him the President is stunned by the events. Unsure of the right way to handle this."

Sara had been looking at Roper's control screen and she frowned. "What's all that, the addresses in Timbuktu?"

"Just something Sean and Daniel wanted."

"What for?" she asked.

Roper's delight in a certain civilized villainy rose easily to the surface. "Oh, they thought they might enjoy a day or two's fun in the Falcon."

"To Timbuktu." She was aghast. "Are they out of their minds? What does Ferguson think of this?"

"He's so busy, they didn't want to bother him."

"Well, they bother me. Let me guess—they're not going alone."

"Right as always. They plan to snatch Hunter, take him to Timbuktu, and have him point out all the crooked officials with their hands in the till."

"Stupid idiots," she said. "I need a bulletproof vest, the right clothes, and weaponry. Don't you dare allow them to leave without me."

"I wouldn't dream of it," he told her, as she ran out and went upstairs to her room, where she dressed quickly in a light khaki shirt over a bulletproof vest, khaki slacks, and desert boots, adding a flick knife in a sheath that she always wore around her right ankle, a Colt .25 with hollow-point cartridges that she carried in a rear belt holster, a shoulder bag with necessaries, Ray-Bans against the desert glare, and a crumpled khaki hat.

When she went down, Dillon and Holley were waiting in the computer room, suitably attired, and Dillon said, "Sorry, my love, it didn't occur to us that you'd like to come along."

Roper laughed, and Sara said, "Come off it, Sean, you lying toad."

Dillon turned to the other two. "I ask you, a nice Jewish girl, a rabbi's granddaughter, is that any way to speak?"

"Go on, get out of here," Roper said. "I'll take the blame with

Ferguson. Two days, and don't worry about Hannah, Sara. Tony will take care of her. Here are the MI5 notes on Mali."

SINCE WEBER WAS still, as it were, hiding out, the only hope Hunter had of finding him was driving down to Charnley, which he did, only to discover that Weber wasn't there, so he sat in the rented Mercedes, waiting and hoping.

The German, approaching in his old Volkswagen, paused on the hill, saw the Mercedes in the courtyard, and called the Master.

"I'm about to meet with Hunter."

"Find out what he wants and let me know as soon as you can," the Master said.

Weber coasted down the hill, drove through the gates of the airfield, and braked beside the Mercedes. Hunter got out, and said, "Hello there, I wanted to have a word with you. The thing is, I think I've been a damned fool in a lot of ways, and I want to put that right. What I'm trying to say is I'd like to have some sort of partnership with you. Everything aboveboard, I promise."

Weber was astonished—it was as if a different man were speaking. "Well, I'm not certain of anything at the moment, Colonel. I could well be interested, but give me a chance to open the office and I'll be back."

"Of course," Hunter said, smiling.

In the office, Weber was already talking to the Master. "It's weird, that's the only word for it. I don't know what's happened, but he's a different man. Quietly spoken, extremely polite. Do you think he could be in shock or something?"

"Remarkable," the Master said.

"It's like he's had a complete personality change."

There was no further conversation because, with a sudden roar outside, just like before, the Falcon swooped in to land beside the two parked Dakotas.

The airstair door opened, and Dillon said, "God bless all here," and walked with his hand outstretched to Hunter, who was standing beside the Mercedes.

In the office at the window, Weber said to the Master, "It's the Falcon pilot and a woman. They're all wearing desert dress."

"Interesting. Get out there and find out what they're up to."

THERE YOU ARE, COLONEL," Dillon said. "I'm sure you remember meeting us at the American Embassy," and the answer he got was surprising.

"Yes, indeed, Mr. Dillon, but especially you, Captain Gideon. I found the account of your combat in Helmand province to be incredibly moving. Your Military Cross was well earned."

Before Sara could reply, Dillon, who was slightly deflated, said, "Well, you really cocked things up at Hedley Court last night."

"I agree. It was one of the most stupid actions of my worthless life. I made a thorough fool of myself, something I've been prone to do for quite some time, and I'm not certain at all whether I can survive the consequences of my actions." He took a deep breath. "But how can I help you?"

Dillon was more than a little confused by the way the situation seemed to be going, and it was Sara who stepped in.

"We're headed to Mali for a couple of days, Colonel. I've been looking at MI5 reports about the corruption of government officials there and the illegal trading in Muslim artifacts."

Hunter shook his head, smiling. "I don't know where MI5 got such information, but it is not correct. There are other parties involved, of a much more criminal nature, and then ISIS, of course, which has to replace its war chest."

Sara had never seen Dillon so taken aback, so she took command because it was the obvious thing to do.

"We intend to go and see the situation for ourselves, and your experience would be very useful. I wonder if you'd consider coming along to give us the benefit of your knowledge?"

"Nothing would please me more. I'm yours to command."

She turned to Holley. "We can take off whenever you like, Daniel." She smiled at Weber. "I'm presuming I can interest you?"

"It's not possible for me, I'm afraid, but I wish you well," he said, and watched them go up the steps and enter the aircraft. Everything seemed to hang for a moment before the Falcon's engines burst into life and they roared down the runway and lifted off.

Weber waited until the sounds vanished into the distance, then he called the Master back. "Well, there they go, just like bosom buddies," he said. "Do you think it's genuine?"

"Hunter, you mean?" the Master said. "Only time will tell. One day or two, and we'll know soon enough," and he switched off.

WITH DILLON AND HOLLEY at the controls, and Sara and Hunter strapped into their seats in the cabin, the Falcon had climbed to thirty-five thousand feet and was cruising on automatic while Holley discussed the route with Dillon.

"Bay of Biscay, Spanish mainland, across the sea to Algeria, and then south over the Sahara. So easily said, but those are huge distances, several thousand miles, six and half hours."

"And landing at Timbuktu?" Dillon asked.

"That's where the action is. There is an airport, but I prefer the old airstrip at Fuad that's ten miles out from Timbuktu in the desert. It's a leftover from the French Foreign Legion days, but the military find a use for it in these troubled times, so refueling is available. This baby will be almost empty after six and half hours."

"You're sure they'll welcome us?" Dillon asked.

"Oh, yes, the Algerian foreign minister stands for a lot around there."

"Which means that as you are his special envoy people know better than to give you a bad time."

"Something like that," Holley told him. "But we do have a small military presence there, commanded by a pal of mine, a Major Caspar Selim. He's an army intelligence man. Interesting how many Arabs went to Sandhurst Military Academy."

"While IRA roughnecks like us," Dillon said, "had to make do with a Gaddafi training camp deep in the desert."

"Once in, never out," Holley commented.

"I echo that," Dillon told him. "If only because it's a bit bloody late in the day to nurse any regrets now. Why don't you go have a chat with Sara and the colonel? Tell them all the good things you've been discussing with me and leave out the bad. I'll take the Falcon off automatic for a while."

Holley went out laughing and Dillon took control, leaning back, thoroughly enjoying himself, when suddenly his Codex buzzed, and Ferguson said, "Enjoying the flight, Dillon?"

"I have to be honest, General, it has a lot to commend it."

"I'm sure it has, and if Daniel is willing to put his highly expensive aircraft to such good use, I'm delighted. On the other hand, it would be nice to have been asked."

At that moment, Sara looked in, a plastic cup of coffee in one hand, which she passed to Dillon, who said, "I have the General on the line."

"Morning, sir, I hope we're not being too outrageous. Colonel Hunter is proving to be a mine of information."

"Is he, by jove. What on earth has got into that man?"

"It's as if he's been shocked into a complete personality change, and, my goodness, he's being helpful. Before we left, Giles Roper passed on to me all the MI5 reports on Mali and the corruption of government officials. They implied a link with Havoc, and the Dakota full of Muslim artifacts that Weber flew into the U.K. seemed to confirm it."

"So what are you saying?" Ferguson demanded.

"What interested Hunter was that Weber's contacts had much more of a criminal background and nothing to do with officialdom."

"I thought al-Qaeda was involved in all this?"

"That's not strictly accurate, General," Sara said. "The revolution operated under the black flag of al-Qaeda to win the war, but the ordinary foot soldiers were the peasant variety, who stole everything in sight and had no idea that they were despoiling Muslim treasures."

"Which is where the true thieves and villains stepped in," Ferguson said. "Stuff worth millions peddled around the world to the highest bidder."

"All very sad, really, sir, when you think of it. Not what Osama bin Laden intended at all."

"Careful, Captain Gideon," Ferguson said. "Just remember which side you're on, and take care—you're sailing into uncharted territory. And don't forget we need proof about the villainy."

She said to Dillon, "I suppose you got that?"

"Every word. You were good, but he had a point. All you need is a head-to-toe black burka and face veil. Just remember to leave your eyes exposed."

"Damn you, Sean Dillon," she said, and returned to the cabin, where Hunter was reading a magazine and Holley lay with his seat tilted back, eyes closed.

Hunter said, "Is all well with you?"

"I think so, I'll take a rest. I suspect it will be a pretty grueling trip," and she lay back, tilting her seat also, and tried to sleep.

SHE CAME AWAKE with a start to discover Colonel Hunter sleeping and no sign of Dillon or Holley. She lay there looking up at the ceiling, then realized why she had awakened. Her Codex was trembling.

She said, "Who is this?"

The Master said, "Ah, there you are, Captain. I trust the trip is proving agreeable."

"How do you know about it?"

"Weber. He is concerned that you may be entering the circle of danger, as bullfighters call it, the one that offers only death in the afternoon. You must forgive him. He's a great fan of Hemingway."

"As it happens, so am I."

"Then promise me that you will take care at all times in Timbuktu. It is a wicked and dangerous place. I particularly urge you to guard yourself against a man called Doctor Aldo Florian. He owns the Astoria Hotel, popular with the French Foreign Legion a century ago."

"Then it would have also been a house of pleasure," Sara said.

"Of course, but a superior establishment."

"Is he al-Qaeda?"

"Allah forbid! There is not a kind bone in his body, and his code resembles that of a Mafia godfather."

"And you deal with such a man?"

"But of course. Remember the old saying: Keep your friends close and your enemies closer."

"So why would it matter to me what kind of man Florian is?"

"Because he controls the illegal worldwide traffic we've been discussing. The whole of North Africa, Europe, the U.K., and America. It's increasing exponentially."

"That's a big word," Sara told him. "Don't tell me that the mighty al-Qaeda can't do something about it?"

"Our day will come, of course, but we have other things to control, ISIS to put in its place."

"Of course," she said. "Their success must annoy you terribly. How do you like being outdone by upstarts?"

"Nobody outdoes us, Captain. We are the aristocracy of terrorism."

"I see," she said. "You mean you do it with style?"

He burst out laughing. "Oh, I like you, Captain Gideon."

"Even though I'm a Jew?"

"We are all people of the book," he said. "We just use different books. Take care, Captain. We'll speak again."

She lay there thinking about the call. Hunter was still asleep, the Falcon droned on, and as she adjusted her seat and sat up, Dillon ducked into the cabin. He opened one of the cupboards, revealing three large flasks of coffee and plastic mugs. Hunter pushed himself up, his sleep disturbed.

"Coffee, you two?"

"Yes, please," Sara said.

"Having a little kip, were you?"

"No, but I was having a very informative chat with the Master."

"I won't say are you kidding," Dillon told her, "because you never do."

Hunter said, "What did he want?"

"He urged me to watch myself because Timbuktu is such a wicked place, and to take care with Doctor Aldo Florian of the Astoria Hotel. Florian seems to be a kind of godfather, responsible for the worldwide illegal trade of Muslim artifacts. You'll be interested to know that al-Qaeda has no interest in that kind of trade."

Holley stepped out of the cabin. "Don't panic, I've put it on autopilot. What's going on?"

"The Master's been having a chat with Sara," Dillon said. "Apparently, he's told her that al-Qaeda isn't interested in the illegal trade."

"That doesn't surprise me, Sean. They've got bigger fish to fry."

"Like taking over in other countries, you mean?"

"Yes, but that's because from a religious point of view they believe their system is the most important one in the world," Holley said. "And they believe it was Osama's gift to them. Of course, the Vatican would dispute this, but that shouldn't bother us, as they proscribed the IRA years ago. I bet you can't even remember when you last went into a confessional box, so have a cup of coffee and shut up."

"Aye, aye, Captain," Dillon said, accepting the coffee. "But we can't get away from the fact that we need to find out as much as we can about Florian and his organization, especially how it's affecting the U.K."

"And we will." The Falcon lurched slightly, slapped by wind, and rain bounced off the windows. "But not now," Holley said. "I really think I'm needed back on the controls."

THERE WAS A REFRIGERATOR, a microwave for snacks, even a television, although the signal varied considerably, but they'd run into bad weather and a darkening horizon.

"Are we okay on time?" Sara asked.

Hunter said, "We left at ten, so we'll be arriving at five-thirty."

"So it should be pretty dark?"

"No, Captain Gideon," Hunter told her. "Very dark in a way that only the desert can be. Does that worry you?"

"No. I fought in Afghanistan, remember?"

"So did I, but coward that I am, I kept my head down. However, I believe what everyone from Lawrence of Arabia on has said: There is no other desert in the world like the Sahara. So cold, so bitterly cold at night, so incredibly lonely, and yet tribesmen and their families still travel with their camels and donkeys from one place to another in a journey that never seems to end."

"An ancient way of life, but who is to say it is wrong?" Sara said, and opened her shoulder bag. "Are you armed?"

"Why do you ask?"

"I get the impression that Timbuktu is a rough old town, and my impression of Florian is pretty harsh. He may not carry a pistol in his pocket himself, but I'm sure he'll be surrounded by people who do."

"You are, of course, completely right," he told her.

"I thought so." She unzipped the shoulder bag and took out a silenced Colt .25 and a small box of ammunition. "Hollow-point cartridges. I come from a hard school, Colonel Hunter. In our business, we don't aim to wound, only to kill. Whether you feel you can act in that way is your business."

"Never fear, Captain, this is exactly what I need," and he started to load it.

She passed him a rear belt holster. "The Colt fits nicely into one of these. Easy to draw when you need to."

She turned and found Dillon standing just outside the cockpit door. "What are you two up to? Preparing for war?" he asked.

"I suppose we are," she said. "From the sound of things, Timbuktu is the town where it pays to take care."

"Which should be interesting," he said, and went back to join Holley.

LATER, AS SHE SAT looking down at the desert below stretching into infinity, Sara felt engulfed by the vastness. They were still cruising at thirty-five thousand, but soon Holley started to take the Falcon down until the network of trails and roads became clear, making ancient routes, vehicles and camel trains visible, villages here and there, and then Timbuktu, rearing up out of the desert on the horizon like some fairy-tale city, the light blue sky of the day already tinged with the darker hue of night. It was impossible not to be excited by the look of the place as they descended.

They passed over the desert, lower and lower, until Fuad greeted them in the distance, the big surprise being the electric lights that marked out the runway and shone in welcome from the windows of the concrete flat-roofed buildings to one side, the oil tanks clearly visible.

A scattering of people watched as Holley dropped the Falcon in. He turned it around at the far end of the runway and started back to the oil tanks. "Fill her up, Sean, that's what I want in case anything untoward occurs and we need to get out fast."

Most of the spectators were Arabs, but they spotted a SandCat in desert camouflage with a crew of five men in army uniform manning it, a general-purpose machine gun mounted on it.

A uniformed major came to greet them as the airstair door opened, and Holley went out and greeted him with an embrace.

"Caspar, how goes it? What's happened to the Tuareg robes?"

"Too theatrical for the chief of staff. He feels simple khaki uniforms are more appropriate."

"How bloody boring is that?" Holley said.

"Well, orders are orders, you know how it is."

"I'd like you to meet Captain Sara Gideon."

"My goodness, but I know all about you." Caspar gave her a hug. "One old Sandhurst hand to another."

"I've heard a lot about you, too," she said. "Have you meet Colonel Samuel Hunter?"

Caspar shook hands. "No, I missed you when you were last here. I was fifty miles out at an oasis. The usual nonsense. Throat cutting between families. Can't have that."

Behind him, a small team was supervising the refueling, and Holley said, "All top quality, I trust?"

"Come off it, Daniel," Caspar told him. "When have I given you less? By the way, as your trip is completely unexpected, I'm afraid you're going to have to manage without me for two or three days. I'm needed at El Hajiz. Murder this time. I'll be off first thing in the morning."

"That's nice for you. We've no fixed plans. We could stay a couple of days or climb on board and clear off now."

"Well, that's up to you, old son. Where will you stay if you remain here?"

"The Astoria," Holley said.

"Well, that's as good as you'd get anywhere else in Timbuktu. Watch your pockets where Florian is concerned. I'll let him know you're in town and need somewhere to lay your weary heads. You can borrow one of our people. I've got to go and check up on my men now. I may see you later, I may not. Be sure to carry a weapon at all times."

THE JEEP WAS a workmanlike military vehicle in khaki green, ALGE-RIAN DEFENSE FORCE stamped across the hood in Arabic, and the pennants that flew on either side were small Algerian flags.

"With luck, this should be enough to frighten off any kind of troublemakers, and I know that you've all taken Caspar's advice to arm yourselves, so we will sally forth to experience a thousand and one Arab delights, a finger on the trigger at all times," said Holley.

The military Jeep had been an excellent idea—the people in the crowded narrow streets jumped to one side to avoid it like the plague. There was a warmth flowing like a current through those crowded alleys, and everything was varied. There were many women in black burkas and face veils, but just as many were flaunting faces of haunting beauty wrapped in the chador, the obligatory head scarf for women, and yet more women revealed faces of exceptional beauty framed by dark and lustrous hair flowing down over bare shoulders.

The Astoria was four stories high and stood in a courtyard at the end of a surprisingly wide alley. An entrance gate stood open, a large black man on either side wearing the same white uniform and green turban. There were cars parked inside the courtyard, and Holley drove in and paused.

The man on the left called to his friend. "More stupid Western-ers for the casino, but I could think of something better to do with the woman."

Holley said to Dillon, in Arabic, "I believe I've got something that needs scraping from my shoe."

Dillon said, "You're mistaken, my friend, he is the dung on my shoe."

Their perfect Arabic bewildered both men, and things were made worse when Sara joined in, also in excellent Arabic, and said, "They are not sure whether to play with themselves or say sorry."

The one on the right raised his hand to her, and Hunter grabbed his wrist with remarkable speed, and said, also in Arabic, "No way to treat a lady."

There was a great booming laugh, and they turned to see a very large man in a fez and a fawn linen suit, the armpits damp with sweat.

"It's a pleasure to hear such fluent Arabic and I'm grateful you haven't shot both of them. It's so difficult to find good people these days. I'm Doctor Aldo Florian. Come in, my friends, Caspar told me to expect you. Colonel Hunter, of course, I had the privilege of meeting when he was here before. You must excuse Ali and Selim."

"Quite a place you've got here," Holley told him, as they entered the foyer that extended into the casino, where every table seemed to be occupied. There was also a dining room with a four-piece group in a corner playing standards.

It was noisy and active and not what one would have thought of in such a location. "You look uncertain, Captain Gideon. Not what you expected of Timbuktu? So let's adjourn to my private quarters, enjoy a glass of champagne, have something to eat, and get to know one another." Florian turned, taking it for granted they would follow, and led the way.

There was a large mahogany desk, a computer on it, and all the usual bits and pieces needed to run a business, perhaps the most essential being the huge leather swing chair into which Florian sank as Holley and his friends followed him in. They were followed by Ali and Selim, who positioned themselves on either side of the door, both having produced machine pistols from their large coat pockets.

"Do you protect all your guests in such an extreme way?" Sara asked.

"These are dangerous times, Captain Gideon, and Timbuktu a particularly wicked place. I would have thought Colonel Hunter would have made that plain to you. Be seated, please."

The room was a welter of overstuffed divans, draperies hanging everywhere, everything touched by a perfume that was cloying and sickly. A woman in a black burka and face veil appeared from behind a hanging tapestry pushing a trolley, an open bottle in an ice bucket on it and four glasses.

"Krug champagne." Florian waved a hand. "A personal favorite."

"Yet there is no glass for you," Sara said in English, then in Arabic to the woman, "Take the trolley away. We are here on business, not pleasure, and do it now."

The woman didn't even hesitate and withdrew with the trolley, and Sara said, "So let's get down to business. Colonel Hunter, acting as an agent for British and American interests, has visited Timbuktu in past months to try to discover who is behind the ruthless plundering of Muslim treasures during the recent upheavals in Mali."

"And what would I know about that?"

"According to Colonel Hunter, everything there is to know."

"I knew you were trouble the moment you came in," he told her, producing a Walther quickly from a drawer in front of him. "We're making millions selling Muslim artifacts all over the world. Do you think I'll stand by and let you expose us? We prefer the quiet life in Switzerland."

As Florian fired, Hunter shoved Sara to one side so quickly that he received the bullet himself, which ploughed into the left side of his chest. Dillon, on his feet in an instant, shot Florian between the eyes, driving him backward over the swing chair.

At the same moment, Holley turned to Ali and Selim, who both dropped their machine pistols to the floor and ran out. Sara was already examining Hunter's wound. He had closed his eyes in shock.

She looked up at the others. "A serious business. He needs a top surgeon and a decent hospital."

"Well, all he'll get here while the authorities are arguing over the rights and wrongs is more medieval than anything else," Holley said, mobile phone in hand. "Caspar, we're in bad trouble and we've got to get the hell out of here. I'll explain when we get to Fuad, but make sure the Falcon gets a swift departure, and I'm going to need half a dozen of those army medical battle packs. Don't argue. We're leaving now."

A moment later, they were going, Holley and Dillon supporting Hunter between them, Sara following, her hand on the Colt ready in her pocket, but they had in no way disturbed the general hubbub of the casino, and there was no sign of Ali and Selim on the door.

In a matter of moments, they were driving out of the gate, Holley at the wheel.

AT FUAD, it was raining the warm night rain of the desert as Caspar's medical sergeant examined the wound. "This is a bad one, sir," he said to Caspar. "The bullet has ploughed through on the left side of the chest, but I think it has splintered the shoulder bone. All this is very close to the heart."

"Do you think he can survive the best part of seven hours on that Falcon?" Holley demanded.

"Our battle packs are those used by American Special Forces. He'll be bandaged tightly and given plenty of morphine. But only Allah can say whether he can survive," said the sergeant.

"Will there be any problems with air-traffic control if we want to leave now?" Holley asked.

Caspar said, "Florian was a disgusting human being in every way. Get on that plane and I will tell aircraft control that it's a request from the Algerian foreign minister himself. A speedy journey, my friend, and may Allah guard all of you, particularly a brave man named Colonel Samuel Hunter."

THE FALCON SOARED into the night, Holley staring into a multiplicity of dials, Dillon glancing back at the lights fading rapidly as they climbed to thirty-five thousand and leveled off.

"And so we say farewell to Timbuktu, city of romance and adventure. If ever a city looked like a movie set, that did. So, who do we call, Roper or Ferguson?"

"Roper," Holley said. "And if he thinks it should be Ferguson, he'll say so."

ROPER WAS IN THE COMPUTER ROOM having a chat with Hannah, who was able to stay the night because Blake and Cazalet were staying over at Highfield Court, and they were both surprised when Dillon came on the line.

"Where are you?" Roper demanded.

"Winging our way back as fast as we can."

"You didn't last long. What went wrong?"

"Oh, a particularly obnoxious character named Aldo Florian tried to shoot Sara, but the good Colonel Samuel Hunter flung himself in the way and took the bullet for her. It's bad, Giles, through the left chest area, chipping the shoulder bone and too damned close to the heart."

"Then why isn't he in hospital?"

"Because getting the hell out of there seemed the smart thing to do after I shot Florian between the eyes."

"Let me get this straight," Roper said. "Hunter has saved Sara's life?"

"You'd have to see him to believe it. He's no longer the idiot who shot his mouth off to Cazalet. He jumped in to cover her and took Florian's bullet without hesitation."

"And then you shot Florian?"

"And legged it back to the plane, where we got some military first aid from Holley's chums, then got the hell out of there. Scores of millions these bastards are making, and Florian indicated they've been using Switzerland. I heard that just before I shot him. MI5 will be pleased."

"The Muslim Council will be more pleased than anybody," Roper said. "But never mind that for the moment. What do you need?"

"Permission to land at Farley between two and three in the morning. If Hunter's still alive, he'll need instant treatment, so alert Professor Charles Bellamy and Matron Maggie Duncan to be ready. He is a brave man; he did take the bullet and saved Sara's life. What about Dolan?"

"He passed on, I'm afraid. But I still don't understand the change in Hunter."

"He's a different man. You'll obviously pass all this to Ferguson."

"Of course."

"Try to get him to take it easy for the next few hours," Hannah called. "Sean, tell Sara I love her."

"Of course I will, and we'll see you soon." Dillon turned to Holley. "I'll go and see how they are. I'll bring you a coffee."

He went into the cabin and found Sara sitting beside Hunter with a basin of water and a hand towel. "How is he?" Dillon asked.

"A bit of a temperature. His forehead is rather warm." She wiped it carefully.

Dillon said, "I've been talking to Roper. He'll see to everything, Rosedene, Bellamy, and Maggie Duncan. Hannah told me to say she loves you."

"Bless her," Sara said.

"Dolan died, which is unfortunate, but Roper still can't get his head around the change in Hunter. What about you?"

"I can tell you I had several talks with him before he placed his life on the line, and I found him a different individual from the man who'd harassed Cazalet from the audience. Maybe a psychiatrist would have a suggestion why that might be, I don't know. But I'll tell you one thing: He was a true hero to do what he did for me."

"And you know what?" Dillon said. "I agree with that statement completely," and he poured two cups of coffee and took them into the cockpit.

Sara sat there, carefully wiping the colonel's forehead. Her phone buzzed, and the Master said, "Praise to Allah. I was distressed to hear what happened. How is he?"

"The wound was point-blank and did considerable damage. He's on lots of morphine and swathed in battle packs. We have made arrangements to treat him at the highest level."

"Which means that hospital that Ferguson provides for his people, Rosedene. I shall pray for you."

She took a deep breath. "I shall never understand you, you know."

"Don't let it worry you. We'll speak again. Try to get some sleep."

Which she did, of course, out of it for a couple of hours, awakening to a panic at finding Holley bending over Hunter. "Oh, my God," she said. "How is he?"

"I've taken his temperature and it's high, which you must expect, and he's sweating profusely, but we must also expect that. I've just made fresh coffee and filled the flasks, so keep drinking it. It will help, I promise you. I'll get back to Sean. We're expecting heavy rain."

He went out, and Sara sat there on the stool beside the seat they'd tipped back so that Hunter could be laid out on it. She was not conscious of having fallen asleep again, only that she'd leaned over, her cheek against the colonel's body, when suddenly she was conscious that they were landing.

THE WAITING AMBULANCE with Bellamy inside greeted them, as did Tony Doyle in the Subaru, Hannah his only passenger. She threw her arms about Sara at once, and Sara burst into tears. They scrambled into the vehicle, and Holley and Dillon followed.

"God bless you, Tony," Dillon said. "I can't wait to get back to bed at Holland Park."

"Well, you'll have to. Professor Bellamy insists that everyone in the party come in for a full checkup. Regulations."

"To hell with regulations," Dillon said.

"Just look on the bright side, Sean," Holley told him. "As I recall, they do a very nice breakfast at Rosedene."

HUNTER WAS RUSHED OFF for X-rays, and Maggie Duncan put an arm about Sara.

"There's only one place for you, bed. You look like a walking corpse."

"I don't know about Daniel, but I feel like one," Dillon told her. "Having said that, we all drank too much coffee on the trip so a nice cup of tea would go down a treat before we retire. It's an old Irish remedy that our friends across the Atlantic have failed to learn."

"Well, go and wait in reception, and I'll have one of the girls bring some from the kitchen, but after that, it's bed for the three of you." They did as they were told and were drinking tea when

Bellamy appeared in theater scrubs looking grave, Maggie standing behind him,

"Go on," Sara said. "Tell us the worst."

"That army sergeant was good, and right on the button with his diagnosis. Severe damage to the upper area of the lung on the left side. He must have pushed you down, Sara, and received the bullet at point-blank range. You were quite right; he certainly saved your life."

"Yes, I was aware of that, Professor."

"Slight tearing to the left side of the heart and considerable splintering of the left shoulder bone. I'll do what I can, but it's going to take some of my best work."

"How long?"

"Between three or four hours in theater and probably a year of therapy after that, but, for God's sake, Sara, you look as if you might faint at any moment. Bed for you."

Maggie stepped in and put an arm around her. "Just through this door, room three." As they moved, Maggie looked over her shoulder at Dillon and Holley. "Four and five for you, and don't be stupid, let it happen."

IT HAD RAINED most of the night in London, drifting across Mayfair and rattling the shutters of Kate Munro's bedroom in the early Victorian town house called Munro Place at the end of Green Street, with its wonderful views across to Hyde Park.

Originally the home of a great-aunt, a well-known suffragette in her day, it had passed on through the family with the proviso that it should never be sold, only inherited, and the death of Kate's parents on a Spanish holiday brought ownership to her, the good thing being that she had lived there since childhood. The fact that soaring London prices meant that it was now worth millions was something to be endured, especially when one considered that the narrow flagged path giving access to the rear garden was barely wide enough to park Kate's Mini.

A maiden aunt, her mother's sister, Molly, had moved in while Kate went to St. Hugh's College, Oxford, where she studied geography, geology, and archeology, enjoying life in the open air and managing to describe her travels well enough to create a reputation as a freelance writer whose work was sought after.

The events at Hedley Court had been unlooked for. She had not attended with the intention of writing a piece. She'd simply been interested in hearing Cazalet, and then the disturbance with Hunter had happened and her instincts as a journalist had taken over.

She did not work full-time for the *Spectator* but had seen a number of her pieces published by it and had been certain the editor would be happy to consider her work again. In fact, she had already knocked out fifteen hundred words and intended to get straight on it after breakfast.

She turned on the old-fashioned tea maker beside the bed, then crossed to the window to pull back the curtains. In spite of the wind and rain and early morning traffic of Park Lane, the view of Hyde Park never ceased to give her joy, and as the kettle whistled, she turned, feeling good, and went and made her tea. She raised the cup to her lips, and her mobile buzzed.

She picked it up with one hand as she sipped. "Kate Munro," she said.

"I was very impressed with your question for President Cazalet. It was quite thoughtful."

"Well, thank you."

"And then that strange American Colonel Hunter and his rage. I've never seen anything like it. Are you actually writing about it for the *Spectator*?"

"I'm freelance, but they have published me in the past. Tell me, who is this?"

"People just call me the Master, Kate," he said. "But rest easy, I'm not a crank."

"Well, I think you might be, my polite friend, so I think I'll switch off at this point."

"And miss out on the most remarkable story of your career?"

"What do you mean?"

"What if I told you that Hunter is in a private hospital called Rosedene as we speak—that he'd been shot in the chest yesterday in Timbuktu and flown back last night in a private Falcon jet, nursed all the way by Captain Sara Gideon of the Army Intelligence Corps, one of General Ferguson's people."

She hesitated, and then said, "Who the hell are you?"

"I've told you. Now let's see how far you get with the information I've given you. I'll call you again later."

Kate went straight downstairs to her study, found her smartphone, and sat behind the desk. The door opened and Aunt Molly looked in.

"Breakfast?"

"Not right now, love. I'll let you know."

Molly withdrew and Kate looked up Rosedene hospital and there it was. Private referrals only. No reference to medical staff.

She phoned anyway, and when a woman answered, Kate said, "I'm trying to trace a friend, but I'm not sure whether I've got the right hospital. A Colonel Samuel Hunter."

"This is a private establishment, and I'm afraid we can't give out that kind of information."

"Thank you," Kate said.

At Rosedene, Maggie Duncan pressed a button that put her straight through to Roper.

"I just received a query asking if Hunter is here."

"I'll get right on it," he said.

But Kate Munro had moved on, looking up Captain Sara Gideon, and was astounded at what she found. She was moving on to Ferguson when Molly looked in. "It's on the table now. Anything else can wait."

Kate followed her along to the kitchen to find perfect scrambled eggs and toast. "Nothing better," Kate said. "Ian Fleming used to eat it three times a day. Just the food for a writer."

Halfway through, her phone buzzed and Kate answered.

"How are you doing?" the Master asked.

"I called and they said they've no knowledge of a Samuel Hunter. Didn't seem the kind of place to tell me if they did, though. Sara Gideon, she's a remarkable lady, only lives minutes away from me, as it happens. So where you are going with this?"

"Did you know that Colonel Hunter was an official presidential aide?"

"He's what?" Kate said. "That's terrible."

"I thought so, too. But what if it was a plot by British Intelligence people to make him look like some sort of bad guy so the really bad guys would be fooled? I believe I know why and who, and I'm willing to give it all to you. Hunter a true American hero, and you could be part of all that, Kate. You'd be famous."

"Notorious, more like. Why should I believe you? What's in this for you?"

The Master started to reply when the front doorbell sounded.

She went and peered out of the window. "My goodness, there's a wonderful old Daimler out there, an army staff sergeant at the wheel and a woman army captain in full uniform. The man holding the umbrella for her wears a trench coat, a slouched hat, and looks dangerous. Do you think they've arrived to save me?"

"Something like that, although I don't think it was intended. I'll say good-bye for the moment, Kate. We'll talk again."

MOLLY CAME IN to say she'd answered the door. She was quite excited. "There's a very nice army officer asking to see you. Very smart she is, a captain, and I've never seen a woman wearing so many medal ribbons. The man with her is Irish. I heard him talking to her."

"Well, let's have a look," Kate said.

Her aunt ushered them in, Dillon leaving the umbrella in the hall. Sara, holding her hand out, said, "Captain Sara Gideon, Miss Munro. May I say I admired the part you played in Hedley Court when President Cazalet was making his speech."

"Well, that's nice, but what's this all about?" Kate demanded. "Are you MI5 or 6?"

"No, although we use them when it's necessary," Sara said. "We serve under the Prime Minister's warrant to take care of problems of intelligence for him."

"I had no idea such an outfit existed," Kate said. "Is it legal?"

Dillon broke in. "It's been working successfully since the Second World War. It serves irrespective of political party, and people have died meeting its demands. It's commanded by Major General Charles Ferguson, and all that is privileged information. You could be arrested for disclosing its existence, and there is no mention of it online although some people used to refer to it as the Prime Minister's private army."

"And who are you?" she said. "Another soldier?"

"You have no idea how funny that is," Dillon told her.

"Don't mind him, he likes shocking people, but don't let him. You phoned Rosedene and inquired after Colonel Hunter?" Sara asked.

"Yes, I did, and I was told there was no one of that name there. I deduce from the way you are acting that there is."

"Yes, and fighting for his life, as it happens."

"After taking a bullet meant for you point-blank in his chest."

"How do you know that?" Dillon asked.

"I had a strange call on the phone this morning," Kate said. "An older guy who thought I'd done well at the speech. He praised me to the skies, then turned a bit odd. He tried to make me believe that Hunter was obnoxious at the speech on purpose as part of a plot by you people."

Sara was nonplussed. "Did he give you his name?"

"Not really. He made a big deal of it, but when I asked him for a name, he just said that people called him the Master."

Dillon said, "There you go, Sara. He's returned to haunt you. If you and Kate got your heads together and shared notes, then maybe the rest of us could make sense of what's going on."

"Sean, he's playing with us. I don't know why he's trying out this story, but maybe he thinks that by pitching it this way it'll keep us from looking too hard into his business. After all, it makes Hunter into even more of a hero—me, too, in a way. All the press attention—I'd be famous. Maybe he was trying to buy me off with that. And you, too, Kate."

Dillon said, "Can you be bought, Kate? I wouldn't have thought so."

"Not a chance." And just then Kate's smartphone buzzed. She answered it and found the Master.

"Are they still there, Kate?" he asked.

"Standing right here."

Sara held out her hand. "Give me the phone." Kate did and Sara turned it on to speaker. "What a fool you made of me on the flight back. All that soft soap you handed out as if you were concerned."

"But I was and am. That is the civilized way we would like to behave except that we serve on different sides in a war, don't we? And that means that one has to kill people. You did, didn't you, Sara, when you fired that heavy machine gun in Afghanistan? What was your score? Forty?"

"Go to hell," she said, and Sara switched off and turned to Kate. "General Ferguson would like to see you if that's convenient. Would that be a problem with your aunt?"

"Not at all; she only visits me now and then. Has a cottage in West Sussex, Aldwick Bay, just along from Bognor Regis. I love it so much that whenever I get the blues I jump in my old Mini and drive down there."

"There is no such thing as an old Mini," Dillon said. "I tell myself that every time I get in mine. Of course, it's supercharged."

Kate said, "So is mine."

"Well, there you are, then, obviously a lady of taste and discrimination. I allow Sara and my cousin to use mine." He turned to Sara. "You could start a club."

"Never mind that," Sara told him. "We've business to take care of. General Ferguson would very much like to meet you, Kate. That would be at our safe house in Holland Park. It wouldn't be out of the way to call in on Rosedene first."

"That's fine by me," Kate said. "I'll just tell Aunt Molly what's happening, then I'll get ready."

AT ROSEDENE, Maggie Duncan was unable to see them for a while. A young nurse informed them that a trauma or two had erupted, but she'd be available soon. In the meantime, coffee would be provided in reception.

"This is nice," Kate said to Dillon.

"Small, but superbly equipped," Dillon said. "It's run by Professor Charles Bellamy to take care of people damaged in our line of work."

Tony Doyle, sipping his coffee, said, "He put you together a few times."

"I'm happy to say," Dillon told him.

"A lot better than trying to get the nuns to take you in or the village doctor when you were on the run."

"The first time I was shot was in Belfast, all of nineteen, and I thought I was bound to be lifted," Dillon said.

"So what happened?" Tony asked.

"You know the British Army never stopped ambulances, so the Provos sent me and four others down to the border in one, where we could cross to a convent run by the Little Sisters of Pity. The mother superior, a surgeon who'd trained at London University, was first class."

Kate said, "You mean you were in the Provisional IRA?"

"Probably its top enforcer," Tony told her.

Kate looked at Sara. "I don't understand."

"You're not meant to. One of our best chaps is a convert from al-Qaeda; I shot forty men in Afghanistan. We find it takes all sorts."

At that moment, Maggie Duncan appeared wearing theater scrubs. "Sorry, it's been all hands to the pumps today, and Professor Bellamy is busy reassuring two or three patients. He'll be with you soon, but come along the corridor and have a look at Colonel Hunter through the viewing window."

He was festooned with tubes and electronic lines, fluid of one kind or another pumping into his body. There was a slight humming, the room dimly lit, and there was a corpselike look to him.

"What are his chances?" Sara asked Maggie.

It was Bellamy who answered as he came up behind them. "Not good at all, I'm afraid. It wasn't until I opened him up that I discovered Florian had been using hollow-point cartridges. I hardly need point out to you, Sara, the appalling damage such rounds can cause."

"We'll stay in touch," Sara said. "This is Kate Munro, a new friend, and we've got to have words with Ferguson, so we'd better get moving."

As they went back to reception, Philip Hardy entered. "I thought I'd better show my face. How is he?"

"Professor Bellamy can tell you that," Sara said. "He's still here." She turned to Kate. "I'm sure you remember Ambassador Hardy from Hedley Court. This young lady is the journalist who asked President Cazalet why he'd left Harvard."

Hardy shook her hand. "And thank God he did. He saved my life more than once in Vietnam. I'll go see Bellamy. I'm pressed for time."

Sara turned to Kate. "Are you okay?"

"Oh, you know how it is," Kate told her. "I've met one of the few women in the British Army to be awarded a Military Cross, the top enforcer of the Provisional IRA, and the American ambassador, and am about to have words with the general commanding the Prime Minister's private army. Just another day, I suppose."

"Not quite. You also get the army's finest bomb disposal officer,

Major Giles Roper, winner of the George Cross, and though that's as good as it gets, it also earned him a wheelchair. He's the man who traced you so quickly."

"That's it," Kate said. "I give in, so let's get moving to this Holland Park place."

It astounded her when they got there, the grim walls and electric gates, all rather intimidating, but Roper's computer room with its multiplicity of screens she found quite amazing, as she did the man himself, sitting in his wheelchair and devouring a bacon sandwich while reviewing the world.

"You asked Jake Cazalet exactly the right question the other night," he said. "Because his answer told us so much about him, and the ability to extract such information with accuracy is what good journalism is all about."

"Why, Major Roper," she said, "I suspect that praise from you is praise indeed, if slightly overdone."

Dillon said, "There you go, Giles, the lady's got the measure of you straightaway."

Ferguson entered at that moment, followed by Sara, who had gone to get him. "Don't listen to him, Miss Munro," he said. "Dillon, as you'll find, seldom takes life seriously for very long, but let's get down to business. The approach the Master made to you was the first time he's been in touch?"

"Absolutely," Kate said. "He called me out of the blue and told me how good I'd been at Hedley Court. I asked him for his name, and when he said that people called him the Master, I decided he was a crank and told him I was cutting off. That was when he launched into the whole Hunter affair and what a big deal it could be for me if I became involved. He said I'd be famous in America, on television. Everything. He told me about Rosedene, Captain Gideon."

"So what did you do?"

"Checked that Hunter was at Rosedene and that Captain Gideon existed, and he phoned me back, and we were talking when she and Dillon arrived at my house. I didn't know who they were at the time, so he cut off."

"And that was it?" Ferguson said.

"No, he called me back later, and when Captain Gideon realized he was on again, she took the phone and gave him a bad time." She shrugged. "That's it and I've not heard from him again."

"Well, thanks for being so frank."

"Look, General," she said. "I want to be reasonable about this, and I'm not averse to serving my country, but what's going on here?"

"We are not fighting just ISIS these days," he said. "But also al-Qaeda. Their Grand Council is based in Europe, but they have what they call Masters based all over the world controlling events at a local level."

"Can't you do anything about them?"

"Yes, we can, and we have disposed of a couple. Finding this one is proving particularly difficult."

"What do you want with me?"

"I'm not certain. If he gets in touch with you again, you must let us know. Your aunt lives with you, I believe?"

"Only now and then. She's gone back to her cottage in West Sussex."

"I can't say I'm happy about that," Ferguson said. "You should have someone there, especially overnight. Somebody who knows what they are doing."

"And is capable of shooting the hell out of anyone who tries to gain access," Dillon put in.

"And who would you suggest, Sean?" Sara asked.

"Well, as I mentioned to Kate, I have a cousin on the other side of the park at the Royal College of Music. Nineteen years of age and a genius. You wouldn't happen to have a piano in the house, would you?"

"Indeed I do. In the garden drawing room, there is an old upright Bechstein. I don't play, but Aunt Molly does."

"Well, there you are, a sign from heaven indeed."

"I'm sure she'll be excellent company, but aren't you forgetting the security part?"

"Not where Hannah's concerned. My cousin was raised from childhood in the depths of the Irish countryside during the Troubles. She was handling a pistol at twelve, carries a Colt .25 in her handbag, and sometimes uses a stick because, like Sara, she limps, in both their cases because of enemy action."

"I'm speechless," Kate said.

"You'll be able to write a book about it," he told her.

THE LAST HANS WEBER had seen of Colonel Samuel Hunter was his departure from Charnley in the Falcon with Dillon, Holley, and Sara Gideon. He was unaware of the events in Timbuktu or the fact that the Falcon had already returned. He had locked up at

Charnley and moved to Hatherley Court, to await developments, which was where the Master found him.

Weber listened in amazement to his account of events.

"So Hunter's prospects don't look very good?"

"Not really, in spite of his being in the hands of a great surgeon. Although I'm not suggesting he should be assisted into the next world, his demise would certainly be a relief to a wide range of people."

Weber was horrified but didn't say so. "What do you want me to do with the Dakotas?"

"Nothing is the answer, not at the moment. MI5 are aware of the first load of Muslim artifacts brought into the country, yet they haven't arrested you and haven't closed Charnley down. You can still leave it open for small aircraft and the like. There is a living there, so carry on as normal while we see how the other business works out. I'll speak to you when I need to."

ON HIS BARGE at the Quai des Brumes in Paris, the Master took a glass of red wine out to the stern and sat in one of the cane chairs, considering the situation. Weber was a faithful servant, events had shown that, and he could still be so in the future.

Colonel Samuel Hunter had morphed from a rather bad man into a gallant hero, which would have made him totally useless for any future machinations the Master had in mind. On the other hand, that didn't really matter now as his life touched the edge of death at Rosedene despite Professor Bellamy's best work.

Which left Kate Munro. A disappointment, really. It had started well. After all, he had offered her so much. Quite staggering professional opportunities that it would be stupid to refuse, but that was the problem with young women. So unreliable. He sighed. He decided to try one more attempt to make her see reason and reached for his phone.

The garden at the back of Munro Place was small but charming, a small stone-flagged terrace leading to a lawn, flower beds, and two cypress trees. It was possible to walk around from where the Mini was parked, but French windows gave access inside, and when the Master phoned, Kate was sitting at the garden table. She was enjoying a cup of coffee while Dillon, who'd brought her home from Holland Park, went off to pick up Hannah so they might meet.

When her phone buzzed, she answered it without a thought but recognized the voice at once.

"There you are, Kate, a remarkable day, I would think, and full of surprises. Hunter still hanging on to life, I hear."

"Look, what do you want?" she demanded.

"An answer to my offer of fame and fortune and an entry into the big time, New York, Washington, CNN."

"Absolutely not."

"Don't be silly. You'd be crazy to turn down such opportunities with your talent."

"Oh, I don't know. I'd rather write about you, I think. Now that would be an eye-opener. A sure best seller. Whoa, I could even sell the movie rights."

"You are an intelligent woman, my dear, so you can't be serious."

"Why not?" she demanded.

"Because I see I am wasting my time where Hunter is considered. He will probably die anyway, and if you try to investigate me, you'll be signing not only your own death warrant but also Aunt Molly's, I promise you."

"I'll see you in hell," she told him grimly, and switched off.

Dillon and Hannah came around the corner, and he said, "What was that about?"

"The Master again, one threat after another. So this is Hannah? I've heard a lot about you."

Hannah shook her hand. "That's a top smartphone you've got there. Could we listen to what he said just now?"

"Of course." Kate picked up a tray. "As you're Irish, I'll go and make some tea."

When she came back, Dillon was coldly angry, but Hannah was calm and collected. She opened her shoulder bag and took out her usual weapon, which she placed on the table between them.

"I've killed with that gun on several occasions. The circumstances of my life have made it necessary. It is a silenced Colt .25, and I fire hollow-point cartridges with it because they are more destructive than any other kind. I find it easy to administer justice that way, as I was the victim of a car bomb in Northern Ireland that left me crippled, the same affliction that Sara Gideon suffers from as you may have noticed."

"Yes, I have," Kate said. "So what can I do about this situation?"

"Sean and I will take you back to Holland Park now to the shooting range, where we'll familiarize you with the same weapon as mine and make sure you know what you're doing if you have to. The stopover tonight is fine by me, by the way, so I suggest we get moving."

THE GARDEN OF THE SAFE HOUSE boasted a large bunker from the Second World War, with targets of soldiers brightly illuminated. Roper was practicing there with Sara when they arrived. He was firing an unsilenced Beretta, the noise terrible in the enclosed gallery. He stopped, and he and Sara turned to greet them.

"There you are," Roper said to Kate. "So you had trouble when you returned. Sean sent me the audio from your smartphone, the argument you had with the Master. Not nice."

"An understatement," Kate said. "The threats to me are bad enough, but to include my old aunt Molly is despicable."

"Well, let's see if we can teach you to be able to retaliate when it becomes essential," Roper said. "We'll make it simple. Each of us is to use the same weapon, and we'll make it our standard-issue Colt .25."

TWO HOURS PASSED and it was amazing how quickly Kate got the hang of it and the lack of sound made a huge difference. "I can't believe I'm doing this," she said to Hannah. "And the silence is so eerie."

"Some people prefer the sound of the weapon when it's not silenced," Hannah told her, "because of the frightening effect."

"And what about you?"

Hannah pulled a lever and six charging soldiers stood up straight. She raised her silenced Colt and very deliberately shot the first one in the head, then did the same to the other five.

"There you go," she said. "Six men dead, and silently. Now that's really scary, don't you think?"

"I'm shivering all over," Kate told her.

"You did really well," Dillon said, and passed a shopping bag to her. "A present for you from the Wilkinson Sword Company. A nylon-and-titanium bulletproof vest. I'm wearing one now, and so is Hannah. It will stop a Colt .45 fired at close quarters. In your present circumstances, I'd put it on at your earliest convenience. Ferguson would like to see us in the computer room, so let's go there and wait for him."

IN FACT, Ferguson was already in the computer room with Blake Johnson and Cazalet, and the Daimler waited outside with Tony Doyle at the wheel.

"It's going to be a long weekend. President Cazalet, Blake, and I are needed in New York for a series of secret meetings with anti-terrorism people regarding a new way of meeting the ISIS threat. That means you'll have to stand in at Highfield Court, Captain Gideon, with Dillon and Holley," Ferguson said.

"Which leaves Hannah to back up Kate Munro," Roper said.

"Are you suggesting I'm not up to it?" Hannah asked.

"Shame on you, Major Roper," Kate told him. "She shot six soldiers through the head on the shooting range. What on earth has a woman to do to prove herself?"

"Enough of this nonsense," Ferguson told them. "I have every faith in our Hannah, and I'm sure you couldn't be in better hands, Miss Munro, so let's get out of here, gentlemen," and he led the way.

SADIE HAVING BEEN left on her own at Highfield Court, Holley and Sara made tracks to help her, and it was left to Dillon to give Hannah and Kate a ride back to Green Street.

"Would you like to come in?" Kate asked him, when they got there.

"I could check inside the house if you like."

"Holy Mother of God, Sean," Hannah said. "We've each got a Colt .25 about our person. Poor weak women we might be, but I think the two of us together might just manage any man who tried to jump us."

"Would you shut your gob, girl, and here's me only conscious of my responsibility for you as your cousin. I'd hate to think of you getting into the kind of scrape that might require Mr. Teague's assistance. After all, it's been known."

"Get out of it before I brain you," she said, hurrying in after Kate, then turning to slam the door. "Damn you, Sean Dillon."

"Don't be silly, you adore the man, but then who wouldn't. He's a charmer. Your cousin, you say? What about your parents?" Kate asked.

"Killed in that car bomb near Belfast when I was fourteen. Stone dead on the instant, the both of them. I was the survivor though I have to hobble around some days with a walking stick. It varies."

"I'm so sorry."

"It's strange, but that's what people always say. I wonder why that is?"

"Because they can't think of anything else."

"Good answer. Where's this piano you mentioned?"

"Just through here." Kate opened a clever folding door, obviously Victorian, and disclosed a charming sitting room with an outlook on the garden and an old black Bechstein upright piano in an alcove.

Hannah sat down, flexed her fingers, and launched into a Bach prelude, very fast, very showy. Kate was astonished. "That's absolutely brilliant."

"Oh, I can do Cole Porter, too, but I'm not sure who for. These days, the kids have never heard of Bogart, never mind Fred Astaire."

She dropped into a sofa, and Kate sat opposite on a stool, and said, "What on earth did Sean mean about Mr. Teague and for you not to get into the kind of scrape that might require his assistance?"

"Well, Mr. Teague is the boss of what we term the Disposal Team. We call them in when there's a body, or maybe two, that needs handling."

"You mean he's an undertaker?"

"Not exactly. What you might call a private undertaker. Cremate a corpse, you'll have about six pounds of gray ash in an hour."

"But is that legal?"

"No, it's not. Ferguson decided years ago that too many bad guys, terrorists and people of that ilk, were getting away with it, courts failing, so he brought in summary justice. We knock them off, and Mr. Teague cremates them."

"But that's terrible," Kate said.

"Well, the ones I was responsible for were absolute bastards, I promise you. You're entitled to your opinion, but I'm only nineteen and I've been involved with death and destruction for most of my life, and am aware of what so many bad people are capable of that I see things differently. I hope it won't spoil our friendship."

Kate jumped up. "No, dammit, I won't let it." She looked at her watch. "Let's have some fun, it's only half past eight, and fifteen minutes' walk down Park Lane is one of the best hotels in the world."

"You mean the Dorchester? Well, I'm with you there."

"Well, let's adjourn to the Dorchester bar, see off a bottle of champagne, and indulge in one of their amazing light suppers."

"Now you're talking," Hannah said. "No need to change, so let's get going."

AT THE DORCHESTER, they found a quiet night and thus managed to get a booth not too far from the bar. The pianist nodded to Hannah and smiled warmly.

"Would he let you play, do you think?" Kate asked.

"Musicians, particularly pianists, treasure their fiefdoms. I wouldn't be welcome."

"Well, that doesn't seem right."

"I'm too good, and that isn't ego. It's the rules of the game," Hannah said. "And that doesn't apply to just music but also the other arts. Journalism, too, I'd think."

"You're not wrong there."

"Now, allow me to introduce you to Dillon's favorite champagne, Krug. We'll split a bottle, and I'll let you choose what we have to eat."

Which turned out to be lobster with a French salad, Jersey Royal potatoes, and chopped onions, followed by a milk-chocolate soufflé.

"Isn't it strange when something is so disgustingly wonderful?" Kate said.

"You certainly can turn a phrase—an essential gift for a good journalist! The meal was excellent, the company amazing, so God bless the good work, and we'll take our time walking back."

"I hope this is the beginning of a beautiful friendship," Kate said. "So this meal's on me," and she gave the waiter her credit card.

"Fair enough," Hannah told her, as her Codex sounded. She held it to her ear and the smile faded. A few moments later, she nodded. "Thanks for letting me know, Giles."

She turned the phone off, her face grave. "Hunter has just died. Heart and lung damage just too much. Bellamy will be devastated."

Kate nodded, and they walked out, their evening turned more somber.

It was warm and sultry as they walked along Park Lane. A man came up behind them wearing a French beret and a belted anorak, but he stepped off the pavement and passed them without a word, walking fast, and turned to the right.

They watched him, but he seemed to be no threat, and they carried on to Green Street, pausing beside the parked Mini while Kate unlocked the front door. They entered the house, and Kate led the way into the drawing room, switching on the garden lights, then opening the French windows, and stepping outside, Hannah following.

"My goodness, it's warm," Kate said. "I think I'll make some tea."

As she turned to go inside, the man with the French beret stepped out of the rhododendrons and grabbed Hannah at pistol point from behind, an arm about her neck.

"The Master wants you two dead, but he didn't say how, so I'm going to enjoy myself." He nuzzled Hannah's neck, and said to Kate, "Don't worry, sweetheart, I'll get around to you later."

"I don't think so, you piece of shit," she said, as she pulled out her Colt .25 from her pocket, leveled it, and shot him between the eyes. Hannah stepped back, allowing the corpse to fall to the ground.

Kate stood there, the Colt hanging from her hand. "So easy," she said. "I can't believe I could do that."

"Well, you did," Hannah said. "And it was a damn sight better than what he intended for us."

"What a criminal he was," Kate said. "As for the Master . . ."

"It would be a pleasure to see him face-to-face," Hannah said, and phoned Roper. "Giles, we need the Disposal Team at Kate's house."

"What happened?"

"A very obnoxious hit man turned up, sent by the Master. He managed to grab me and made it clear he had rape on his mind as well as murder, so Kate shot him dead."

Roper said, "Thank God we gave her that training session on the firing range. Sit tight, and Teague will be with you soon."

———

TIPPED OFF BY ROPER, Dillon was in his Mini and on the way to Green Street within minutes, arriving before Teague and his people did. It was Hannah who answered the door, and Dillon hugged her fiercely.

"Are you all right?"

"Yes, cousin, but he isn't."

She led the way into the drawing room and indicated the corpse covered by an old raincoat on the terrace.

"And Kate, how is she?"

"Making tea in the kitchen," Kate said, looking in. "I'm getting more Irish by the minute."

"And he definitely said he was acting under the Master's instructions?"

"Kate will confirm that."

"Which she does, Sean," Kate said, and a tall man with silver hair and wearing black overalls came around the corner with three other men also in black overalls.

"Ah, it's you, Sean, come to help the ladies out?"

"A bad one this, Mr. Teague," Dillon said. "A paid assassin who also had rape on his mind. I know his boss, and there will be a reckoning. You've met my cousin, Hannah. He had her under his gun, but her friend Kate Munro managed to shoot him."

"Well, God bless you for that, Miss Munro," Teague said, as his men carried the body back around the corner to the hearse.

"So there you are," Dillon said. "Two hours and all that will be left is six pounds of gray ash. Don't allow the fact that you had to kill that foul man give you a problem, Kate."

"It won't. Here's what does: The Master told me to expect this kind of retribution to follow when I refused to go along with his mad plans for Hunter. He said he'd make me pay and also see that something happened to my aunt Molly."

There was a nasty silence until Hannah said, "Do you think he meant it?"

"No doubt," Dillon said. "He's just tried to organize a double murder and the one who shot his hit man was you, Kate. Now he'll want revenge, and that's a short step to Aunt Molly."

"We must phone and warn her," Hannah said.

"She wouldn't know what I was talking about. She's a sweet eighty-two-year-old who attends parish church on Sundays and is nice to people because she always has been. She lives in West Sussex. What am I wasting time for? If I put my foot down in that Mini of mine, and knowing the back roads like I do, I can be there in two hours."

"Well, I'm coming with you," Hannah said.

"And I'm going to follow you," Dillon put in. "Don't worry, I always keep an overnight bag in the car."

He called in to tell Roper what was happening, who said, "Keep a pistol in your pocket. I've got a bad feeling about the Master. I think he's getting desperate."

"I've been killing men since I was nineteen," Dillon said. "He's welcome to bring it on."

Hannah and Kate emerged from the house and clambered into

the Mini. Kate switched on with a roar and started to move, and Dillon went after them.

THERE WAS NO QUESTION of traffic difficulties getting out of London, as those didn't exist as far as Kate was concerned. She plunged into a maze of back roads that would bring her to Brighton to follow the Channel coast, aiming for Bognor Regis and Aldwick beyond.

She drove like Stirling Moss in his prime, Dillon had to acknowledge, but he hung in there on her tail even when, about twenty miles out of Brighton, it started to rain hard, only stopping when they reached the outskirts of Bognor Regis and turned along the front. There were beaches and seafront on their left, and at the far end, the road took them out to typical English countryside and then a small parade of shops, and beyond that, the spectacular pillared entrance to the Aldwick Bay estate.

Hedge End was larger than expected for a cottage, high hedges surrounding the front garden, which explained the name, and a large closed gate that opened automatically to Kate, and Dillon followed her through into an ample courtyard where an old Volkswagen was parked.

A young man was standing at the bottom of a tall hedge ladder while another stood on the small platform at the top, trimming with an electric cutter. On closer inspection, they were twins, wild black hair disheveled, denim shirts damp from the rain.

As the girls got out of the Mini, the door of the house opened and Aunt Molly appeared at the front door, obviously surprised, and hugged them in turn.

Dillon got out of his car, produced a packet of cigarettes, and lit one. "Do you use these things?" he asked the workmen. He got an eager response and tossed the packet to the youth at the bottom of the ladder, followed by a matchbox. The one on top slid down the ladder expertly to join his brother.

He said to Dillon, "I'm Eric Haran, this is my brother Faldo. We're helping Miss Molly out. Her gardener fell from the ladder and broke his ankle."

"Well, that's kind of you."

"But she has been wonderfully good to us. We're students at Chichester University, which isn't very far from here."

"I know," Dillon said. "It's getting quite a reputation these days."

"Our general interest is archeology, and we just started a field trip—a long weekend on the beach to further our studies in pale-ontology."

Hannah joined them. "I bet you don't know what that is, Sean."

"It's the study of fossil animals and plants, and such remains are often found on beaches on English Channel coasts. Some of the fossils are thousands of years old."

"I'm impressed, Mr. Dillon," Eric told him.

"You mustn't be. There was an excellent article in the *Times* a week or so ago that explained it all very well."

"I wish I'd seen that. Well, as I said, Miss Molly helped us out. We arrived early this morning with pup tent and sleeping bags, hoping to camp out for a few days, and then that torrential rain turned up."

"And Molly came to the rescue?"

"Couldn't have been kinder. She has allowed us to bunk in the old boathouse at the rear of the cottage."

"Well, there you are," Dillon said. "There's still a lot of kindness to be found in this wicked old world," then he added, in excellent Arabic, "What are you, Palestinian, Libyan, maybe Egyptian?"

Eric smiled and answered in English. "Egyptian, but Coptic."

"Just like Omar Sharif," Dillon said. "Who changed his name and religion when he married a Muslim."

"Exactly, but Egypt is no place for Coptic Christians these days."

"True. I'm surprised to find you here at all. How have you managed?" Dillon asked.

"We were very lucky," Eric said. "We have an English grandmother."

"Ah, so under filial law, you could get U.K. passports. That must have made you think Christmas had arrived early. Now, you'll have to excuse me; I really have to go and say hello to Molly."

Hannah, who had stood listening to the whole exchange, said, "What's going on, cousin? I know you. Do you think they're phonies?"

"Their stories are plausible, even the bit about the field trip. Students constantly get involved in them even if it's only an excuse to climb into your sleeping bag with a girlfriend. But knowing my name was a fatal error."

Hannah gasped. "Really?"

"As sailors used to say in the days of sail, me darlin', big ships sink themselves on small rocks. Let's go inside."

"Just remember that Molly doesn't know what's been going on," Hannah said. She led them into the kitchen, where they found

Kate and her aunt enjoying coffee. Dillon made a huge fuss of Molly, kissing her on both cheeks.

"You've been having an exciting time of it, Molly, all that rain, then your gardener falling and breaking his ankle."

"Yes, Eric was holding the ladder at the bottom, and then it slipped, and Oscar slid all the way down, and an ambulance came and rushed him off to hospital in Chichester. He's going to be fine."

"I'm sure he is, and it was a good job Eric and Faldo were around to care for you. After all, you'd no idea that we were going to drop in on you for the weekend like this."

"I had suggested to the boys that a good old-fashioned hot pot might be nice, but that would have been for three, now we'd be six."

"Is that a problem, Auntie?" Kate asked.

"Oh, no, dear, I've got plenty in the larder, but I'll just go and check that everything's right with the bedrooms."

The moment she had gone, Dillon took out his Codex and called Roper. "A couple of names for you to check out, Giles."

"Got it. I'll call you back."

"What's going on?" Kate demanded. "Is there something wrong with them?"

"I'd like to hear what Roper's got to say, but I've never been so certain. I now believe that the threat to harm Molly was just a ploy to bring you two into the circle of danger, where you'd be finished off for good."

"And you?" Hannah asked.

"Oh, me, they'll just have for afters, but let's see what Roper has to say."

Before Kate could comment, Roper called back. "Tell us the worst, Giles," Dillon said.

"These brothers exist and do have British passports and an English grandmother who's respectable. But Chichester's never heard of them."

"Very stupid, that, and bound to come out," Dillon said.

"But understandable if whatever they are up to has been planned in a rush. I talked to Dr. Ali Sharif. Sharif runs the MI5 safe house at Tenby Street. He would like them presented for interrogation at your soonest. He suspects them of terrorism."

"The things I do for England," Dillon said.

"That's what you're paid for," said Roper.

"No, it isn't. By most people's standards, I'm a wealthy man, as you well know."

"Well, this is your chance to give something back to society."

"And Miss Molly's good old-fashioned hot pot tonight?"

"My heart bleeds for you. I've discussed this with Ferguson, and if Kate's listening, he feels you should find an excuse to bring Molly back to London tonight."

Kate answered at once. "I hear you, Giles, and I'll see to it."

"Okay, it's up to you now, Sean. But then it so often is."

"And that's supposed to make me feel good, is it?" Dillon said, but Roper had gone.

The two women were stunned. "But how on earth do we explain any of this to Aunt Molly?"

"Leave it to me. As far as those two, I'll take them in charge, as the police say, and spirit them away to London. It's a long-standing habit of mine to keep handcuffs on board my car. I'll stick them in the backseat shackled together, and even do their ankles. Very uncomfortable all that way."

"I'd say that's an understatement," Kate told him.

"Well, cruel 'ard I am. Dickens would have loved me." He took out his Colt, ejected the magazine, then rammed it home. "As it has started to pour with rain, I'd better get on with it. They're not in here yet, so I'll try the boathouse. I'll pick up my handcuffs from the Mini and one of those umbrellas from the stand."

Kate and Hannah followed, watching him take the umbrella, put it up, and start walking to the boathouse. Hannah said, "Who does he think he is, Wyatt Earp? Is there a back entrance?"

"Yes, there is," Kate said.

"Well, maybe I can do some good there." Hannah took an old oilskin from the stand. "Don't worry, I'll be right back," and she went out into the rain.

Kate was just about to go after her when Aunt Molly called down. "Are you there, Kate? Come and help me to make up some extra beds."

Kate hesitated for a moment, reluctantly watching Hannah setting out along the beach before turning behind the boathouse, then her aunt called down again, and she turned and mounted the stairs.

ERIC HARAN STOOD, the door open no more than a foot, and peered out clutching a Walther PPK. Faldo sat at an old table beside a pungent oil stove, the same weapon as his brother lying in front of him.

"What are we going to do?" Eric asked.

"The Master has made it clear he wants him dead. We'll have to shoot him."

Hannah had been easing the old-fashioned bolt on the rear door open and stepped inside, her Colt ready. "Now, that's not nice," she said. "Not nice at all."

She shot the Walther off the table and invited Faldo's brother to drop his, which he did, looking stunned, and she held up her Colt, and said, "Silenced mode, always a shock," and then raised her voice. "Sean, where the heck are you?"

The door swung open and he walked in. "I was waiting for you to finish, oh great one," and he flung a pair of handcuffs on the table. "But if you'd care to do something useful, cuff 'em, as they say in cop shows."

At the same moment, a mobile rang in Eric's pocket, and Dillon reached for it quickly and switched it to speaker. The Master's voice was clear. "Is this Eric or Faldo?"

"It's neither, you chump, just your old friend Sean Dillon. Eric and Faldo are in handcuffs, I'm afraid, facing a journey to London."

The Master sounded amused. "Why, Eric, you and your brother seem to have let me down badly. All debts will be paid in full. My deepest respects to your grandmother, who will be delighted at the news, but for how long, I wonder?"

Eric, a new strength in his voice, said, "Our grandmother has nothing to do with this business."

"Too late to think about it that way now," the Master said. "There is a debt here that must be paid."

"A debt on my part, too," Dillon said. "Because I intend to execute you."

"What a stupid man you are to think that you could do that. I don't deal in fantasy, but in reality. I can cause calamity right there in London or in the White House itself, little man."

"You must be mad," Dillon told him.

"Well, we shall see what I can accomplish in the next few days. Look for me."

FACED WITH the ignominy of being trounced by a female, the brothers argued angrily in Arabic as they were urged into the rear seats of Dillon's Mini to have their ankles manacled. They calmed down after stern words from Dillon in Arabic.

"What's going on?" Hannah asked.

"Each has been blaming the other for praising Osama online and allowing the Master to come into their lives. I've just now told them that their U.K. passports are going to be canceled and they will be sent back to Egypt. It's frightened them to death, which is why they are suddenly behaving themselves."

"Do you think there's any chance of their being sent back?"

"Doubtful. I think Dr. Ali Sharif will have plans for them. But if you knew what life is like in an Egyptian jail, you'd know how the prospect terrifies. They'll be good boys on the trip back to London."

"You can be a proper bastard when you want to be, can't you, Sean?"

"Hannah, these people are all the same, foolish puppets of men like the Master, spreading death and destruction like you faced the other night. I'll tell you, cousin, I've made a personal vow that I will see the Master dead one way or another."

Kate came running from the cottage clutching an umbrella. "Just go, will you. It's difficult to make sense of what's happened, but it would help if you went. I can't imagine that we're likely to be threatened by any more of the same ilk, so I'll take my time convincing Molly that Mayfair might be good for her again."

And as they took to the road, Hannah said, "Frankly, I can't see Aunt Molly being anywhere near as happy in London as she is in the Aldwick estate. It's a lovely place, you can see that straightaway, and violent fools like you and me aren't welcome."

"Save all your anger for the Master, Hannah. We'll get him one of these days."

Eric Haran, who had obviously been listening, said, "But you'll never catch the Master, Mr. Dillon. He is just a voice that comes and goes without warning. That is how he entered our lives. A voice from nowhere telling us we were needed by al-Qaeda."

"And you believed that?"

"Yes, but now I'm not so sure. This Dr. Ali Sharif. Is he a good man?"

"He used to be in your shoes. Believed in al-Qaeda, but then Ferguson turned him. He's quite good at interrogation. Don't try to lie to him. He has a brilliant mind, and you would be foolish not to listen to him. As for me, I have one important piece of advice for you. Never go anywhere near Egypt again. Don't even travel on a plane that might have to make a stopover. You could be in the worst prisons in the world and drinking water out of the lavatory bowl before you know it. They never forget and they never forgive. And if Sharif offers you a job with MI5, grab it with both hands."

TENBY STREET SAFE HOUSE had been a Victorian primary school in its day, a grim-looking establishment that offered ample accommodation to meet the requirements of MI5. It was London's turn to be flooded by heavy rain, and in response to Dillon's mobile call, Dr. Ali Sharif waited under an umbrella, flanked by four military policemen in waterproof capes, who had the boys out of the Mini in no time and hauled them inside.

Dillon and Hannah stayed in the car, and she handed Ali Sharif the two Walthers. "You'll need these for evidence," she said.

"Did they fire these at you?" he asked.

"I persuaded them otherwise."

He smiled and held out his hand. "You were so kind to me when I thought I was going to die in Rosedene last year."

"It's good to see you looking so well. These two are silly spoiled boys, so please kick their backsides and make them see sense."

Dillon said, "The Master called in on Eric's mobile as we were cuffing them. He cursed them for letting him down and threatened their grandmother. He then tossed a torrent of abuse my way, hinting that not only might he pull his party tricks here but also in Washington."

"A big claim, Sean, do you believe him?"

"Yes, but first let's watch out for Eric and Faldo's grandmother."

"I'll see to it, Sean, I promise you," Ali said, and went inside.

"There goes a great and good man," Dillon said. "He fell for Osama bin Laden's message but saw through it and survived the assassin's bullet that al-Qaeda sent his way."

"I agree," Hannah said. "Where do we go now?"

"Report in to Roper at Holland Park, see if Maggie Hall has some dinner for us tonight."

"I suppose it would help to ease the pain of losing out on Aunt Molly's hot pot. Holland Park it is, driver," Hannah said. "Let's get out of here."

"At your service, ma'am." Dillon switched on the ignition, slammed down a foot, and roared away.

ROPER WAS DELIGHTED to see them, Tony Doyle brought tea, and Maggie Hall was offering fish pie for dinner.

Roper said to Hannah, "I haven't seen you since you and Kate had your evening out at the Dorchester. How are you after your little adventure there?"

"Excellent. The moment that man got me from behind and leered at her over my shoulder, Kate shot him."

Roper said, "Ferguson wants her for MI5 at least but is playing with the idea she might be good for MI6. He's looking on her as his discovery. What do you think?"

"She's certainly got the makings," Dillon said. "It may be a curse in some ways, but we can't avoid who or what we are. To do what Kate Munro did, and at night, her willingness to kill on the instant—you can't teach that." He switched topics. "Something to discuss with you, Giles."

"Okay, fire away," Roper said.

"When Hannah and I were arresting the boys, the Master called on Eric's mobile. He puts on that suave approach, as if amused at your stupidity, poor fool that you are. He told Eric and Faldo they'd let him down, so there were debts to be paid, and hinted that their grandmother could be one of his targets."

Roper said, "Well, he would. All part of his unlovable approach. You've mentioned this to Ali Sharif, I hope?"

"Of course," Dillon said. "He said he'd take care of it."

"And he will. Didn't you notice anything different when you dropped the boys at Tenby Street? About the military policemen?"

Dillon thought. "It was pouring with rain, and they were swathed in heavy-weather gear, but there's nothing unusual about that."

"Well, thanks to Ali Sharif's new approach, the soldiers under that heavy weather gear are Ghurkhas."

"Why, that's wonderful," Hannah said.

"And controversial," Roper told her, "but we'll see."

"The Master said something else, too," Dillon said. "I threatened him, and he implied that I was a stupid man to think that I could harm him. He said he didn't deal in fantasy, but in reality— and that he could cause calamity right here in London or in the White House itself."

"But he's insane, surely?" Hannah asked.

Roper nodded slowly. "I'd like to think so, but perhaps not. What did you say to him, Sean?"

"Oh, I told him he must be mad."

"And what was his response to that?"

"He said he'd see what he could accomplish in the next few days. The trouble is, Giles, he's not just a fantasist, this guy, as he's proved by his actions so far. Where's Ferguson?"

"He, Cazalet, and Johnson are up to their eyes in the antiterrorism discussions."

"Oh, well, I'll just have to do something myself," Dillon said. "I'll give Alice Quarmby a call."

"And why would you do that?" Roper asked.

"Because the great and the good, struggling to save the world, tend to see only the big picture, leaving a great deal behind. Like Blake, for example, and his secretary of many years, who struggles to run the Basement while he's not there."

"What are you saying?"

"Alice Quarmby is my friend, too. I'll tell her how the Master boasted about White House calamities."

"Excellent," Roper said. "Take your choice. Phones all over the damn place in here."

IT WAS NOON in Washington. Alice Quarmby sat at a table outside a coffee shop, a shopping bag loaded with groceries at her feet.

Her phone rang, she hurried to turn it on, and Dillon said, "How's my girl?"

"Never mind that, Sean, how's my boy?"

"I hardly see him. He and Cazalet are pulled in to serve on one committee after another in a futile attempt to save the world from I don't remember what anymore."

"You sound depressed."

"I am, I suppose. I was recently involved in a phone exchange with the Master."

"How did that happen?"

"Never mind how, but he made a rather disturbing remark to me. He boasted that he could cause calamities here, which he has, but also in the White House itself if he wanted to. Would you believe that?"

"The times we live in, I'd believe anything, Sean. On the other hand, the clown could have been boasting."

"No, this guy is for real. Just hear what happened to my cousin, Hannah, and her friend the other night."

She listened while he told her, and when he was finished, she said, "What an evil son of a bitch he must be. You've got to get him some way, Sean."

"Oh, we will, but I just thought that with the swine mentioning Washington I'd like my friends to know, if only to remember to keep a gun under the pillow."

"I do that, never fear, but I'll see the President hears about it. Take care, Sean, and thanks."

ROPER SAID, "Good stuff, I liked that. A real sense of theater. You should have gone on the stage."

"Don't listen to him," Hannah said. "He's taking the mickey."

"Now, would I do that?" Roper asked, and Sara walked in wearing her black suit and looking strained.

"Hello, love," Roper said, and to Dillon and Hannah, "Our American chums were taking Colonel Hunter home from Rosedene. How was it, Sara?"

"They're sending him home as a hero, soldiers in uniform to handle the coffin, a forest of umbrellas from the American Embassy. I felt embarrassed at being the only one of our people there, but Ferguson and company are too busy with ISIS."

"And Hannah and I were getting fired at," Dillon said.

"So I heard. You're really going to have to do something about that. As for me, I could do with a drink."

"What an excellent idea." Holley, in a tracksuit and with a towel around his neck, joined them.

"There's a magnum of Cristal in the small icebox, Hannah. If you wouldn't mind," Roper said.

Hannah didn't. Dillon uncorked it. Sara found five glasses, and Roper poured and gave them the toast. "My dear friends, to love and friendship and to what comes next, which we'll face together."

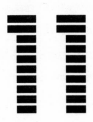

HANNAH BORROWED THE MINI and sped up to Highfield Court, where she persuaded Sadie, much against her will, to return with her for dinner at Holland Park. They went in for seven o'clock, had settled themselves to Maggie's turtle soup, when there was the roar of a Daimler arriving. A few moments later, Ferguson walked in with Blake and Cazalet.

"Well, hello, stranger," Sara said.

"I thought we ought to look in on you. I know you've had a hell of a time, but so have we. My God, but that soup smells good." He raised his voice. "Henry, get in here. This is better than the Garrick."

Frankel hurried in and sat down opposite Blake and Cazalet.

"I'm sick of having a mobile phone. The Cabinet Office won't leave me alone." He started on the soup. "It's like nectar, and fish pie to follow, I understand? You do realize what a treasure Maggie is?"

"As a matter of fact, we do," Hannah said.

"Good, because you'll really need to keep your strength up, ducky, what with all these people you seem to go around shooting. That episode the other night after your meal at the Dorchester was quite something."

"That's old news," Dillon said. "You should have seen her shoot someone's Walther off a table this morning. Annie Oakley couldn't have done better."

Cazalet said, "It doesn't sound as if you're finding much time for your piano, Hannah."

"Mr. President," she said. "I appreciate that the demands of the great and the good, and sometimes the not so good, take up all your time these days, but meanwhile, we've been guarding the wall."

"Now then, Hannah," Ferguson said. "Just let it go."

"No, I won't, General. The assassin who tried to murder me and Kate Munro the other night boasted that he was acting under the Master's orders and that he intended to rape us. Well, he made a mistake, just like the two fools this morning who we turned over to Tenby Street. Just like the Master himself and his threats."

She had the attention of everyone now, and Ferguson said, "We'll discuss this later."

"But later is too late, sir. I heard the Master say that he would cause calamity not only in London but also in Washington. When Sean told him he must be mad, he said we would see what he could accomplish in the next few days."

There was complete silence until Blake said, "Have you spoken to anyone about this, Sean?"

"Yes, I had words with Alice Quarmby. She told me she would speak to the President."

Ferguson said, "Hannah, I hear what you say, but there is a bigger picture to all this."

"I know, sir, but you know my family background. It's the foot soldiers who take the heaviest burden." And with that, no one could argue.

AFTER DINNER, Roper said, "If you could give me a full account of what happened with these two young rogues you passed on to Ali Sharif, Hannah, it would help my records. Do you mind if we do it now?"

"I'd be happy to."

"Then if you gentlemen will excuse us." And he rolled out in his wheelchair, Hannah following him to the sanctuary of the computer room.

"Was I out of order saying what I did, Giles?"

"Not at all," Sara said from the doorway, as she joined them. "I particularly like that phrase about us guarding the wall."

"Yes, I thought that particularly apt," Roper said. "But their problem is they don't know what to make of you. Even Ferguson isn't sure. I, however, haven't got the slightest problem. Do you, Sara?"

"Not a bit," Sara said, then put an arm around Hannah and kissed her cheek. "They broke the mold when they made you."

Hannah almost blushed. "What Dillon said—do you think Alice Quarmby has spoken to the President yet?"

"I can't say," said Roper. "But I know she will. She told Dillon she would."

"So we wait and see," Hannah said. "Which just about sums life up at the moment."

WHICH WAS VERY MUCH how it looked to Alice Quarmby, for several attempts to see the President had failed. Even her friendship with his secretary, Elsie, had got her nowhere.

So she had gotten some food from the White House canteen, consumed it alone in the Basement office, and tried to clear her desk, which was always a problem with Blake being away. She decided to try the Oval Office again and saw Elsie making for the powder room, so she took her chance, tapped on the door, and went in. And she was lucky, because the President was working at his desk, quite alone, and looked up, startled.

"Why, Alice, it's you. Did we have an appointment?"

"No, Mr. President, I'm here quite illegally and behind Elsie's back because I was desperate to see you."

"Well, you are here, so what's this about?"

"The Master, sir. Things have been getting out of hand in the U.K."

"Well, nobody's telling me that. I hear damn little from Blake, in fact, no reports at all."

"State affairs are beyond my remit, Mr. President. What I do know is this dreadful man has been responsible for a great deal of death and destruction—and he's now threatening to do the same to Washington."

"Who says so?"

"Sean Dillon. He phoned me at noon and asked me to speak to you, which I now have."

Behind Alice, Elsie opened the door and peered in, and the President waved. "It's all right, Elsie."

She withdrew, and the President said, "Let me make one thing clear. I have enormous respect for Dillon, but the Secret Service and the FBI will need more than that to go on."

"All I know is he means to try something, and he's an evil creature capable of anything. He put a hired assassin on to Dillon's young cousin and her girlfriend the other night, but they were armed and blew him away. He could easily be planning the same kind of thing for the streets of Washington."

"Alice, I'll speak to the right people; I can do no more. Tell Elsie on the way out that I sent for you. It will make her feel better."

Which Alice did, but as Elsie couldn't understand how it had happened, it didn't help at all, and Alice returned to her office to clear her desk and get ready for home.

She answered her phone when it rang, thinking it might be Blake, so the sound of the Master's voice was a shock.

"Oh dear, Alice, you have been a naughty girl. So now we've got the President discussing your information with the Secret Service; the FBI; the Washington, DC, police. Have I left anyone out? It won't help, you know. It certainly won't help you. So why don't you go home now and think about where your stupidity has led you."

She had seldom felt so tired yet so angry, and she took out an Australian drover's coat and a rain hat once owned by her long-dead husband, then locked the office door and went upstairs.

A green Lincoln was parked outside the entrance, the driver standing under the cupola, a tough military-looking black man she'd known for years.

"And how are you, Kilroy?"

"Could be worse," he said. "Are you sure you're not setting out on an Australian cattle drive?"

"It's a thought," she said. "But I doubt whether I could find enough romance in me these days."

A shabby Ford work van drove past, a roughly painted sign on its side that said ANY JOB TAKEN. A driver peered out and then continued on, turning from view as Alice Quarmby walked straight through the heavy rain toward her Mercedes.

There was the roar of an engine, and the Ford van jumped out, drifted sideways, and bounced her at some speed. Then it turned around and drove very fast down to the exit.

A Secret Service man had appeared in the entrance, but Kilroy said, "Get an ambulance," then scrambled into the Lincoln and drove to where Alice lay.

She made no sound and there was no blood on her face—it was as if she were in a deep sleep. Old soldier that he was, Kilroy opened the drover's coat and found blood on her left side and, gently sliding a hand down her left leg, was aware of a fracture. It was then that the ambulance arrived from MedStar Washington Hospital Center and took Alice away, and then the police arrived, grateful for Kilroy's description of the guilty vehicle, its number, and his opinion that the driver who glanced out appeared to be of Middle Eastern appearance.

As for the President, he was consumed with guilt at not having treated Dillon's information more seriously. Most difficult of all was to have to explain it to Holland Park. It was Roper who took the call.

"I'm sure you appreciate how terrible I feel about Alice Quarmby. She's being treated at the finest trauma center in Washington, but I feel mortified that I didn't take Dillon's warning more to heart when Alice brought it to me."

"We've all miscalculated the Master to some extent, Mr. President," Roper said. "I'll let General Ferguson know what's happened, and Blake. I think this will hit him particularly hard."

WHICH IT DID, and Cazalet and Ferguson made the decision to drop Blake from the Cabinet Office committee and have him return to Holland Park and await events. Blake was completely stressed out, and his friends—Holley, Dillon, Hannah, and Sara—were being particularly careful with him. Suddenly Roper sat up. "Fox News coming up now. An attempt to murder White House staffer Alice Quarmby by—here we go—Muslim youth Wali Hakim, who crashed in flames while being chased by D.C. police. Hakim was known to have an interest in al-Qaeda and ISIS, and was in police files in New York and Washington. Alice Quarmby remains heavily sedated in the trauma center at MedStar Washington Hospital Center."

"News at least," Hannah said. "And hope in it."

Dillon's Codex sounded, and the Master said, "So here we are again, Mr. Dillon. Alone, are you, or with friends, or perhaps you haven't any left, after stirring up the wretched Alice as you did?"

Blake exploded then. "You are not fit to mention her name!"

"Oh, yes, I am, and I'm winning, Mr. Dillon; it's time you realized that. The young Wali Hakim was a martyr for our cause. There are others like him. We can't be beaten," and he switched off.

BLAKE WAS DISTRAUGHT, and it was obvious to all. "You know, my mother died of cancer when I was twelve years old, so it was my Dad and I until I lied about my age at seventeen and ended up in Vietnam. Then years later, when I inherited the Basement, I found this icon named Alice Quarmby came with it, 'the old broad,' as she described herself, serving one president after the other over the years. A White House institution. God help me, I don't know where to put myself."

Holley said, "Well, I do. In Washington, D.C. I have a perfectly good Falcon jet at Farley Field, and we can make the flight in five and a half hours if we push it. Is that okay, Major Roper? I understand you to be in command here when no one else is around."

"True," Roper said. "So my orders are to get the hell out of here before I change my mind, and, yes, I'm aware you'll need a second pilot, so that's obviously you, Dillon, and no arguments from the ladies, please."

"Who's complaining?" Sara asked, as Holley, Blake, and Dillon left quickly and Dillon's Mini roared to life.

"Just shut up and allow me to send Farley Field my orders for the flight. What a shame. I'd always had hopes of making colonel, but you can't have everything."

"I always thought you were special, now I know you are," Hannah told him.

"So are you two on the same wavelength over this?" Roper asked Sara.

"Absolutely," Sara said. "But I do think you should send a message to the White House notifying the President that Blake is on his way—which, ironically, is exactly what the President has been wanting for some days. I don't think General Ferguson would argue about that, so you may be a colonel yet."

"For the first time, I can see why you are in the Intelligence Corps, Captain Gideon," Roper said. "I'll follow your orders at once; I'll also request the hospital to expect a visit at, say, ten o'clock Washington time. Since the request is from the White House, I'm sure they'll comply."

"Excellent. My final advice is: Don't speak to Ferguson, just send him a text. Once he's read that a time or two, shocked though he may be, he'll realize he has no option but to agree."

"Your advice is noted, and at the rate you are going, I expect you to make major sooner rather than later."

Hannah said, "Do you have any orders for me, sir?"

"Yes," he said. "Take Sadie home to Highfield Court, lock yourself up in the conservatory, sit down at the Schiedmayer concert grand, and get practicing."

"At your command, oh great one," she told him, and left.

———————

THE FALCON HEADED OUT over the Atlantic at forty thousand feet, Holley at the controls. Dillon sat beside Blake in the cabin, trying to cheer him up without much success.

Finally, he gave up trying. "I'd get some sleep, old son," he said. "I'm needed in the cockpit. Have an Irish whiskey, extend your seat, and lie back. You'll be asleep in no time."

"I don't think so," Blake said.

"Pull yourself together or you won't be fit enough to see Alice, you clod, and you don't want that, do you?" Dillon told him harshly.

He joined Holley in the cockpit, who said, "How is he?"

"Terrible," Dillon said. "I've never seen him like this. How's the weather?"

"Rain, wind, the chance of storms in the mid-Atlantic."

"Well, that should be fun," Dillon told him.

"You can imagine you're a Spitfire pilot in the Battle of Britain if you like while I check on our cargo and have a coffee."

"I'm a Hurricane man myself," Dillon said. "They shot down more planes than the Spitfire."

"And not many people know that," Holley said, and went out.

Dillon eased back in his seat and his Codex buzzed. Roper said, "I've heard from the White House. The President will be happy to see Blake, you, and Holley when you get in. Any way the White House can help, they will. He's also asked me to assure you that Alice has the tightest possible Secret Service security at the hospital."

Holley returned and eased into the other seat.

"How is he?" Dillon asked.

"Half asleep."

Dillon passed his Codex across. "I've just recorded a conversation with Roper that ought to make him feel better."

Holley listened, and said, "That should do the trick."

"I could do with a cup of tea and a sandwich. I'll let him listen to Roper and we'll see if it works," Dillon said, and went into the cabin. He passed his Codex to Blake.

"Message for you from Roper. It might cheer you up."

And it seemed to straightaway. "Thank God," Blake said. "Remember the Master saying to us that Wali Hakim was a martyr for the cause and there were others like him? It made me think of Alice in a hospital bed at the mercy of a lot of different people, but to know that the Secret Service is guarding her is a great relief."

"Well, hang on to that feeling," Dillon said. "And try to get some sleep, because that's exactly what I intend to do for an hour."

So he dimmed his light, tilted his seat, and closed his eyes.

A BRISK TAILWIND helped with the final approach to the American coast, and it was nine-fifteen when they landed at Reagan International, where they were immediately waved in to where several Mercedes waited with men in black raincoats and good suits at the ready, the Secret Service on display.

Blake knew them, of course, and it seemed to have an effect on him at once. A man named Murphy was in charge, he sped them past customs, and in fifteen minutes they were on their way.

Murphy sat in the front seat beside the driver, and the three in from England behind. "Good to see you, Blake," he said. "And have I got news for you. A couple of hours ago Alice, God bless her, opened her eyes and started to ask questions."

Blake was shocked. "Is that for real?"

"Absolutely. She's got some hip and leg damage, but the docs are saying that, mentally, she's the Alice we know and love. But you'll see for yourself soon."

Blake seemed to choke a little and gasped for air, and Dillon patted him on the back. "Take it easy and breathe deeply. You'll be seeing her in minutes, so pull yourself together."

ALICE WAS IN A PRIVATE ROOM, two very obvious security guards seated outside. A doctor in scrubs stood watching while a young nurse helped Alice drink through a straw. As Murphy led Blake, Dillon, and Holley in, Alice ejected the straw, joy on her face.

"The things an old broad like me has to do to get your attention. Is President Cazalet with you?"

"No, he's needed too much by Number Ten Downing Street. I'm here only because Holley's a rich bastard and offered the use of his Falcon."

"Well, I must say I'm touched to have two such outstanding members of the Provisional IRA standing at the end of my bed. Is this allowed, Mr. Murphy?"

"For you, anything is allowed as far as the White House is concerned, Alice."

"With a name like Murphy, how could he not approve?" Dillon said. "I'm sorry my warning didn't work as I'd hoped."

"Not your fault, Sean. Just put the Master down once and for all, and do it for me, that's all I ask."

"You have my word on it," Dillon said.

"That's good enough for me." Alice turned. "But you shouldn't be here. I love you, Blake, you're like a son to me, but Jake Cazalet needs you in London. It's your duty and you owe it to your country. I'll be fine. The doctors will confirm that. I don't want to see you again until this Master creature is stamped out once and for all. Now off you go to the Oval Office, where I'm told the President is waiting to have words."

Blake laughed out loud. "Well, you always did say you were a tough old broad."

"You can bet on that," she said. "So you and your chums can oblige me by getting the hell back to London."

MURPHY SAT UP FRONT AGAIN with the driver as they left for the White House. Blake was a different man, cheerful and smiling again in spite of the torrential rain.

"It's great to be here," he said to Murphy. "I've been away too long."

"We've all missed you, Blake, and now you tell me it's straight back to London."

"When your country calls, what can you do?" Blake said. "But I miss Washington. Look at that, demonstrators this late and in this weather. That's Pennsylvania Avenue for you."

"Crazy people," Murphy said, and told the driver to try the East Entrance, which they did, and they found a Secret Service man who escorted them to Elsie waiting at her desk outside the Oval Office.

"It's good to see you back, Blake," she said. "Can I ask how she is?"

"Broken bones, but fresh as a daisy otherwise," Blake said. "She sent you her love."

"That's nice," Elsie said. "The President's waiting, and he wants you also, Mr. Murphy." She opened the door to the Oval Office, announced them, and Murphy led the way in.

The President said, "Is everything supplied for the return flight?"

"So I am told, Mr. President," Murphy said.

"Excellent. Just wait outside."

Murphy went out, and the President said, "I was going to say hello, Blake, it's been a hell of a long time, but I've something much more important to say to you. Alice told me, Mr. Dillon, that you had asked her to make clear to me the threats the Master had made about his intended behavior in Washington. I made the huge mistake of not taking it seriously. The guilt I feel for this is beyond description."

Dillon said, "The depravity of the Master is considerable, Mr. President. It's not your fault. Anyway, we've just had the pleasure of finding Alice awake and active again."

"Particularly with her mouth," Blake told him, "and if I might make a suggestion, nothing would thrill her more than a visit from you."

"That's a great idea, I'll see her tomorrow." The President was smiling now. "You always come up with an answer. That's why I miss you so much, but I realize now that the work you and President Cazalet are engaged with in London is of crucial importance."

"It's good to know you support us in this way, Mr. President."

"And you, Mr. Holley, special envoy for the Algerian foreign minister now, I hear. It's good to see you, too. Now I'll say good-bye to all of you, and have a safe flight back."

The door opened, Murphy appeared and shepherded them out, walking them through the convoluted corridors of the White House to where the Mercedes waited to take them back to the airport.

Holley checked his watch. "Half past midnight. I've never spent such a short time in America."

Dillon said, "At Holland Park right now, Maggie Hall is serving full English breakfast."

Murphy said, "What about the full Irish, Sean?"

"Ah, you'd have to go to the Europa Hotel in Belfast. They do the best in the world. I often dropped in during the Troubles. Roper had to call in there a time or two to defuse bombs, but we never met. Ironic, that."

"Who's Roper, then?" Murphy asked.

"Probably the greatest bomb disposal expert during the Troubles," Dillon said. "He's been in a wheelchair for years. It was a woman who got him in the end. A real crazy after revenge. A great man. He was awarded the George Cross."

"I don't understand," Murphy said. "You were on different sides."

"In the end, me old son, you could say we were all on the same side, but you would have needed to go through it to understand that."

The Mercedes turned into the airport and drove straight to the Falcon through the torrential rain and pulled up at the airstair door. Dillon shook hands with Murphy.

"Look at it, the romance of flight. If we go down in the middle of the Atlantic, it was a real pleasure," and he opened the car door and ran for the steps.

HOLLEY LET DILLON take the flight up to thirty thousand feet, climbing gradually all the way to the Maine coast, then up to forty thousand feet as they moved out over the Atlantic. Blake, the non-pilot, made himself comfortable with a pot of coffee in the cabin. Remembering Roper's nocturnal habit, he tried calling him on his Codex and struck gold.

"Good to hear from you," Roper said. "What on earth is behind this extraordinarily quick return journey?"

"Well, it appears that Alice is going to be all right. She was in some kind of a traumatic state, little evidence of life besides breathing, when it seems she suddenly opened her eyes and started asking where she was and what had happened."

"So how is she?"

"Well, her hip and left leg are fractured, but she's sitting up in bed in a private hospital room with the White House Secret Service in charge of her security."

"But what are you doing coming back so quickly?"

"Oh, she told me it was my duty to stay with Jake Cazalet and continue the fight with the Master, so she suggested we go straight back to where we came from. The President agreed and sent you his regards."

"You're making that up," Roper said.

"Only the bit about the President. I didn't want you to feel left out!"

"Thank you. I leave you to attempt to rest for your five hours of flying in the happy knowledge that according to the weather reports on my screens very severe storms are expected in the mid-Atlantic. I wish you joy and try not to worry that Ferguson and Jake Cazalet were not exactly thrilled to hear of your trip."

"Which you were kind enough to permit."

"So we're all in trouble. I look forward to seeing you," and he switched off.

IN THE BARGE on the Quai des Brumes, the Master sipped coffee and considered the quick trip to Washington with a certain perverted enjoyment, because, although Daniel Holley was an enemy, the élan with which he'd been able to offer a friend the use of one of the most expensive jet planes in the world was quite admirable.

The only thing more extraordinary was the thought of Alice Quarmby sitting up in bed and drinking through a straw. More bungling. It was infuriating. It was time to find some good news, and his thoughts turned to Pound Street. He wondered how the new imam was surviving. Not easy being the new man, especially since he'd lost his strong right arm, Omar Bey, the one they called the Beast.

A few minutes later, Imam Yousef Shah was sitting at his desk when he got a call. He was shocked, as always, by the quiet voice.

"There is one God and Osama is his Prophet. This is the Master, concerned by your problems. Has there been any word about Omar Bey?"

"Nothing," the imam said. "I have discussed the matter with Scotland Yard, but they merely shrug their shoulders. As far as they are concerned, he had a bad reputation for violence and met someone who was worse. Do you have some thoughts on the matter?"

"The man Dillon we have spoken of, I believe him to have somehow put Omar Bey into the river. It is a favored method of his and the gangsters along the Thames. With strong tidal currents, anyone who goes in is swallowed by the sea eventually."

"What can we do about this man?"

"I am thinking about it now. I'll be in touch when it is time to strike."

DILLON AND HOLLEY were in the computer room with Roper when Sara and Hannah arrived from Highfield Court.

"Well, that was a memorable trip," Sara told them.

"Yes," Hannah said. "And great news about Alice!"

"Blake was thrilled," Holley said. "But all that activity proved too much for him. He's sleeping his head off in the guest wing. Ferguson slept over, too."

"General to you, Major," Ferguson said, as he entered. "The heroes return, is that how you see it?" He sighed. "Well, I suppose it was in a way. On the other hand, it was a gross breach of discipline, so don't do it again."

Roper looked suitably serious. "Of course not, General."

"Just so we understand each other. Get the Daimler ready, Sergeant; I'm needed at Downing Street."

"At once, General," Tony Doyle barked, and was out like a flash.

"That's what I like to see, good order and military discipline. What about you, Hannah? Why aren't you at college?"

"I'm dropping her off, General," Sara told him. Hannah started to say something and stopped.

"Excellent. I see your birthday is coming up, Sara."

"Yes, General."

"Rather more impressive, it will also be a celebration of your fifteen years in the army." He turned to Roper. "I think that calls for a party, don't you, Major?"

"I certainly do."

"Well, see what you can arrange with the Salters."

He left, the Daimler roared as it drove off, and Roper grinned, and said to Sara, "Will you want a cake?"

THE MOMENT THE sound of the Daimler had faded into the distance, Sara said, "It won't be a very big party, though. My grandfather left for Israel yesterday, and Kate Munro and her aunt are still down in Sussex. So I have just Hannah and Sadie."

"And Giles, Daniel, and me," Dillon said. "And to show you we all love you, Daniel and I will take care of dropping Hannah off at college and carry on to see Tad and Larry Magee."

"I've kept telling you all," Hannah said. "It's half term. I don't have any classes. However, I'd be happy to see the Magees again."

"I thought they might like to come to the party."

"So we'll go and ask," Hannah said. "And see you lot later. Come on, Sean."

As they turned out into the main road in the Mini, Dillon said, "What do you think you are, a marriage broker or something?"

"So Sara and Daniel were once an item." Hannah shrugged. "Nothing wrong with trying to help a friend."

THEY TURNED OUT of Park Lane into Curzon Street and paused for the gates to swing open. Tad opened the door to them, smiling. "What a surprise. Larry's going to be delighted." He kissed Hannah on the cheeks. "Molly's gone home to Ulster. The funeral of an old girlfriend."

They went through to the conservatory, where Larry dropped his newspaper, forced himself up, and embraced Hannah.

"You're still giving college your full attention, I hope?"

She grinned. "Well . . . most of the time."

Dillon said, "She lends us the occasional hand."

"But surely Hannah has got better things to do."

"Than fire a pistol?" Dillon shrugged. "There was a stupid boy waiting to blow my head off the other day in the depths of Sussex. She went in the back door and shot his weapon right off the table."

"When she should have been playing Bach," Tad said.

Hannah grinned. "Or Cole Porter. Now, if you'll point me toward the kitchen, I'll make us all a pot of Irish tea while Sean tells you why we're here."

When she brought the tea back, the matter had already been discussed, and as she poured, Hannah said, "General Ferguson is the one who suggested the Salters' place. I think it's for a special reason, but I'm not going to speculate."

"You've got me wondering now," Dillon said.

Tad laughed. "All very intriguing, so we'll be there if only to find out what it's all about."

"We'll see," Hannah said. "But would it be all right for me to inquire how things are at Drumore House? My visit there was pretty remarkable."

"You'll be interested to know that Eli's proved an impregnable wall where Finbar is concerned. The big man has grown even bigger, in a way. Since I transferred ownership to him to keep it in the family but out of Finbar's grasp, Eli has become more than able to control Finbar."

"And the legend of the *Maria Blanco*?" Hannah asked.

"Hugh Tulley, the IRA chief of staff for County Down, is still alive, but the original story is still the same, and the whereabouts of the boat itself a mystery."

"We have to accept that there's no answer," Dillon said.

"Or there's something so simple that it is eluding all of us?" Hannah said.

"Well, I'm damned if I know what it might be," Tad declared.

Dillon got up. "We'll see you at the party, but now duty calls. If the Master tries it on with you again, let me know. We can compare notes."

ROPER WAS ALONE when they returned to the computer room, Sara and Holley having gone off for a drive around the countryside.

"Are the Magees coming?" he asked.

"Wouldn't miss it," Hannah said. "Have you spoken to the Salters?"

"Not yet, but I thought we'd call round this evening to the Dark Man. With any luck, Dora's hot pot will be on," Roper told her.

"That suits me," Dillon said. "I'll take you in the back of the van. What time?"

"Let's say seven. I bet Sara and Daniel will join us," Hannah said.

"That's fine. Now I'll give myself an hour in the steam room. I suggest you sit down at the dining-room piano for an hour, Hannah. Half term or not, you need to practice."

GEORGE MOON HAD BEEN AWAKENED early by the drumming of heavy rain on the cabin roof of his motor launch, the *Moonglow*. The heating system had packed up, and when Moon rolled over, he realized his bedclothes were damp.

Cursing, he got out of bed, searching drawers for fresh clothes, his wardrobe for a decent suit, a small insignificant man scrabbling for his steel spectacles that had fallen to the floor in the night. As he straightened, Moon's mobile buzzed again.

"Who the hell is this?" he demanded.

"You sound annoyed, Mr. Moon," the Master told him.

"On a morning like this, the London waterfront is not exactly the Riviera. Most uncomfortable." Moon hesitated, his door open to the deck, and told himself to stay calm. "What do you want?"

"To remind you that only a few days ago I deposited seventy-five thousand pounds in your bank account."

Moon took a deep breath. "Yes, I remember, so again, what do you want?"

"Some civility, you nasty little man, or I promise you'll regret it. So struggle up the steps from the pier, knock on the door of the pub, and talk to your disgusting cousin Harold, who I expect to put to work for me tomorrow night. And remember this: For the kind of money I'm paying, I suspect Harold would be happy to dispose of you in the Thames, too."

Which was undoubtedly true. Moon took comfort in the fact that he had an original Walther PPK loaded for action in a hidden drawer of the old Victorian desk in his cabin. He quickly checked that it was still there, then went out into the heavy drizzle, put up his umbrella, and mounted the steps to the pub, where Harold opened the door.

"There you are. I thought I'd lost you." Moon noticed he seemed a trifle strained. "Dirty morning. You get in and I'll see to your usual."

"The Master called," Moon said. "He wants to speak to both of us."

"Really?" Harold said, and his tone made it plain to Moon that something odd was going on, and it put him on high alert and even more grateful for the Walther in the desk drawer.

Moon's mobile buzzed, and the Master said, "To business. Harry and Billy Salter are hosting a birthday party at their restaurant, Harry's Place, the night after tomorrow."

"I like it," Harold said. "I've got a few scores to settle with the Salters. Do you want us to smash them up?"

The Master said, "No, something more subtle. Get a gang of young villains to frighten the hell out of them. Shake them up a bit. And one thing more. I understand that Harry Salter's proud of the *Linda Jones*, an old Victorian Thames boat he's spent thousands renovating. He keeps it on the end of the jetty outside the Dark Man. Sink it."

"I could sail up there in the inflatable," Harold said. "I'd love to see the bastard's face when it goes down. The Thames is forty feet deep off that jetty. And since you mentioned the young villains before, I've already put together a posse of very bad lads indeed," he added. "They'll be led by a guy named Barry McGuire, who got ten for manslaughter and was released after five—which was a big mistake from society's point of view."

"And you?" the Master inquired.

"I'll be visiting the *Linda Jones* in the inflatable."

Moon asked, "Is Harold's plan to your liking?"

"Certainly," the Master said. "In fact, it would seem to cover everything except you, who don't seem to be doing very much."

"I drive the inflatable. It's the same type used by the River Police and rather complicated for Harold, but not for me. You forgot to mention that, Harold."

"All right, then," the Master said. "Get to work. There will be a fifty-thousand-pound bonus for wrecking the party and sinking the boat. Nothing for failure," and he switched off.

There was silence for a moment, and then Harold said, "We're in the money here all right."

"So it would appear," Moon said. "In fact, it all looks too easy."

"You worry too much," Harold said. "Just leave it to me."

IT WAS SEVEN-THIRTY when Dillon drove up to the Dark Man in the people carrier, Hannah, Sara, and Holley up in front, Roper in his wheelchair in the rear with the hydraulic lift that lowered him to the ground.

There were lights along the jetty to the *Linda Jones* tied up at the end. Looking across the Thames was always a pleasure, with Big Ben and Parliament in the distance and the sudden fast charge past of a riverboat ablaze with lights.

They went into the Dark Man and sat in their usual corner booth, joining Harry and Billy. Joe Baxter and Sam Hall, Harry's minders, kept an eye on things from the bar. Roper, with hair hanging almost to his shoulders these days, sat in his wheelchair like some medieval king with his bomb-scarred face.

Harry called, "Dora, my love, those two bleeders at the bar can stick to their beer. Cristal for us. Will there be enough hot pot to go around?"

"If not, there's lovely chops or a really nice salmon."

"Dora, you're a treasure," Sara told her.

"Well, you've got to be to get any respect around here."

"Bloody nonsense," Harry said, "but never mind that. I couldn't be more pleased to get the booking for your birthday, Sara, just surprised it came from Ferguson. I never considered him a sentimentalist."

"Hannah thinks there's something going on. It's not just her birthday. She'll be celebrating fifteen years in the army," Roper told him.

"Well, that sounds like a bleeding sentence to me," Harry said. "Here's to you, Sara. Any special guests?"

"The Magee brothers," Hannah announced.

"God help us," Harry said to Billy. "We'll have to put our good suits on, but seriously, I've got nothing but respect for those two."

"And distaste for their father," Hannah said. "Who can go to hell as soon as he likes. Implied I was a crippled tart so I pushed the barrel of my Colt into his mouth and splintered his teeth."

"My God," Harry said. "I must remember not to offend you."

Hannah said to Billy, "How is Hasim these days?"

"He's really come on, learning to crew the inflatable. It's the same type the River Police use, so it's quite technical, but he's really taken to it. Hasim's mother died and Dora never had a son, but she does now, a beautiful Muslim Cockney, and she adores him. Thinks I'm teaching him bad ways."

"And you are?" Hannah asked.

"Dammit all, I'm in MI5, Hannah, got my warrant card just like you," Billy told her.

"Enough said." She burst into laughter, and then the door banged open and Hasim walked in, his naval storm coat streaming with rain, and he pulled back his hood, ignored the group in the corner booth, and went behind the bar and stood talking to Dora. He was obviously excited, and she glanced across, then pushed him into the back room.

Harry said, "See what's going on, Billy."

Billy did, following them into the back room, finally emerging with Hasim, whom he brought across. "Tell Harry what you told me."

Hasim said, "Do you remember my friend Caspar Hassan, Mr. Salter?"

"Yes, I do. A third-rate petty thief who specialized in breaking into old folks' houses. They gave him eighteen months and he deserved more."

"He's going straight now."

"Don't make me laugh. He'll be a thief till the day he dies."

To everyone's shock, Billy took his uncle on. "Just shut up, Harry, and let the kid talk. It's important."

Harry scowled. "Well, it better be good."

"Oh, it is," Billy said. "And I've not even heard the half of it."

"Well, come on then," Harry said. "Just put us all out of our misery, for God's sake. What's the story?"

"I was at Wally's looking for somebody to try a few rounds with in the ring. I go in now and then when I've got time."

"I know, young punks pretending to be hard men. I've told you before, you're better than that trash."

"Okay, but it was different tonight. This old geezer called George Moon was there. A right creepy specimen, believe me, and he had his cousin with him, an oaf named Harold who really did believe he was the terror of the neighborhood. He got in the ring with me once; told me not to worry, he'd go easy on me because I was a Muslim."

"The bastard," Dora said.

"So what did you do?" Harry asked.

"Knocked him down, so he said he'd slipped and got out."

"Bravo," Harry said. "But where is this leading?"

"Moon and his cousin were recruiting a posse to make trouble at the party."

"You're sure about this?" Billy asked.

"I know what the plan is because Caspar told me. They intend to turn our customers over in the car park. There was a lot of drink taken and loose talk, and this stupid idiot Harold was boasting away. Said there was plenty of money in it because they were doing it for a man called the Master, who was very rich, and Moon told him to shut his mouth."

There was silence for a moment, and Roper said, "How did you fit in to all this? Didn't it occur to these people that you would warn Harry?"

"The only person who knew I worked for Harry was Caspar, and whatever you think, he's going to stay quiet. He's just another Muslim to these guys, like me, the Muslim Cockney with a brown face, always despised by those kind of people, but there's stuff I haven't told you yet. Make your mind up if you want to know, because I want to sit down and eat."

"Go on then, tell us the worst," Harry said. "Burn down the Dark Man?"

"No, all those fire engines would make too much fuss. They've got a big inflatable like we have, the same model as the River Police. The word is that Harold is useless with it, but Moon is a dab hand."

"That pompous idiot," Billy said. "I find that hard to believe. What's his intention?"

"To sink the *Linda Jones*."

Harry's face seemed to change completely, dark with astonished anger. "He's what?"

"Like I said, his target is the boat according to that stupid ponce Harold. He said you'd been king of the river long enough and it was time someone put you in your place." Hasim shrugged. "I'm sorry, but according to Caspar, that's what Harold was saying."

"Put me in my place?" Harold said. "I'll crush him like a maggot, him and his miserable cousin. I'll destroy them."

Hannah jumped straight in. "No, you won't Harry. We're all going to consider this carefully at a council of war. But in the meantime, Hasim isn't the only one who's hungry."

Harry gave a great barking laugh, and said to Dora, "What a girl, putting me in my place when I needed it. I knew she was trouble the first time I met her on that horse farm of hers."

THE MEAL WAS AS GOOD AS USUAL, Dora made to blush with the compliments, and then they got down to business over tea and coffee.

"We need a plan of campaign," Hannah said, as Dora was pouring. "First of all, do we still have the party?"

"If we don't," Dillon said, "it means these sods have won and I'm not having that." He turned to Holley. "What do you think?"

"All this aggro in the car park doesn't worry me. Moon won't hand out pistols to his young thugs—too dangerous—so I don't see them as a problem, not with all of us ready for them."

"Fine," Hannah said. "This leaves us the *Linda Jones*."

"I'll take care of that," Billy said. "Moon's old motor launch is chained to the jetty. I'll take some bolt cutters from our workshop and slice through the chains easy as butter. Sinking that launch would be a cinch. Hasim will help with the inflatable."

"Now that I like," Harry said. "What a clever sod you are, Billy."

"So I guess the party is on," Sara said. "Is it private, or do we keep the place open? It's your restaurant, Harry."

Dillon said, "I don't think we should risk the safety of any bystanders just in case the Master has something else up his sleeve."

"Pure evil," Hannah said. "A few days ago at Holland Park, a suitcase was delivered for President Cazalet and it turned out to be a bomb. Major Roper sat in his wheelchair in the rain with Staff Sergeant Doyle holding an umbrella over him, and he defused it. And a girlfriend and I were stalked to her home by a killer hired by the Master to rape and murder us. While he was trying to throttle me, my friend managed to shoot him dead. The Master boasted on his mobile of having been responsible."

There was a silence for a while, then Sara said, "Harry, I think we'll make it a private party. Is that okay with you?"

"Absolutely."

"And the aggravation the Moons are going to cause?"

"Bring it on!"

WHEN THE BIRTHDAY EVENING rolled around, Hannah wore the fabulous black silk Givenchy evening suit that Sara had bought her when they plundered Harrods one day. A black-ribbed shoulder bag complemented it, perfect to carry her Colt .25 and spare ammo.

When she appeared, Sara was in black, too. "My goodness, we look like sisters."

"Well, I think of myself as your younger sister."

"Which I never had, but now I do. So, as your big sister, let me check you over. Are you carrying?"

"Of course."

"And your bulletproof vest?"

"Every girl should have one," Hannah said.

"Then let's get moving."

THEY RENDEZVOUSED AT HOLLAND PARK and were surprised to find Roper resplendent in a black-velvet jacket, Victorian-style, his long hair tied with a bow, a silk scarf at his neck. Tony Doyle, in dress uniform, was pouring a glass of Cristal.

"My goodness, Giles, you look like Oscar Wilde come back to haunt us."

He raised his glass. "And you two look absolutely smashing. Happy birthday, Sara."

They went to give him a kiss, and Dillon and Holley entered, both wearing black tie. "What about us?" Dillon demanded.

"Wonderful," Sara told them. "You look like gangsters in an old Cagney movie. Now have a drink and then, since everybody's here now, we'll be off."

Dillon noted, "They say it'll be raining later on. That should be uncomfortable for all those thugs Moon has taken on."

"Well, bad cess to him, as we say in Ireland," Hannah announced. "And let the battle begin."

GEORGE MOON ALREADY had the light on in the cabin of the *Moon-glow* at the jetty below the old pub. He had changed into a Harris Tweed suit against the penetrating dampness of the Thames evening, and the sound of rain tapping against the roof gave little hope of any improvement.

In his wardrobe, he pushed a couple of suits and some hanging shirts to one side and opened a cupboard, which revealed a small safe stuffed with packets of banknotes. He took one out, a thousand pounds in twenties, and slipped it into his breast pocket. As he moved to find a raincoat, his mobile buzzed.

The Master said, "Just checking in. It's a foul old evening out there. I hope it doesn't keep the customers away."

"There won't be any," Moon said. "The sign outside says it's a private party, so it'll be just them. Twelve or fourteen people at the most."

For once, the Master exploded. "That wasn't what I intended. I wanted much more damage than that!"

Moon was beginning to get weary. "Look, the bad weather isn't my fault, or the small dinner party. Besides, Barry McGuire has been in touch. Only eight or ten men have turned up. He's parked an old bus beside the river just beyond the restaurant and is awaiting orders, but they won't hang around long. This isn't what they signed up for."

"And not what I've paid for," the Master told him.

This surprised Moon because, in a way, it showed a weakness

in the man that was almost childish, so he said patiently, "There's nothing to be done about the weather, but we can still do some damage to the partygoers. More important, no one expects Harold and me in police waterproofs belting along the river and doing the dirty on the *Linda Jones*."

The Master was more in control now. "Deeds, not words, Mr. Moon, that's what I expect. I've invested a great deal of money in you, and it'll be not just me but also al-Qaeda you will have disappointed if you don't get the job done."

"The *Linda Jones* goes down; you have my word on that," Moon said.

"If it doesn't, you're dead."

The mobile clicked off; Moon shivered, stomach hollow, and sat down to think about it, then called McGuire on his mobile. "How many have you got in the bus now?"

"Only seven; the rest have jumped ship. What do you want me to do?"

"I'm not letting this opportunity pass. Give it half an hour, then drive the bus into the courtyard of the restaurant and draw them out. There's only a handful in there. Rough them up good."

"This is becoming a bad joke," McGuire said.

"Nobody's laughing, McGuire. You're getting paid, so get to work."

The door opened and Harold entered wearing yellow oilskins. "We set?"

"Oh, sure," Moon said. "Let's see. I've just had the Master on, full of threats. The whole thing is a cock-up because Salter made the birthday party private and closed the place to outsiders. It's pissing down rain. Oh, and if the *Linda Jones* doesn't sink, we're dead. How's that?"

"Oh, stop whining. Put your waterproofs on, you git. Run me up to the Dark Man, and I'll sink the *Linda Jones* for you," and Harold turned and went out.

AT THE DARK MAN, they were getting ready to leave for Harry's Place. Dora looked very dapper, her blond hair fresh from the beauty salon, pearls at her neck, wearing a knee-length black dress and pumps.

"You look the business, girl," Salter said, and kissed her cheek.

"Why, Harry, I didn't know you cared," she told him. "And I've never seen you look smarter."

"Well, I would in a monkey suit, girl," he said to her, and as Joe Baxter and Sam Hall also wore black tie, added, "We look like Al Capone and some of his boys on a bad night out."

At that moment, Billy and Hasim emerged from the storeroom behind the bar wearing black wet suits and cowls.

Dora said, "I don't like this at all. He's only a young lad."

"I'm as good as Billy driving that police inflatable," Hasim said.

"And so he is," Billy told her. "He's not going in guns blazing, but he's there to pick me up quickly if I end up in the river. I trust him completely."

"The really great thing about this is that they haven't got the slightest idea that we know about their intention to sink the *Linda Jones*. They're coming upriver to find the pub in darkness and easy prey." Harry smiled. "But it's Moon and Harold who'll be the prey."

"And afterward, you get straight on up to Harry's Place," Dora said, putting an arm around Hasim and kissing him.

"For God's sake, leave the lad alone, Dora," Harry told her.

He gave his nephew a brief hug. "Take care, Billy, come back safe and try not to kill anybody this time."

They drove away, and Billy and Hasim stood there holding flood lamps dipped to the ground, rain bouncing off their wet suits.

Hasim asked, "What now?"

"Follow me and I'll show you," Billy said, and led the way along the jetty to where the *Linda Jones* was tied up.

He stepped over the stern rail under the canopy, followed by Hasim; opened the saloon door; and reached for the switch. Light came on under the stern canopy, and it was strangely comforting with the rain drifting down.

"We'll wait for them here," Billy said. "Not with the lights on, of course."

He switched off and gazed down the river, lights winking in the distance, and Hasim said, "Are you sure they will come?"

"Absolutely," Billy told him. "Nothing has ever been more certain."

13

HARRY SALTER'S RISE from gangster to multimillionaire had been the product of his discovery that there was more money to be made from business than criminal enterprises. All along the Thames, decaying warehouses had been resurrected as offices or blocks of flats, and occasionally something personal like Harry's Place.

On a good night, there would be a queue at the restaurant, people hanging in there hoping they might get in, but not tonight. Only Fernando, the Portuguese head waiter in his white tuxedo, stood in the arched entrance at the head of the steps, flanked by two waiters in white monkey jackets, each clutching an umbrella.

They hurried to meet the Dark Man party as Harry led the way in. "Are we the first?"

"Yes, but there's a bus parked up in the car park," Fernando said. "I checked it out, pretending to be an attendant, and was told to go away in quite colorful language."

"Did you recognize anyone?"

"Barry McGuire seemed to be in charge. There were only seven of them, typical yobs."

"Not McGuire—he's an evil bastard, that one. Good, we know what to expect. We'll see you inside."

The restaurant was designed in an art deco style, white the predominant color, a bar and a piano beside a dance floor, small and intimate tables dotted around it, and booths against the wall.

Fernando led the way to the bar, seated Harry and Dora, Baxter and Hall taking up their stations. The head waiter heard other voices and hurried off to meet Roper, who was followed by Sara, Hannah, Dillon, Holley, and Tad Magee.

"I can't believe this weather," Sara said. "Tad is leaving his Aston Martin in the hands of an attendant to park in the courtyard. I hope it'll be all right."

"I don't think it'll come to any harm there, the way things are shaping up," said Harry.

"And why would that be?"

"The Master must be cursing the day he put his trust in that fool Moon and his cousin Harold." Harry filled in the blanks for them, and when he was finished, said, "So instead of Moon and an unruly mob putting the fear of God into my customers, we're left with one bad bastard, McGuire, and six or seven third-raters sitting in an old bus in the car park putting away too much whiskey because they don't know what else to do."

"And Billy and Hasim?" Dillon asked.

"Guarding the *Linda Jones* in case that clown Harold tries to do his thing. He and Moon are right up the creek without a paddle. So let me say happy birthday to Captain Sara Gideon." He hugged her. "Shot and shell, fifteen years in the army. A truly remarkable lady."

Roper's Codex buzzed at that moment. He listened, then held up his hand. "Can I have quiet, please? Ferguson would like a word. I'll put it on speaker."

"It's impossible for us to get away; it really grieves me," Ferguson's voice said. "Your service with the British Army has been truly remarkable, wounded and decorated, a veteran of every conflict your country has served in, and I couldn't respect you more, Major Gideon."

Startled by his mistake, Sara hurriedly corrected him. "Captain, General."

"Not if you can be bothered to read the Army List today, Major Gideon."

The party exploded with delight, Hannah flinging her arms around Sara, then others reaching out to embrace or kiss her, and Roper pulled her over and did just that himself. "Bless you, Sara, for everything about you. Not to have read the Army List shows real style."

"Listen to that," Ferguson said. "The voice of Lieutenant Colonel Giles Roper confirming that he doesn't read the Army List either."

For once, Roper was speechless as the group erupted again around him.

"Go on, have your fun, and I'll see you soon," Ferguson said, and switched off.

"Cristal for everybody!" Harry said.

BARRY MCGUIRE was an angry man and not just because he had been drinking heavily. He could handle that, but what he couldn't handle was the fact that everything had gone wrong. Nothing had happened like it should have, and he saw his money flying out the window. The other men drank and argued, but were careful not to offend him, for it was a known fact that he'd killed a man and done time for it.

He sat at the back of the bus staring morosely out of the window at the rain falling in a dark curtain, dimming the lights on the other side of the Thames, when his mobile phone jolted him.

"This is the Master, Mr. McGuire. I'm sure you've heard of me. You must be very disappointed. No big money here, I'm afraid. George Moon and Harold got it very wrong."

"They certainly did, the bloody morons."

"Well, let me tell you what to do to improve matters. First, cause a ruckus. Tell your friends to have a go at the cars in the courtyard. Draw out the people inside. They'll be armed, I'm sure."

"And so am I," McGuire said.

"Don't be stupid. Dillon and company would kill you dead without a thought. If that's what you want, I suggest you make arrangements with your undertaker. I don't care what happens to the other morons, but if you want to make a great deal of money, listen closely."

Suddenly, McGuire was alert and alive again. "So what can I do?"

"Get these few louts you have, cause problems with the cars, as I said. You say you have a weapon. What is it?"

"A Belgian Leon automatic."

"Hardly a Walther PPK, but it will do. Fire a few shots in the air to get things moving but don't get involved yourself. Here's what I want you to do. Not much more than a mile down the river is Moon's old pub. His motor launch, the *Moonglow*, is chained to the pier. The pub is his office and Harold sleeps there, but Moon always sleeps in the launch."

"So what?"

"Harold, being the rat he is, has told me that Moon has a fetish for cash in large amounts and has a secret safe somewhere in the old launch."

"I don't believe it. How would Harold know?"

"Because they have a relationship that might shock you, and when Harold needs cash, Moon always gets it for him from the launch, for which he has the only key."

"So what are you expecting me to do?"

"What you do best. After all, you did serve five years in prison for manslaughter. With a gun in your hand, I'm sure you'll have no difficulty in making them see reason. If they're not at home, I'd wait."

McGuire said, "If it's so easy, why don't you have a go yourself?"

"I don't waste my time that way. Now I've answered your problem. They are having a wonderful time in the restaurant while you and what's left of the original scum decay gradually. I suggest you get on with it."

McGuire sat there, thinking about it for just a moment, and then said, "Listen to me, idiots, we're just wasting our time sitting here while that lot are enjoying champagne and caviar in the restaurant. Let's show them we're here!"

He got the bus door open, scrambled down, and made for the courtyard. When he glanced back, they were following.

IN THE RESTAURANT, Hannah was seated at the white Bechstein, working her way through some favorites, when she was shocked by the sound of angry voices outside and sudden gunfire. Everyone in the room sprang to their feet, Harry first to the French windows of the terrace that revealed the melee in the courtyard. McGuire, having fired three or four shots in the air, had departed.

Two men had also cleared off, which left five determined and very drunk individuals with fence posts in their hands to be used as crude clubs as Harry, Tad, Dillon, and Holley faced them.

The leader, a red-haired man with a bloated face, raised his fence post high as he stood behind the Aston Martin. "I'll show you what I think of this car."

Dillon drew his Colt on the instant and shot the lobe off the man's right ear. The man cried out, dropping his post, and so did the others. Dillon approached the man, took out a handkerchief, and gave it to him.

"Hold that against it. Try your stupidity again and I'll kill you." He turned to Harry. "Get Fernando to pack them into one of your vans, take them downtown, and drop them at one of the hospitals. Let's get on with the festivities, shall we? I could do with another glass of champagne."

UNAWARE OF EVENTS at Harry's Place, George Moon and Harold sat at the kitchen table in the pub dressed in their oilskins and drinking their second hot toddy. The rain pounded down, the wind that had stirred up rattling the windows. There was a reluctance to move on the part of both of them and even more reluctance on the part of George Moon to answer his mobile when it rang.

The Master said, "A night for farce or villainy, it would seem. It was a total disaster at Harry's Place; Barry McGuire and his men dispersed. No reply when I try calling him. Remember that line about the Scarlet Pimpernel, is he in heaven or is he in hell? In this case, I suppose it's hell."

"Look, this whole affair has been a disaster," Moon said. "It's nobody's fault. Let's just regroup and think of a new plan."

"A new plan? Oh, my dear Mr. Moon. If I want, I can have you kidnapped and deposited in a Middle Eastern prison, where you will share a cell with fifteen people. Should I do that?"

And it was Harold who intervened, crying hoarsely, "For God's sake, shut up, George, and let's get on with the rest of what we're supposed to do."

"How sensible," the Master said. "I suggest you do exactly that, or you will come to regret it very, very much."

He was gone, and Moon stood up wearily. "Nothing to be done except go."

"Exactly," Harold said. "So come on. No point in taking that jerry can of petrol with us. Not much chance of a fire in this weather, but I've brought this just in case we meet anybody."

The weapon he held was an Israeli Uzi submachine gun.

"An ugly weapon," Moon said. "But I suppose that sometimes there's no choice."

They went out into the storm and descended the steps to the jetty, where the motor launch was jerking against the chains, the inflatable bobbing beside her. They stepped in, Harold cast off, and Moon switched on the engine, which responded with a deep and hungry roar, their lights cutting into the darkness as they forged ahead.

BARRY MCGUIRE HAD ARRIVED after a long walk on foot, his light overcoat soaked and useless for such weather. From the pub, he had seen them boarding the inflatable in the pool of light from the single lamp standard on the jetty. He started down the steps, shouting, but the inflatable was already turning away.

He descended to the bottom of the steps, cursing, approached the door of the motor launch, tried stamping at it without success, so he gave in, went up the steps to the pub, and had better success with an assault on the kitchen door.

It was warm in there, and he struggled out of his sodden overcoat and jacket; went to the bar, where he purloined a bottle of whiskey; and returned to the kitchen to sit by the ancient potbellied stove in which a fire burned.

He sat there, enjoying the heat, and suddenly noticed a felling axe propped in a corner behind the stove, reached for it, weighing it in one hand, wondering how long the door to the motor launch would stand up to it. Well, he'd soon see.

IN GOGGLES AND HOOD against the rain, George Moon loved every minute of piloting the inflatable. Strange in a man who was a timid soul in so many ways, yet he could respond to every demand of this craft and always had done.

Other boats did pass by, but not many, for it was black and dirty enough to encourage most folks to stay home, and there was the rumble of thunder to go with the rain now.

On the *Linda Jones*, Billy and Hasim drank coffee and waited, and it was Billy who suddenly said, "They're coming."

"How can you be sure?"

"Twelve or fifteen years of doing this kind of thing with a gentleman called Sean Dillon, a grand master of the art of skull-duggery."

"You think a lot of him, don't you?"

"I sure do. I was a real bad guy when I was your age. I'd been to prison twice, just a small-time hoodlum, and Harry couldn't control me."

"And Dillon did?"

"Absolutely. He made me face the error of my ways, all right." He raised a hand. "Listen. They are coming now." He took a Colt .25 from an inside pocket and handed it over. "You've been shown what to do with one of these on the firing range at Holland Park."

"And what about you?" Hasim said.

"Oh, I've got one as well, but they'll be here in a couple of minutes, so we'll surprise them." He switched on the stern lights of the *Linda Jones*, and as Moon did the same to his engine, the inflatable drifted in.

Hasim was already holding the Colt at waist level, and Billy was drawing his. "You can stop right there, Moon," he shouted.

Harold pulled out the Uzi, and Billy slipped on the wet deck, his shot going wide as the other man's bullet sliced across the top of his left shoulder.

Harold raised the Uzi for a second shot, and Hasim fired quickly, catching him in the chest, knocking him back into the well of the inflatable, and Moon revved up his engine, swung the inflatable around, and sped away.

"Oh, God, it hurts," Harold moaned. "Get me back to the pub." And Moon, terrified in a way he had never been before in his life, tried to control the bouncing inflatable.

"YOU'RE SHOT," Hasim said to Billy, who was taking an American battle pack from his pocket, opening it with his teeth, and tightening it in place.

"Don't worry about me," he said. "Top speed, Hasim, get after them." And he leaned forward, clutching the grab rail, conscious of the severe pain of his wound but denying it. "They can be going to only one place."

A moment later, the engine stopped dead, and Hasim cursed and started to go through the checklist in his head.

HAROLD COULD NO LONGER STAND and had slumped onto the rear bench, clutching his chest, blood oozing through his fingers. Moon coasted in, scrambling out and tying up the inflatable at the bottom of the stone steps leading up to the jetty. He gave an arm to Harold, and with great difficulty, they made it, but it was apparent that the steps up to the pub were an impossibility, so Moon took out his key and unlocked the cabin door of the motor launch.

"You need to lie down, love," he said to Harold. "You wait here, and I'll find you a doctor."

"Waste of time," Harold said. "I'm dying and something is wrong here. The boat is rolling all over the place. Why is that?"

"Because somebody seems to have cut the chains," Moon said. "We've only got a single line holding us in. Rather dangerous in weather like this."

The door to the saloon was flung open, and McGuire stepped inside, holding his Belgian Leon automatic at the ready.

"I've been waiting for you to get back. The Master had words with me. I must say you look in a damn bad way, Harold."

"He's dying, poor soul," Moon said. "A young Muslim boy shot him. Mind you, Harold managed to shoot Billy Salter."

"Well, the only thing I'm interested in is the secret safe somewhere on this boat that's crammed with money."

"It's a lie," Harold said.

"And even if it wasn't, I wouldn't tell you," Moon added.

McGuire leaned forward, poked with his gun at Harold's left

kneecap, and pulled the trigger. Harold didn't cry out, only slumped, and Moon said, "What a cruel man you are."

"Oh, that's nothing to what you'll get if you don't show me where the bloody safe is damn quick."

"No need to get nasty," Moon said. He got up, went to the old Victorian desk, opened the secret drawer, and turned with the Walter PPK in his hand. "No cash, you bastard, but you can settle for this."

Moon pulled the trigger; McGuire did the same as he was hurled backward by the force of the PPK, his own bullet striking Moon between the eyes, knocking him back against Harold so that they tumbled to the floor together.

It was perhaps ten minutes later that the other inflatable coasted in and discovered the carnage and Hasim said, "What happened here?"

"It doesn't matter," Billy said. "It just did."

"So what are we going to do?"

"If we were Vikings, we'd burn the boat. We are not, but we can open the seacocks and send them below."

"If that's what you'd like, but you're not fit to do that. I'll handle it, and you go and wait in the inflatable," which Billy did, suddenly more tired than he had ever been, Hasim coming down the steps and the *Moonglow* already settling in her last resting place fifty feet below.

Hasim started the engine and turned the inflatable toward Harry's Place.

Billy said, "So you've killed your first man."

"He was trying to kill us. No problem. He shot you and was going to shoot you again."

"Dora won't be pleased."

"She'll have to get used it. I'd like to be like you and work for MI5. I know I haven't had a fancy schooling, but my Arabic is fluent. Do you think they'd be interested in me?"

"Hasim, they'd grab you with both hands."

"Well, that's what I want, but never mind for now. What you need is Rosedene and Professor Bellamy. Your face is wet with sweat, so let's get you back to Harry's Place."

THEIR ARRIVAL WAS MET with dismay when the circumstances were made clear. Roper, who was titular head of operations at Holland Park, took it upon himself to have Billy immediately placed in Bellamy's charge for, as the professor pointed out, it was the fifth occasion in fifteen years of service that Billy had suffered a gunshot wound.

As Bellamy said to Roper, "You of all people, suffering as you have done over many years, should appreciate more than most human beings that there is a limit to the amount of violent trauma any individual can take, and Billy Salter is only thirty-five years of age."

"And seems more concerned about young Hasim being forced to kill for the first time at nineteen," Roper pointed out.

"A brave young man, who I understand has his eye on MI5. Do you think this likely?"

"I imagine so. His fluency in Arabic alone makes him invaluable."

"Then I would have thought that Dr. Ali Sharif and his people at Tenby Street safe house might provide what he's looking for. This won't give him a problem with the Salters at the Dark Man?" Bellamy asked.

"Absolutely not," Roper said. "They are the only family he knows. Can I ask how long Billy will be hospitalized?"

"Five or six weeks with appropriate therapy."

Roper laughed. "Well, he won't like that."

"Well, he'll have to. Congratulations on your promotion, by the way. Long overdue. How's your health? Any problems?"

"Oh, fine," Roper told him. "Except that I'd like to have various new bits and pieces, but as you aren't Dr. Frankenstein, I know it is impossible."

Bellamy said, "Giles, in all my years of experience in the medical profession, you're the bravest man I've ever known."

"Come off it, Charles, now you're trying to flatter me."

"Of course I am, old lad," Bellamy told him, "but now you'll have to excuse me. Duty calls," and he moved on.

LATER, TONY DOYLE, Hannah, and Sara were in the computer room when Roper's Codex came to life and the Master's voice echoed around the room.

"Lieutenant colonel now," he told Roper. "My sincere congratulations. I believe you're my favorite adversary."

"And that really does worry me," Roper told him.

"To be honest, I have a fondness for you all. George Moon and his cousin Harold were stupid people who deserved what they got, and Barry McGuire, a murderous thug. Billy Salter has always killed with style, and Hasim is set to follow in his footsteps. MI5 will be delighted to have him."

"All right, mister," Hannah called. "You're supposed to be able to tell us everything, but most of the time you're talking about things we already know."

"My dear girl, here goes. With the support of the White House, President Jake Cazalet is about to be named to chair a committee based in New York to investigate the spread of ISIS in the Western world. Both Johnson and Ferguson will be going over for it, and Lieutenant Colonel Roper will then be in charge of Holland Park. Have I missed anything out?"

Hannah said, "Giles, is that true?"

"Not as far as I know, but I've a feeling it's going to be."

"Excellent," the Master said. "I've told you that our information service is superior to the CIA's, but you won't listen. But never mind. We will speak again, I'm sure."

Sara said, "Can't you speak to Ferguson, Giles? If it's true, we're all going to be affected. I think we're entitled to know."

"I expect he'll do it in his own good time, but protocol is every-thing to old-timers like him. I'll see what Blake has to say when I ring him."

Which he did, starting with the obvious inquiry when Blake answered. "How's Alice getting on?"

"Well, it has only been a few days, remember, and from what I understand, it's going to be a pretty drawn-out process. I've spoken to her several times and she's cheerful enough."

"That's good. Of course, you'll be able to visit her when you go over for Cazalet's ISIS committee."

There was a pause, then Blake said, "Who the hell told you that?"

Sara cut in. "The Master, Blake. Hannah and I were sitting here when he phoned Giles."

"This is a breach of security on a monumental scale," Blake told her. "I must discuss it with General Ferguson," and he switched off.

"Well, that's put the cat amongst the pigeons," Hannah said, and Roper's phone system positively rattled.

Ferguson said, "It's outrageous the way this bloody man keeps popping up. How in the hell does he do it? A Cabinet decision made at the highest level, not even announced in the press or BBC, and here we have him cheerfully calling you, Giles, and passing the time of day."

"Having said that, the important question is where does he get his information from, General."

"Well, we'll just have to try harder to find out. Having said that, yes, it's true that Blake, President Cazalet, and I depart for New York tomorrow. You, Lieutenant Colonel Roper, are now in command at Holland Park. Major Gideon, you're number two and I wish you well."

Sara said, "As we do you, General, and every success in New York." But by then, Ferguson had gone and there was only silence.

"There goes an angry man," Hannah said.

"You can understand why." Sara shrugged. "When Ferguson was a young subaltern, war was a magnificent game played according to the rules. My fifteen years in the army were different. Definitely no rules in Ireland, or Bosnia and Kosovo, and Afghanistan could be hell on earth. The most unbelievably awful game in the world."

"Then why play it?" Hannah asked.

"Because of a fascination that's been there since Roman times and beyond. It makes the rest of life incredibly boring," Sara told her.

"Which it probably is for most people."

"So much more sensible to go and get yourself blown up," Roper said. "I can really recommend that."

"So what do we do about the Master?" Hannah demanded.

"That's the wrong question," Roper said. "The question should be: What is he doing about us? That's his game, you see."

AND HE WAS PLAYING it now, calling up Hans Weber at Charnley, who immediately recognized the voice and was actually pleased to hear from him.

"How's business?" the Master asked.

"I'm making a living. Plenty of private pilots are happy to find a home for their plane and the chance to fly. What's the word on the Dakota flights?"

"There's no future trying to make a living from selling religious artifacts. Even thieves recognize it is an affront to Islam."

"No longer a future for Havoc, then," Weber said. "That first and only Dakota flight from Charnley. All that Islamic stuff from Timbuktu. I couldn't possibly meet the demand with one flight filled with ancient books and manuscripts. Every dealer in London and Paris was begging for more, and then MI5 stepped in. I thought I was going to end up in the Tower of London."

"You got off lightly, I think," the Master said.

"I'm sure of it. I still have the money in my bank account, and it's a lot."

"The Intelligence Act says you may be arrested and imprisoned as the judge advocate sees fit."

"How long for?"

"As seems appropriate. Thirty years is common."

"Which means they'll keep me because I may be useful."

"That's what intelligence outfits do."

"Ah, well, I must take my chances. May I stay in touch?"

"Of course, you have my number."

ON THE QUAI DES BRUMES, the Master drank coffee under the canopy over the stern of the barge, thinking of Weber. A good man who could have extracted a lot more than he had done out of Timbuktu, but when it came right down to it, he couldn't bring himself to do what was necessary.

A different kind of man, someone of a piratical disposition, a Finbar Magee, for example, would have grabbed at the opportunity to ravage Timbuktu or anywhere else when it came right down to it. The way things had gone at Drumore House fascinated the Master, so two Magees to choose from, and he made it Eli, who was sitting in that huge kitchen enjoying a glass of red wine and reading the local newspaper when his mobile buzzed.

"Eli Magee."

"How nice to hear your voice. It's been some time," the Master said.

"Who is this?" Eli demanded.

"Why, the Master, of course. Don't say you've forgotten me. You are the master now of Drumore House; Finbar must have been distressed by that."

"That's my affair, not yours. Finbar gets bed and board, and does little in return. An idle and drunken bastard, my cousin, who will mend his ways or get off my property. And you can get off my phone," and Eli switched off.

FINBAR HAD COME into the house from the garden and was approaching the kitchen along the corridor and heard Eli answer the phone. He passed outside, listening to what his cousin was saying, and then he turned away and went upstairs to his room.

He hated Eli, dreamed of killing him, but he quite simply was not a match for the big man. Finbar kept a bottle of whiskey in the bedside locker and he poured a generous glass, sat on the bed, and started drinking; and his phone rang.

The Master said, "Finbar, old friend, how are you? I was just talking to your cousin, and he was very unpleasant about you. I don't know how you put up with it."

"Not much longer," Finbar said. "When I strike, it must be hard. I intend to finish him off for good, and that means dead in the water."

"My dear chap, are you sure about this?"

"Of course I am. I met a man recently in a bar in town on market day who deals in illegal weapons. The police are very hot about that over here, but if you have the right contact, you can get anything."

"And what have you got, my friend?" the Master asked.

"A two-shot derringer with hollow points that will blow my cousin away once and for all, and my sons can go to hell."

"And when do you intend to do this?"

"Soon, very soon, but I want to get it right. I don't want things to drag on now. I can do it. Eli Magee is a dead man."

The Master said, "Has it occurred to you that Eli's going to an early grave may take the secret of the *Maria Blanco* with him?"

"So what? There's Hugh Tulley, IRA chief of staff for County Down, and, sure, didn't he mastermind the whole operation in the first place? I've always said he knows a hell of a lot more than he's telling."

"You may be right," the Master told him. "But promise me you'll take very great care and I'll stay in touch."

ELI HAD NO HESITATION in phoning Tad Magee with the information that the Master had been in touch.

"Kind of creepy and slimy, he was, as if we were friends. Told me I was now the master of Drumore House, and he said Finbar must be distressed. I told him he was an idle drunk who'd better mend his ways or get off my property."

"I see," Tad said. "Does Finbar threaten you?"

"Mainly behind my back, but I'm respected in the community, and people say that they worry about the threats he makes."

"Well, I'm damned if I'm going to have that, Eli. Leave it with me, and I'll get back to you very soon."

DILLON WAS IN the computer room with Roper and Hannah when he took Tad's phone call.

"I need your help badly, Sean."

"Well, I'm sitting here with Hannah and a certain Lieutenant Colonel Giles Roper who is in charge here now with Ferguson's departure for New York."

So Tad told them. When he was finished, Roper said, "I think we all get the picture, but what are you asking us to do?"

"Fundamentally, this is an IRA matter."

"And how do you think they'd have handled it?"

"Hugh Tulley would have sent a top enforcer to Drumore to sort things out, a pistol in his pocket and a readiness to use it if necessary," Hannah said. "I naturally assume this means Sean Dillon swings into action, and let me be the first to volunteer."

"There is a small matter of the college to consider," Roper said.

"You keep forgetting, it's half term. I mean, don't you think that a decent Irish girl like me could be very useful in this situation?"

"Actually, I do, because you've been to Drumore before and know the people involved," Roper told her. "So what's the next step?"

"We'll meet at Barking, the same place as last time, the Chieftain. Any comments, Sean?"

"Billy Spillane who runs the aero club at Dunkelly is a Provo, isn't he?"

"To the hilt," Tad said. "What are you thinking?"

"If Finbar does harbor murderous intent, he'll need a weapon. Perhaps Billy could check with his friends to see if anyone has anything helpful to say."

"I'll take care of it," Tad said. "See you at Barking."

"Our first job with you in charge, Lieutenant Colonel," Hannah said.

"The next thing you'll be suggesting is that we should have a drink on it, but it won't work, because I finished the champagne last night. So, off you go, and try to keep Dillon on the rails if you can."

14

THEY DROVE OUT of Holland Park in the Mini, Hannah at the wheel. "Turn right instead of left," Dillon told her as they exited.

"Why?" she asked.

"Billy Salter," he told her. "I know it's too soon, but I'd like to know how he is."

"You could have phoned," she said. "He's got a Codex, hasn't he?"

"What happened to those two last night was typical of the crazy game we play. Of all people to get shot, it's Billy, fifteen years of service, four times wounded, now five. And the executioner in this case who killed the villain is nineteen."

"So what are you saying, that life is pure chance? It certainly was for me, crippled by a car bomb that murdered my parents but not me, and then there was Sara and those Brigade Reconnaissance Force heroes."

She swung into the Rosedene car park, then they found Harry and Hasim in the lounge having coffee and a chat with Maggie.

"No Dora?" Dillon asked.

"She's in a right old state," Harry said. "I told her not to worry because Billy wouldn't be able to play football for England, but she couldn't see the joke. Said he'd never played football in his life, so I gave up."

"I don't blame you," Dillon said, and Bellamy appeared wearing scrubs and looking tired as usual.

"You seem to be past every damn thing there ever was," Dillon told him.

"A bad night, Sean, and other people persist in sending special cases. Billy is responding well to the removal of the bullet. However, those Uzi rounds are particularly lethal, so I'd rather he wasn't troubled by visitors."

He went back to his office, and Maggie Duncan said, "Which puts you all in the same boat."

"Not Hannah and I," Dillon told her. "We're off to Northern Ireland on business, but we'll stay in touch."

"Business?" Harry said. "I can imagine. For God's sake, Sean, is there no end to it?"

"Not in the world we live in," Dillon said, and turned and put a hand on Hasim's shoulder. "You did well last night. I'm proud of you."

Hannah reached up and kissed Hasim on the cheek. "Welcome to the club."

"Take care," Hasim told her.

"Always do," and she limped away after Dillon.

AT BARKING, they found the usual couple of dozen single-engine planes parked and the Chieftain waiting. Tad was sitting at an outside table of the small café with Pat Ryan and Jack Kelly from Kilburn's Green Tinker.

Tad said, "You'd better sit down. We've got news for you. Billy Spillane has checked around and discovered a dealer from the old days who has done business with Finbar very recently."

"What kind of business?" Dillon asked.

"A rather unusual handgun. A two-shot derringer with hollow points. There's a shortage of these on the market."

"You're telling me," Dillon said. "At close quarters it is absolutely lethal, guaranteed to blow you apart."

"Do you think Finbar knows that?" Ryan asked.

"Well, if he didn't, he will have been told by the guy he bought it from."

"So what's the next step?" Hannah asked. "To relieve him of it?"

"Of course," Tad said.

"And what if he says you can't have it?"

"Well, then, it will have to be taken from him."

"You make it sound really easy," she said. "Do you think it will be?"

"That will have to be handled as it comes."

"It is all very well saying that, but hollow points are probably the most lethal pistol rounds in use. That's why they're popular in many South American republics as a tool of assassination."

"Where the hell does she get her information?" Ryan demanded.

"The horse's mouth," Hannah told him. "Raised in a Provisional IRA household since childhood. Survived a car bomb, which my parents didn't. Various male members of the Flynn family have ended up dead in service to the Cause, and I'm cousin to Sean Dillon, for what that's worth."

"Thanks for including me in your summing up of the the essence of Irish Republicanism during the last thirty-five years of the Troubles," Dillon said to her.

"Think nothing of it. It's just that, because I've managed to learn about Finbar, I think the only real solution to the bastard is to shoot him, and sooner rather than later."

Ryan said to Dillon, "For God's sake, Sean, where did you find her?"

"The truth of it is, Pat, she found me, and I thank the good Lord every day of my life that she did. So with thanks for your support, I think we'll be climbing into our plane and making for Dunkelly and County Down."

TAD STAYED IN THE CABIN dealing with papers from his briefcase, Dillon loosened his tie and took control, and Hannah joined him in the cockpit. The Chieftain roared along the runway and started to climb.

"You really love your flying, don't you?" Hannah said.

"Oh, yes, as the SAS got to grips with the really tough places, like Armagh, in the early nineties, I moved on from Ireland, worked for the Israelis. That's where I learned to fly."

"And Sara implied that Ferguson pulled a dirty trick on you."

"You could say that. I fell in with an international relief group to fly medical supplies into Serbia during the war, drugs for children. I was shot down by a MIG fighter, and Stinger missiles were found under the drugs, the kind of thing that usually got you executed. A setup of course."

"By whom?"

"Brigadier Charles Ferguson, as he was then, who was looking for someone like me to do his dirty work."

"The old bastard."

"A bad word coming from a nice girl like you; but after all, the drugs probably reached children who needed them, the missiles replenished the war supply, and Major Branco, in command of the prison where they shot you in the morning, was able to go to England and join his mother in Hampstead, courtesy of gallant Brigadier Charles Ferguson. So everybody got something, including the children."

"But it could have been so different. They might have shot you."

"Perfidious Albion, love, that's how the English ruled the world for several hundred years. Now I wouldn't mind a cup of tea if you think you could manage."

"And what else would I have to do except serve your lordship?" she said, thickening her accent.

"Try the Abbey Theatre," Dillon told her. "You might have a future. After all, your aunt did."

She went out, Tad moved in, and a moment later, Dillon's Codex alerted him, and the Master said, "This should be an interesting trip. The wretched Finbar is making waves again, I hear."

"Which gives me no pleasure," Tad cut in. "But even less to have to listen to you sticking your nose in again. Yes, a wretched man, but my father and my problem."

"You heard that," Dillon said. "It is obviously going to be a lively day, so I think you should drop out and leave us to it unless you have any information about the fate of the *Maria Blanco*."

The Master laughed harshly. "You won't believe me, Dillon, but I always wondered whether you knew more than you were letting on. The story of the IRA having sent you off to Algeria to train volunteers seemed too convenient."

Dillon glanced over his shoulder and realized Hannah was leaning into the cockpit listening, so he spoke with passion.

"I have my cousin, Hannah, with me now, who has suffered more than most in our country's Troubles. I swear to her that I have no knowledge of what happened to the *Maria Blanco*, but I promise that I will find out while I am there. The mystery has dragged on long enough, so clear off and leave me to land this plane."

AND AS THE DUNKELLY FLYING CLUB loomed below, Dillon dropped the Chieftain in neatly and rolled along to the buildings at one end where Eli waited with Billy Spillane, who was wearing his old flight jacket.

Eli and Tad hugged each other, and then the big man turned to the others, embraced Hannah, and shook hands with Dillon. They sat outside in the café.

"How is he?" Tad asked.

"In his room under lock and key," Eli told him. "I have his wrists shackled during the day, plus his ankles at night."

"Would that be considered a bit harsh?" Hannah inquired.

"Not to Jimmy Leary and Jack O'Dwyer, who I got to help me restrain Finbar when he turned up at the little bar here three nights ago and started taking the place apart. It took six of the boys to hold him down. Jimmy's got a broken wrist, Jack two fractured toes in his right foot from being stamped on."

"Where is he now, a police cell?" Tad asked.

"God, no, we wouldn't do that to the Magee family, but it must be solved. Mad, bad, and dangerous to know sums him up," said Billy.

"I love the quote," Dillon said. "It shows you've read a book."

"We tried to shake the derringer pistol out of him, but he isn't playing. Eli had us round last night; we had Finbar at one side of the big table in the kitchen, tried to get him to tell us where he had the gun, but with no joy."

Hannah said, "You were never active in the IRA, Eli?"

"I never operated in the field. It was felt that my size would be a giveaway. I kept the house and saw to the boys on the run."

"Was Finbar active?"

Tad said, "Tell her the truth, Eli."

"A certain kind of man was common in those days. Big of mouth and claiming to be IRA, when in fact they were often driving a delivery truck for a supermarket. Finbar had a problem with the RUC for illegal possession of a firearm. He got a year in prison and missed out on the twenty-five-million-pound gold robbery involving Drumore House and me."

"You were found manacled in the boathouse, and the motor cruiser loaded with ingots vanished into history." Hannah smiled. "An intriguing story we are all familiar with."

Billy Spillane said, "Hugh Tulley is eighty-four but very fit with it. He'd be happy to meet if you'd like that."

Tad said, "I'd be fascinated." He turned to Dillon and Hannah. "Wouldn't you?"

"Well, considering what we went through together, I think it would be churlish not to see him." Dillon smiled at Hannah. "Who knows, he may have some answers for you."

"Right, then, Billy, bring him along for six and bring one of your cook's light suppers in a basket."

"And what do we do with Finbar?"

"Oh dear," Hannah said. "I thought we were talking all friends together."

"Well, we are," Tad said. "But if the opportunity arises, we'll see. I'm staying with Billy for a while. Eli will take you two onward to the house. See you later."

THERE WAS A VIDEO SYSTEM in Finbar's bedroom that enabled Eli to keep an eye on him. It was as if Finbar knew that he was being watched, and he put out his tongue and shouted. "Go fuck yourself, whoever you are," and he looked old and twisted and evil.

Standing by the fireplace, Hannah said, "Let's wash some of that away. The sun is shining, the Irish Sea magnificent. Let's go along the cliff top."

"Where there is a place not far from the house that is the most dangerous of all. A cliff path a hundred feet up from jagged rocks below. Locals call it the Devil's Jump," Dillon said.

"Well, lead on," she told him. "I'm presuming it never was the Devil making the jump, but some incredibly brave young man doing something extraordinary."

"How clever you are," Dillon told her. "And perfectly right. After the French Revolution, there was upheaval in other countries, and Ireland was one of them. There was a revolution in Ulster, the United Irishmen, led by a man named Wolfe Tone. He was a Protestant, which didn't sit well with a lot of Irish Catholics. The British put him in a prison cell anyway, where he committed suicide, and if you believe that, you'll believe anything."

"But what has that got to do with Devil's Jump?"

"Because, during the revolution, a man was running so hard to get away from the militia that he jumped one hundred feet down into the sea and survived. Local tradition says it was Wolfe Tone."

"What a great story," Hannah said. "Can I look?"

"Of course, but you must promise me not to do anything silly. Over the years, there's been the occasional accident and what might have been a suicide or two. The fencing is not the best. Tad got Eli to put a concrete platform there with a steel railing. There's only room for two or three people at the same time, but the view is fantastic."

And so it was, leaning over to see Drumore House, way below

them on the right, the narrow road, the boathouse, and the jetty. But up here, high on the cliff as it reared up, Hannah was dizzy with pleasure to look at the sea swelling a hundred feet below.

"It isn't dashing in, one wave after another. Why is that?"

"Honeycombed with caves and canyons and deep gorges, all under the water. Highly dangerous to dive down there. Difficult to handle your depth in such fierce currents."

"But you're an expert in that kind of stuff. I remember Sara saying the reason Ferguson wanted you originally was because you'd done great work underwater for the Israelis. Then you went on to discover a German U-boat in the Virgin Islands."

"Well, there you are," Dillon said. "Look at all that fun you've missed. Heavy stuff, Hannah, the world down there is something very special indeed. I remember trying it on my twenty-first birthday, with little training to speak of. I was resting, having been on the run for a while, and a man called Harry Leary, who fished out of a village called Bundy four miles up the coast, gave me a few lessons. He also ran cargoes by night for the IRA."

"It must have been exciting, all that."

"It was, Hannah; I never knew such excitement, with a pistol in my pocket plus a belief you could change things, all the fine young men, as the poet said, and most of them long gone. So tell me, girl, what was it all about?"

"Don't ask me, Seaneen, sure, and I'm only a beginner."

"Then let's get back to see what's going on," and he took her hand, and they walked down the hill to Drumore House, where they found the festivities had just begun.

Billy Spillane's cook turned out to be his daughter, Peggy, who had a restaurant in Omagh and visited him when needed to keep the café at the aero club in order. She had taken over the huge old kitchen table, which was already occupied at one end by Tad and Hugh Tulley, white of hair and seated in a wheelchair.

"Sean, it's yourself," he roared. "And who is this beautiful creature you've got with you?"

Introductions were made while Peggy danced around the table laying a wonderful meal of cold cuts of beef, ham and turkey, salmon and salads, cold beer, red wine, and white in ice buckets. Tad said, "A fabulous spread, you must agree. Harry Leary is on his way, Sean, and bringing his son Tim. I hadn't realized you'd given him a call."

"Great comfort to the Provisional IRA," Tulley said. "Of course, fishing off the *Sealark* like he used to in the old days, using the breathing apparatus. It was all a mystery to the rest of us."

"But not for his son, I think," Dillon said.

Hannah stopped smiling. "Damn you, Sean Dillon. If you are considering going diving in a certain hell hole in search of a mythical *Maria Blanco*, I'm not having it."

"My darling girl, trust me and all will be well." He smiled at Eli. "As fine a spread as I've seen in a long time. May we start? The Learys can play catch-up."

HALF AN HOUR LATER, the Learys appeared and joined in, and a fine time was being had by everyone so there was considerable surprise when Dillon said to Eli, "I haven't told you, but I've found a cure where Finbar's gun is concerned."

There was total silence from everyone, for the scandal of it was known to the entire village, so Tad asked, "Are you certain?"

"Any bet you like, but you must bring him to join us so that he will realize his stupid game is up."

Tad was uncertain. "You're sure?"

Sean turned to Eli. "Remove the irons from his ankles and bring him down."

FINBAR WAS DISHEVELED and unshaven when Eli shoved him into the room, and he stood there, wrists chained so that they were a foot apart, as he stared out through the open French windows. He turned to look them over.

"You bunch of shites. What are you staring at? You can't break me, not even my bastard of a son can do that."

"But I can," Dillon told him. "A two-shot derringer with hollow points. Just one of those would certainly cause the instant death of your own son, and I refuse to allow that. After all, you killed his mother, and that, I would suggest, is enough."

"The smallest of guns." Finbar smiled like the Devil, evil. "You'll never find it in a place this size. It's been tried. He had all his mates looking and getting nowhere. Do you think you can do better?"

Dillon took out what looked like a large mobile phone. "This is a key tool in the bomb disposal trade, but it has other uses, and my friend, Lieutenant Colonel Giles Roper, knows them all. Every weapon is unique as regards the metal used to create it, and the derringer is no different. The device will find it like a dog finds a bone—and we already have a reaction here in this room. As Sherlock Holmes would say, always choose the obvious. The kitchen, on this occasion." He walked to the grandfather clock by the fire, opened the face, and turned with the pistol in one hand and the device bleating in the other.

Finbar howled with rage, grabbed the edge of the tablecloth in both hands, sweeping a good deal of what was on the table to the floor, and then ran out through the French windows, chained hands held in front of him, running at extraordinary speed up the slope toward the edge of the cliff.

Tad and Dillon went after him, Billy Spillane following, but Tim Leary, a younger man, overhauled them easily enough, and called to Finbar, "Don't be a fool. There's only one way down."

"Don't you think I know that?" Finbar had paused beside the platform. "Go to hell, the lot of you," and he dived into space, chained hands out in front of him.

His pursuers walked the last few yards to where Tim Leary peered down into the maelstrom. "Swallowed him on the instant," he said, as Hannah limped up to join Dillon and Tad. "We'd better phone Sergeant Ryan in the village just to keep it official, but he was as mad as a hatter. The whole village knew it. My God, it's hell down there."

"Just the place for you and the great Sean Dillon when he's chasing death or the prospect of it," Hannah said.

Dillon approached her, and said, "Are you ready to go back now? We're leaving."

"Not at the moment, my leg's aching. I'll see you later."

She watched them go, then followed, leaning on her stick and thinking of what had taken place, finally resting on a bench just above the boathouse and jetty, trying to make sense of what had happened.

It was all linked to the mystery of the *Maria Blanco*, the treasure ship loaded with twenty-five million in gold ingots. Thinking about it was doing her head in, so she called Roper.

"Finbar is dead," she said, and explained what had happened and the situation at Drumore. "I just don't buy this account of the *Maria Blanco* slipping out to sea with a cargo of twenty-five million in gold ingots and never being heard of again. I wondered if you could help?"

"So what do you want to know?"

"Could you use your powers to have a look in RUC intelligence files of the period and find out what was going on with that job. Like now, please? I'm going down to Drumore to a very IRA supper that includes Hugh Tulley, the chief of staff at the time."

"For you, anything. I'll call soon. Over and out."

PEGGY SPILLANE WAS making up for the disaster at lunch by providing a rather happier supper. She gave Hannah a glass of elderflower wine and told her to rest, and she found herself looking at Hugh Tulley in a different way, because he'd pulled off the original robbery, a desperate business that had not been forgotten in the village nor had the casualties.

Eli was cheerful enough, probably the loss of Finbar just sinking in, and he was offering champagne from the cellar, but that didn't seem appropriate to Hannah, considering what had happened to

Finbar. And then Roper called her, and she went out in the hall to listen.

"AS IT TURNS OUT, there was no gold in that convoy. It was part of a plot to persuade the IRA to attack, and the details were such that the RUC never wanted to explain it and instead left it to legend, the whole affair classified," Roper told her. Hannah thanked him and went back to the meal.

"You must excuse me," she said. "I've just been filling my boss in on the Finbar tragedy and he was giving me details of the *Maria Blanco* affair." She turned to Tulley. "I don't know how long they sent you to the Maze Prison for, but it must have been a high price to pay for no gold, and don't tell me they didn't let you know that."

Billy Spillane said, "God save us, I used to believe when I was first learning to dive that I might find it down there on the bottom somewhere."

"Well, if you'd asked nicely, Eli might have put you out of your misery and told you there was nothing there."

Eli looked Hannah full in the face and smiled. "You guessed it was me, didn't you?"

"It had to be, Eli," she said. "Nothing else made the same kind of sense."

Tulley said, "It couldn't have been Eli, I handcuffed him myself. I took his spare key."

"I had three or four keys knocking around the boathouse, so when you locked me up again after I'd finished loading the boat, and you cleared off in your truck, I freed myself," Eli said.

"What then?" Hannah asked.

"I checked the boxes and discovered they were empty, which annoyed me, and I took the *Maria Blanco* around to where Finbar jumped and sank her, so in a way, I suppose, he found her today. After that, I handcuffed myself and waited to be found."

"And never spoke of it again."

"That was because Finbar wouldn't leave it alone." Eli turned to Tad. "I hope you'll forgive me."

"I forgive you, you old devil. You've done me a favor. There's a man I know who is going to be very angry when he hears the news about the *Maria Blanco*, so we'll open a couple of bottles of champagne, and you can join me in wishing the worst of health to a scoundrel called the Master."

AT TEN-THIRTY, the guests having departed, it was unusually warm, the French windows standing open, Hannah stretched out in a swing chair reading a magazine while Tad and Dillon sat on either side of a coffee table talking together in hushed voices.

"There should be no comebacks as far as I can see," Dillon said. "The RUC did nothing wrong. They didn't even supply false ingots in the boxes. Just space."

Tad laughed hugely, and Eli came in pushing a loaded trolley. "I think you've had enough of the other kinds of drinks today, so I thought a nice cup of tea and a bun might appeal before you go to bed. I'll leave you to it. Goodnight and blessings."

Hannah got up yawning, crossed to the trolley, and started to pour. Tad said, "You're not supposed to do that these days."

"That covers a lot of things, Tad," and her Codex sounded.

"Give me one guess," Hannah said. "It's you."

The Master laughed out loud. "That is what I like about you, Hannah. Direct and to the point."

She turned to the others. "Who wants to speak to him? The Master."

"I suppose I might as well," Dillon said, and called out, "I wouldn't have thought there was much to interest you at Drumore after today's dramatic events. Empty boxes are the big joke around here. You've got to give it to the old RUC. They certainly made us lose face."

"And is that all you can say?"

"Well, I suppose I could add that I'm sorry for the large number of people who hung on to the faint hope that somehow they'd come across the *Maria Blanco* with twenty-five million on board. It's a big letdown to discover it never existed in the first place."

Hannah clapped her hands slowly. "God bless you for that, Sean. I couldn't have put it better myself. Wouldn't you agree, Tad?"

"I would indeed, Hannah. Life is hard knocks, and I think you are experiencing that, Master, whoever you are."

"How unfortunate to have to hear that from a man who so callously saw his father's end this day. I think it will merit retribution for certain."

"So bring it on." Hannah was angry. "Do your worst. I'm going to bed, and you can go to hell," and she switched off.

"Does that make you feel better now?" Dillon asked.

"I suppose so. What happens tomorrow?"

"You and I fly back to Barking. Tad is staying on here for a while."

"The lawyers have a host of things to do," Tad told her. "It's a new era for Eli, so I want to help him settle in."

"Well, all that sounds perfectly splendid to me, but I still need my bed. I'll see you in the morning."

IT WAS RAINING, a touch of fog in the air, when Eli delivered them to the aero club. Hannah gave him a kiss as he passed the hand luggage to them.

"Take care, big man; it's your world now."

He smiled as he drove away, and they turned to Billy Spillane, who waited in the entrance to the café, and Dillon said, "How does it look?"

"Well, you can see the Isle of Man."

"And how far is that?" Hannah inquired.

"About fifty miles. They have the airport there at Castletown and it's open for business. A quick jump to the mainland and it's clear all the way to London."

"Let's get on with it," Dillon said, and shook hands. "An interesting weekend."

"One I'll never forget," Billy said, as he led the way. "God bless the both of ye."

They boarded the plane; the airstair door clanged shut. "I'll join you in the cockpit if you don't mind," Hannah said.

"Fine by me. Put on your earphones. I'll take the left seat."

She settled in the right, and he switched on. The engines

coughed into life and roared along the runway, lifting them off, and she was aware of the Isle of Man in the distance.

She leaned back, brooding about what had happened for twenty minutes, then, glancing to her right, was aware of a few light feathers of smoke coming out of the engine.

"Should that be happening to the starboard engine?" she asked Dillon.

He glanced sideways and stopped smiling. "No, it damn well shouldn't." He checked the controls. "And the extinguisher isn't responding."

"Should we turn back?" she asked.

"No, we'll do better to make for Castletown airport on the Isle of Man. If I push it, we could be there in fifteen or twenty minutes. I'm calling them now," which he did.

The air-traffic controller was a woman, her voice sweetly calm. "We'll make ready at once to receive you. Good luck."

The engine suddenly belched black smoke, and Dillon told Hannah to get the life jacket from under her seat and put it on.

"What the hell for?"

"In case we have to land in the sea."

"And you can do that?" she demanded, as she struggled into the life jacket.

"Yes, I've done it before." And he called, "Castletown, I'm sure you got that. I'm going to dive to a thousand now or maybe lower because I've just noticed a flicker of flame out there."

The controller said, "If you have to land in the sea, it is on your side this morning. Light winds and small waves, so approach with landing gear retracted, full flaps, and reasonable power."

At that moment, the Chieftain shuddered as the other engine packed in, and Dillon said, "Well, that's a problem in my situation, but as I can spy the airport half a mile away, let's forget water landings and go for broke. I'm coming straight in, trailing smoke, so that should make the evening news on television."

He turned to Hannah. "I think you should go back as far as you can. You'll stand a better chance there."

"No, I won't," she said. "Just get it done, cousin."

The Chieftain emerged from over the sea very low through a curtain of rain and black smoke, dropping down for its entry and bouncing, then down again to continue along the runway pursued by two fire tenders and a number of other vehicles.

They slid to a halt, and Dillon unbuckled his seat belt and reached to do the same for Hannah. Her eyes were closed, and she crossed herself.

"Are you okay?" he asked.

"Just celebrating being alive."

"Then let's go and open the airstair before they take axes to it."

He led the way, she followed with the hand luggage, and he got the door open. The closest fireman reached up to help Hannah and Dillon down to willing hands, which passed them on to a van with a driver and a man named Morgan who was head of some sort of special security and wanted to know their business. As both Dillon and Hannah were able to provide MI5 warrant cards, they soon found themselves in a private lounge.

Dillon said, "Do you need a doctor or anything?"

"Absolutely not. I'm just a little shocked, not only to be still alive but also to also realize what an absolutely brilliant pilot you are."

"I'll leave you with the task of speaking to Giles about that and asking him whether we could have Lacey and Parry fly up from Farley in the Gulfstream."

"And what about you?"

"I've got to call Tad to try and explain what's happened to his lovely Chieftain. The Master strikes again. You were kind enough to praise my airmanship, so that only leaves him. I can't allow that to happen anymore. To finish me in the way he intended meant killing you, and I don't accept that. You're my cousin, but also the daughter I never had, and I refuse to allow such a threat to hang over your head. So call Giles."

Which she did, and Dillon sat in a corner, called Tad on his Codex, who answered at once. "I didn't want to call you with so much going on, Sean, and we knew you were alive. That was some of the most fantastic flying I've ever seen."

"So that's been on the screen already? How can that be?" Dillon said.

"It seems there was a TV camera at work on some documentary up there, and whoever was in charge was smart enough to film the whole thing. They'll sell it round the world. It's left the Master with egg on his face."

"And I'm going to have him one way or another. He can get me if he can, but not Hannah, that's a bridge too far. No publicity at the moment, please."

"Of course not. I presume you had an engine problem, which the experts will discover. The rest is up to the insurers, although I'm not bothered about that. Any help you need where the Master is concerned, you only have to ask."

"You'll be the first I come to." Dillon glanced across the room, and Hannah was holding up her thumb. "I've just had the good word from Hannah that the Gulfstream is on its way from Farley."

"That's good. They should bring you a DFC with it. I'll be in touch."

SQUADRON LEADER LACEY and Flight Lieutenant Parry were wearing their uniforms when they brought the Gulfstream in. There was quite a crowd now and cameras on the go and sudden cheering as Dillon and Hannah were delivered to the flight.

Lacey stood at one side of the steps and Parry on the other, and they saluted as Dillon followed Hannah up the steps into the plane. "A bit over the top," he said, as they followed him in.

"Well, everyone loves a hero, and that's what you are today," Lacey said, as Dillon and Hannah sat down.

"I've already heard from Lieutenant Colonel Roper that a preliminary report indicates that there was interference with the Chieftain's engines. It is a miracle that you achieved that landing. We're all proud of you."

"I appreciate that, coming from someone with your experience and medals, Squadron Leader," Dillon said. "But all I want to do at the moment is get back home to Holland Park."

"I understand. Farley Field next stop," and Lacey followed Parry into the cockpit.

A moment later, the plane started to move, and Dillon, sitting beside Hannah, fastened his seat belt as his Codex buzzed.

He turned it on to speaker as Hannah looked at him inquiringly. He nodded, and said to the Master, "What do you want?"

"Just to say hail the conquering hero."

"You went too far today. That was the second time you've threatened Hannah's life, and that I will not forgive. You are a dead man walking."

Dillon switched off, looked at Hannah inquiringly, and she nodded. "And that's telling the bastard, Seaneen, but lie back now and try to sleep. You look tired."

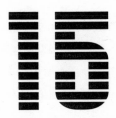

AT HOLLAND PARK, Roper sat in his usual wheelchair in the computer room watching Dillon's desperate flight again when he heard the sound of the Mini arriving outside and Sara walked in wearing her uniform. She looked tired and tossed her cap to one side.

"I'm late. I was due at the Cabinet Office an hour ago, and I've checked in with Frankel, who says he can cover for me, but not for long. Is that tea hot?"

"Of course, help yourself."

Which she did, and said, "How many times have you watched that flight?"

"A lot. One of the most fantastic things I've ever seen. MI5 happened to have a man named Morgan visiting the airport checking on security, and he's made sure there's no hint of Dillon's other activities. A brave private citizen is all. Hannah, by the way, is in excellent condition, and they are on their way back on the Gulfstream as we speak, and shouldn't you be getting down to Number Ten about now?"

"Please, Giles, just give me five minutes. It may be important."

"Okay, love, let's have it. What's the trouble?"

"I had a bad dream last night, which took me back to being on Holley's Falcon en route to Timbuktu. I was awakened in the cabin by the Master calling me on my mobile."

Roper reached for the master switch that turned off all the screens. "Go on."

"The Master said, 'There you are. I hope the trip proves agreeable.' I said, 'How did you know we are making it?'"

"And what did he say?"

"'Weber is concerned that you may be entering the circle of danger. Timbuktu is a highly dangerous place.'"

Roper was astonished. "That's a clear indication that Weber must have a mobile number for him, and he was at Charnley, remember, when you left with Hunter and he knew your destination."

"So what are you going to do?" Sara asked.

"We'll obviously have to arrest Weber sooner rather than later. This could be a real breakthrough. I'll let you know, but you can't leave the Prime Minister waiting, Sara. No Ferguson to smooth things over for him, but you're proving damn good at that and he likes you. They're already talking about making you an ADC to the Queen."

"Okay, I'm going. Give my love to the heroes when they get in, and tell Hannah that enough is enough."

She went out in the rain, and Roper sat there thinking about what Sara had said. It had to be right, and if so, this could be an answer to many things, and then a phone call told him the Gulfstream was due to land at Farley in five minutes. Holley walked in from the gym in a tracksuit, drying his hair on a towel.

"What's happening?" he demanded.

"Not much. Sara's on the run to the Cabinet Office after giving me a possible lead to the Master, and Hannah and Dillon are just about to land at Farley."

"Well, as I notice Dillon has left his Mini in the courtyard, I'll go and pick them up for you."

WHICH HOLLEY DID and found them at a corner table in the café at Farley. "The pride of the RAF expressed their regrets at missing you," Dillon told him. "It seems they have to step in and help out the Cabinet Office when they're short of a plane these days."

"You mean like running some Cabinet minister and his staff up to somewhere really exciting like Glasgow for a speech and luncheon," Holley said. "That isn't exciting; neither is what you two did in that plane this morning because it was more than that. It was magnificent. Never seen anything like it."

"It was Sean who was the pilot, Daniel, not me," Hannah pointed out.

"I told her to go back as far as she could and she refused, sat beside me in the cockpit for the whole thing," Dillon said.

"Well, you know what the Muslims say—it wasn't your time. By the way, Sara was on the run to the Cabinet Office. It seems she is the Prime Minister's new best friend. What may interest you rather more is that she's apparently been able to give Roper a possible lead to the Master."

"Are you sure about that?"

"That's what he told me, but he didn't go into details. I think that comes when we get back to Holland Park. Something to look forward to."

ROPER TOLD HANNAH what Sara had said. "Enough is enough."

"What does she think I am, a child? It's my birthday in two weeks and I'll be twenty years of age. I'm an unusual case, Giles, you can't deny it, and you need me. Who have you got? Dillon and Holley, Tony Doyle. I would also remind you that the Master gave the job of raping and murdering Kate Munro and me to a particularly foul assassin. I'll never be content until he is where he deserves to be. In a coffin."

"As that is definitely how I feel about him, I've no quarrel. Of course, that makes you the only female in our small group as Sara isn't available," Roper pointed out.

"Well, now that's been sorted, could we discuss what's going on here?" Dillon said. "Holley and I shared the flying of his Falcon from Charnley to Timbuktu with Sara and Colonel Hunter as passengers. The Master's first call came as a shock to Sara when he made it clear to her that he knew the plane we were in and the destination. The suggestion is that all this information was supplied by Hans Weber, owner of Charnley Aero Club, the airfield we had started on."

"I believe his working record with al-Qaeda in Timbuktu speaks for itself," Roper said. "So it's in the balance whether he should go to prison."

"I couldn't care less," Hannah said. "All that's important is getting the Master's phone number and, through that, the man himself. So let's keep it simple and allow me to handle Weber."

HANNAH HAD BRIEFLY MET Weber only once, and he didn't recognize her as she approached his front door at Hatherley Court and rang the bell. In horn-rimmed glasses, a scrunched cap, an anorak, and a shoulder bag, she appeared to be a typical student, and he opened the door on a chain and peered out.

"Mr. Clark, sorry I'm late. The Dublin plane was delayed."

"No Clark here; you must have the wrong address."

She fumbled in her pocket and took out a letter. "London School of Economics. I started Tuesday and they gave me this address for accommodation."

He slipped the chain, opened the door to look, and she took out her Colt and rammed it under his chin. "It's the Master I'm after, but I'll kill you if you don't do as you're told."

He was horrified and backed away, and she followed, slamming the door behind her. "My gun is silenced, so if you make me use it, we won't bother the neighbors. What I want from you is the secret phone number you have that allows you to call him. Oh, and don't say you don't know what I'm talking about, or I'll start by putting a bullet in your left knee."

"For God's sake, no, I'll tell you." He held out his right arm, the shirt cuff riding up, and Hannah examined it briefly. "It's a tattoo."

"I never wanted to forget it. I don't know what your problem was with him, but he was good to me."

He sat down on the couch, his head in his hands, and Hannah phoned Dillon and company waiting in the car outside. "I've got him," she said, then went into the kitchen, poured whiskey in a glass, and took it to him. "Listen to me. You can stay out of prison by making yourself useful. That's the way intelligence people do things."

There was a tap on the door, and she opened it to Dillon, Holley, and Tony Doyle. Hannah was copying Weber's tattoo as he held his arm out patiently.

"As the Master's phone number is a tattoo on Weber's right arm, I think Colonel Roper should keep him for interrogation at Holland Park, otherwise MI5 will try to jump in first. Check him out for mobiles, but I don't think you'll find anything. He's being sensible."

"I'll take him off with Doyle," Holley said. "Leave you to follow."

Which they did, Dillon driving. "A good result," he told Hannah. "Now that Roper has that number, he'll run down an address in no time. It is going to be fascinating to find out where the Master lives."

"I suppose so, but I'm so tired because I used up so much of myself breaking down Weber. I was straight out of a concentration camp."

"But it worked."

"Oh, yes, he told me through tears that the Master had been kind to him and that was in spite of my mentioning some of the bad things he'd done to us."

"Never mind. I think it has all been too much for you. Finbar's jump to his death, that nerve-racking flight in the Chieftain, your confrontation with Weber, and now the endgame with the Master."

"It doesn't seem possible in such a brief time," she said.

"Do you prefer to go back to Highfield Court?"

"I can't do that; Giles will have an answer to where the Master is tomorrow. I want to be there for that. It is truly important to me. You do understand?"

"Of course I do. So the guest wing at Holland Park for tonight, I think."

WHEN HANNAH WENT TO BED, sleep was instant, no troubled dreams, nothing at all. When she opened her eyes, there was a light tap on the door and Maggie Hall edged in with a tray.

"There you are, with us again. I've got you some nice hot Irish tea just the way you like it, honey. Everyone's been concerned with your sleeping so long."

"What on earth do you mean?" Hannah reached for the tea and drank some gratefully.

"Well, let's put it this way, it isn't Thursday anymore, it's six o'clock Friday evening, so I reckon you've slept around twenty hours."

"I can't have." Hannah was shocked. "That would be virtually a full day of my life I've lost."

"Well, you have, but maybe you could find it again in the steam room and swimming pool."

"An excellent idea." Hannah tossed the sheets to one side. "Everybody's around, I suppose?"

"Except for Major Gideon. She doesn't seem able to shake off the demands of Downing Street at the moment. Will you be looking for breakfast when you're ready?"

"Hardly the right time of day, Maggie, but, yes, I would. Just give me forty minutes," and she pulled on a robe and rushed out.

ROPER, DILLON, AND HOLLEY had their heads together when she entered the computer room. Roper glanced up and said, "She who was dead hath arisen again."

"A biblical way of putting it, but my priest would approve," Hannah said. "What have I missed?"

"Nothing, it's all waiting for you on the end screen. The Master."

She sat down and the Master gazed at her from the screen, old, bearded, wise, and, most interesting of all, pleasant and kind looking.

"He looks like somebody's grandfather."

"He certainly isn't that, because I know all about him," Roper said. "He's a retired professor of the history of religion at the Sorbonne named Simon Hussein. He has written books on Christianity and Islam, even Buddhism. Looked on as being an authority on Osama bin Laden. A hugely respected scholar. French mother and Algerian father, who was killed in that country's war with France."

"Are you absolutely sure about this?"

"That secret mobile number told our experts all they needed to know about how it operated. Advanced technology has taken steps to make sure it can never be used again as he did. Giving Weber his secret number was a mistake for him, but not for us."

"Which has now betrayed him."

"If you call it that. Don't forget the many deaths he and al-Qaeda have been responsible for all over the world, and just think of his order that you and Kate be raped and murdered. There can be no forgiveness for that, surely?"

"He certainly won't get any from me when we meet," she said. "So where do we go to finish this? Where do we find him?"

"I'm the expert there," Holley told her. "My firm owns a barge moored on the Quai de Montebello on the River Seine in Paris. A special place to live—I stay nowhere else when I'm in town."

"So?" she said.

"There are scores of such barges, and Hussein lives in one chained to the Quai des Brumes not far from me. Heart of Paris and on the Seine. Wonderful place to live, and thanks to the mobile phone, he can roam the world without having to go anywhere himself."

"Well, obviously there's no time to waste," Hannah said. "When are we going to lift him?"

"I wish I were able to go myself," Roper said. "But I'm not, so Dillon and Holley will fly over to Charles de Gaulle in the Falcon, ostensibly on Algerian government business, and deal with him tonight."

"Finish him off for good, you mean?"

"We can't afford to take prisoners. If they knew he was alive, they'd move heaven and earth to get him back, and to be frank, we would be better off without all that fuss."

"I can see that," Hannah said. "So when are we leaving?"

"Just a minute now," Dillon said. "You've done enough. You stay out of this one."

"Then I'll go myself. I've got money, a passport, and an address. Professor Simon Hussein, Quai des Brumes. I'll find him."

"You'd never get through an airport with a pistol on you."

She turned, helpless and angry; Roper stared at her for a moment, and smiled. "If it means that much to you, Hannah, then you can go." He turned to Dillon. "She's earned her spurs. It's my decision, so just get on with it."

AT CHARLES DE GAULLE AIRPORT, Holley landed, and diplomatic privilege allowed him to taxi his Falcon around to the VIP section, where he was permitted to leave with his briefcase not searched, which was a good thing, as it contained three pistols.

"We'll take a cab to my barge and walk the rest of the way," Holley said. Outside the airport, they hailed a taxi that deposited them on the Quai de Montebello twenty minutes later. It was starting to rain, darkness falling, and Holley said, "Hang on, I'll get a couple of umbrellas."

The barge was larger than Hannah had expected, lights on in the prow and stern. "Nobody at home, these lights are automatic," he said, as he passed an umbrella to her and another to Dillon.

"Isn't the security a little lax on those?" Hannah said, as they started walking.

"Well, that one is the property of the largest shipping company operating out of Algiers, of which I am joint owner, and its security is second to none."

"Well, that's fine," she said, as they walked together. "I'm just wondering how we handle Hussein."

"Giles Roper gave me a going-away present. An electronic key the people we're involved with have produced, although Scotland Yard will be unhappy about its potential. If necessary, we'll give it a try, because he might be enjoying an early supper. If so, we'll gain access and wait for him."

WHICH, IN THE END, was what happened on the Quai des Brumes. They found a barge that was a twin to Holley's, the deck lights on but only the dimmest light showing at the stateroom windows. They went down a roped gangplank, and Dillon, a gun in one hand, knocked on the door several times without a response.

"I'll try the magic key," Holley said, but he prepared for somebody calling "Who's there" from the bedroom.

The door opened with ease, and he moved in, Colt in hand,

Dillon and Hannah backing him, weapons ready. There was no response, no one at home in what appeared to be a very comfortable interior—paneled stateroom, plush sofas, many books on the shelves, an extremely advanced television and computer-linked phone system.

A further check disclosed two bedrooms, each with a shower, and a reasonable kitchen. The stern was open to the deck but had a canopy stretched tightly over it, a roof against the rain, and a curtain obscured the entrance from the stateroom.

Holley took down a book to examine, and said, "This has got his photo on the back, the distinguished look."

"Well, it would," Hannah said. "His achievements as a scholar speak for themselves."

She had been crouched at a porthole by the entrance, and now added, "But you can discuss that with him yourself. Unless I'm mistaken, he's approaching now. Walking stick, cap, and a naval duffel coat against the rain."

Dillon rushed to her side to check, looking over her shoulder. "She's right, Daniel."

Holley, who had been pulling the curtain across, opening it to the stern, moved to one side of Hannah, drawing his pistol again, and Dillon went to the other.

A key rattled, the door opened, and the Master stepped inside, immediately discovering Hannah. There was a certain shock but then an instant smile as the door swung back and closed behind him.

"Why, Hannah, it's you. Plus the great Sean Dillon and the formidable Daniel Holley, the pride of the Provisional IRA. Am I to take it this is a hunting party?"

"The best idea you've had yet. Weber sends his regards. He must be a disappointment for you."

He held Hannah's look for a moment, then tossed his cap onto the sofa, followed by his stick, suddenly angry. "What nonsense; you've been searching all over my home seeking God knows what. Disturbing everything. What the hell were you doing in the stern? The doors left open and those beautiful curtains all over the place."

He strode across, reached up to pull them back, and turned, a Walther PPK in his hand. Hannah, who had been waiting for such a move, holding the Colt against her thigh, shot him between the eyes, sending him staggering back through the open door and over the stern rail.

She went out to look, and Dillon and Holley followed. "I felt he must have something up his sleeve, he argued too much, and the second he reached up, I thought he must probably be groping for a weapon."

"Good job you used your silenced Colt. That way, we get going and leave the River Seine to carry him away. The current is more than strong enough here," Holley said. "We'll walk a reasonable distance before taking a cab. We've got the umbrellas. Are you okay?"

"More tired than I've ever been in spite of having spent twenty hours in bed. It's not that I'm sorry I killed him. He was a monster, but enough is enough, I think. It's definitely time for Highfield Court, Sadie's wonderful food, and that marvelous piano of mine."

"Well, hang in there," Dillon said. "Because we've got a Falcon jet waiting at Charles de Gaulle that can't wait to fly you back to all that."

AN HOUR LATER, Holley was sitting alone in the cockpit of the Falcon for the relatively short flight to Farley Field with light rain and winds only, and he was tired and looking forward to his bed at Holland Park. Dillon came in and took the other seat.

"How is she?" Holley asked.

"Asleep," Dillon said. "Her face is as calm and contented as any marble saint in her village church."

"Do you think Roper knew what he was doing when he allowed her to come with us?"

"Of course he did. Her hatred of the Master was so real that he knew he'd get the right result if she was involved."

"And will he want to use her again?"

"He'd be a fool not to, but then he knows he'll have a couple of old-fashioned Provos like you and me to keep an eye on her."

"It sounds good to me," Holley said.

"As long as you remember one thing where Hannah is concerned," Dillon told him. "It's an old saying, but true: The female of the species is deadlier than the male."